One Last Mad Embrace

A novel by Jack Trevor Story

reinkarnation

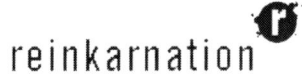

The edition published in 2010 by reinkarnation under licence
from the estate of Jack Trevor Story

First published in Great Britain by Alison and Busby 1970
© Jack Trevor Story 1970

ISBN 978-0-9563689-1-1

All rights reserved. No reproduction, copy or transmission of this
publication made be made without written permission.
No part of this publication may be reproduced, copied or transmitted
without prior permission of the copyright owner

A CIP catalogue of this book is available from the British Library

Printed by Lightning Source

Jack Trevor Story wrote three Horace Spurgeon Fenton novels:
One Last Mad Embrace, *Hitler Needs You* and *I Sit in Hanger Lane*.
Further information about the author and his books can be found at

www.reinkarnationbooks.com

For Maggie MacDonald and
Little-dog, remembering
the long road to Ben Hope.

Is it the hour? We leave this resting-place
Made fair by one another for awhile.
Now, for a God-speed, one last mad embrace
The long road then, unlit by your faint smile
      RUPERT BROOKE *The Wayfarers*

A man is in love with a great many things strewn about haphazardly all over the country. He gets in his car and drives out to them, to have another look at them, and he doesn't want anybody sitting beside him. A man can be in love with streets, plains, mountains, vineyards, towns and cities, or portions of them: with railway tracks, hills, trees, telegraph poles, houses, porches, lawns. County Fairs, morning hours, noon hours, evening hours, night hours. He can go out in search of a fresh assorting and arranging of these things, and of the people of them.
      WILLIAM SAROYAN *The Bicycle Rider in Beverley Hill*

The Dream

I woke up laughing.

The act of laughing is like the act of yawning or sneezing; uncontrollable and deep seated. I woke up laughing so uncontrollably and deep-seatedly that I felt sure that I had been laughing for a long time and that every soul in the big old house on the heath had been lying listening to me and were now waiting to see if I had stopped for good.

Then I had to re-think it all out from the beginning. The dream, I mean. And when I had I started crying because I couldn't remember the girl's name.

Worse; because I didn't even know her now that I was fully awake. I had known her slightly while I was waking up, coming back through that fantasy fringe, those few instants of sleep-time where everything is clear; but now I didn't know her at all. She had gone with the dream.

Then I thought it all through again anyway and I started laughing again, but keeping my laughter as moderate as I could. It was the funniest thing that had ever happened.

It started off, I think, with the girl, and we were in bed. I don't think we were in bed together. There was something more idyllic about it than that. It was the kind of in-bedness that could have been together except that we were transcendently in love. We loved each other with a purity which kept us on the peaks of ecstasy and not in bed together. There was a nearness and a fleshness and an undressness about it that gave us at one and the same time the exquisite pleasures of love and deprivation. That perfect, permanent state that we knew we had it to come.

The girl was very young and I was the same age I am now.

The girl was school age. Some of the beauty and ecstasy and the exquisite pleasure was because of her youngness.

The situation was made more tragic and poignant by there suddenly being in the room with us, crowded and milling and talking to each other, all the people we did not love. Without them we perhaps would not have known how much we loved each other and with what intensity and certainty. I suspect that all the people we had thought we loved were in that room with us, similarly undressed or in the state we thought we had loved them best. But they did not exist to us nor we to them. They were like highly-charged wall-paper.

Now another part of the exquisite pain of loving each other came from that we knew that we were soon going to be discovered by the young girl's parents. The exquisite part of this was that it wouldn't make any difference to our love. Her parents would think it wicked and wrong and everybody in the room, crowded as it was with both our lives so far, would think our love was wicked and wrong—that is to say the world was against us but it wouldn't make any difference. We both saw our love continuing clearly and we saw it perfect and shining, the ecstasy going on to the farthermost tip and end of our lives. She was young and undressed and in bed and waiting for us to marry each other and live happily ever after.

Her mother and father came in together bringing with them a great thunder of discovery and guilt and terrible criminal embarrassment because of our age difference and because we were undressed. I remember very little dialogue at this violent moment. Just the father's anger and outrage coming at me like ugly destructive missiles and demanding to get my trousers on and diminishing and degrading with accusations of unspeakable filth and perversion what until then had been pure and beautiful and inevitable.

The young girl's mother was quite different in her attitude. She was calm because she herself had been a young girl (whereas the father had never been my age or in love, one supposes) and while she got the girl out of bed and dressed her she made me feel that she was enjoying the situation. Therefore I told her as swiftly and sincerely as I could, as though explaining a crime which had not been committed, that I loved her daughter and that her daughter loved me and that we were going to get married as soon as I could get my divorce from the roomful of people.

'Good,' she said.

This is the first bit of dialogue I remember. And the second bit is: 'But she's going away to college in six months and will forget all about you.'

She said this with warm friendliness as though she were on our side but was the reluctant bearer of bad news. And she said it as though she could see clearly to the farthermost tip and end of our lives.

This was the end of our ecstasy.

We left quietly together and met a quaint old lady in busy Oxford Street who asked me if I would like to see her husband's grave. I explained to the girl—who had moved away as people do when accosted by the mentally afflicted—that the old lady was quite harmless and came from Stony Stratford in Northants. I told the old lady yes, I would like to see her husband's grave and she looked bewildered and distressed, searching the busy street with her old eyes.

'I can't find it,' she said.

And then the girl, who I still loved, though hopelessly now, said instead she would show us her brother's grave in the Royal Artillery Hall at the Motor Company.

'How does he come to be buried there?' I asked her.

She shrugged: 'I don't know.' And then she said what was the funniest thing I've ever heard in a dream and woke me up laughing in my shared flat in Hampstead at four in the morning. She said: 'My sister Kim was perfectly normal but my brother is buried at the Royal Artillery Hall at the Motor Company.'

I don't know whether you will see any hint of Ariadne Thing in this dream; of submerged middle-age longings. I didn't at the time.

I didn't until it had practically all come true.

Part One

One

I want you to meet Joan Scattergood.

Joan is a TV producer with the BBC and my agent brought us together over lunch in the canteen at TV Centre; you all know the eyesore by the White City stadium. Like all modern buildings it is designed with the assumption that everybody uses lifts. They don't. I was not surprised to learn from the commissionaire in the North Tower that of the five hundred people working in that building seventy-three have to use the stairs and another twenty-five have to be escorted in the lifts. There were twenty-three flights of stone stairs up to Joan's office on the eleventh floor; I met people, sat and talked to them on the stairs, who were there when I worked on Sixty-Minute Theatre in 1961. Three of us had asthma inhalers. The talk was about the TV playwright George Walter who died during the Guild strike of '65.

'He jumped from this window,' somebody said.

And we talked about other studios and TV centres in relation to us asthmatics and claustrophobics. The building in Broome Road at Teddington, for instance, the old ABC building had stairs that were impossible to find without an original plan of the building. People working there swore there were no stairs. An old actor had got himself locked in the stairs and they found his body during ARP exercises six months later. And once at TV House in Kingsway I got involved in what apparently was a nightly event during the Hiding Place series; that is a race from top to bottom of the building between the two sergeants in different lifts. They had to carry me round to the Kardomah afterwards.

'Horace Spurgeon Fenton?'

Joan Scattergood was smiling at me from behind her big desk, confident that she had got my name right. From the beginning of a relationship with a TV producer till the end your name is likely to be the only thing they'll get right. They know nothing about their job or yours. Nice people, mind you—but where did they come from? So suddenly too? Before television—which is not going back very far— there were hardly enough producers and directors to go round. Suddenly they needed seven hundred and sixty-three—and there they all were. Where did they come from? Watch your television set tonight and then hazard a guess.

'What do you know about Dinah Thing?' Joan Scattergood asked me over the BBC scampi. She was wearing the shortest skirt I've ever seen on a thirty-years-old woman. It proved beyond any doubt that her legs were joined together at the top. It was to show that she was fashion-conscious; she had plenty of feminine attraction and didn't need to have her lunch naked with a stranger.

'It's the UM series,' she said. 'You probably already know about it.'

The UM series was going to be about a pretty Unmarried Mother fighting the good fight in present-day London. Dinah Thing (this is not her real name) had been cleverly chosen to star on the strength of her long-standing Wayward Girl image and the fact that she was a wellknown self-publicised unmarried mother.

'I believe you've already written for her,' Joan said. 'Or something.'

There was no 'or something' about it. Dinah had been in one of the films I had scripted from my own book (*Mix Me a Murder*). I could see that it would be profitable however to leave an open doubt whether I was the father of her child. There is always this search for depth in TV series.

'We want to show the stigma and then get rid of it,' Joan Scattergood said.

I said: 'For every unmarried mother there's an unmarried father somewhere.'

I say this whenever the opportunity comes up but this was probably the most useful time I ever said it. She commissioned three sixty-minute scripts on the sketchiest of story ideas, none of which I intended to use and all of which came from my old

Caxton Drake—-Detective series of pulp books. They would pay me six hundred and twenty pounds each, which meant that I could raise a five hundred pounds advance before opening my typewriter. I was back in business.

There was to be an inauguration party at Joan's house with the object of the writers meeting the script editor, each other, the stars and cast, the PA girls and Assist. Stage Manager girls (all good chaps); talking character, unifying mood ideas, creating continuity gimmicks, collecting telephone numbers and getting drunk.

'I thought it might be a nice idea if she brought her actual child along,' Joan Scattergood said.

'Wot chew avin' fer sweet, dearie?' the BBC's head waitress asked me and I told her.

'After all, an illegitimate child is also a person in his own right,' Joan was informing me, 'and I want these episodes to be not simply romantic and domestic adventures but also to have some kind of philosophical dimension . . .'

It was because she said 'his' own right that I wasn't expecting a girl; and it was because she said 'child' that I wasn't prepared for Ariadne.

The Scattergoods live in Highgate. Lived in Highgate; they've probably moved house twice since we did UM. Like so many people these days they didn't have a home, they had a property. To someone who never owned more than a typewriter and a guitar in his life the house looked an ordinary bay-windowed terraced Victorian villa with six yards of front garden and a box hedge. Not so; it represented every spare hour and every spare penny of their married life. They had fitted a new front door, box seats under the windows, torn down a wall to make a through lounge. Doctor Paul Scattergood's hands felt like a navvy's when we were introduced.

'And this is all coming down,' Joan Scattergood said as we did the inevitable tour. The box room was going to be a bathroom, the scullery a bedroom and the kitchen a nursery.

'I didn't know you had children?' Dinah Thing said.

'No, we haven't. Well, it wouldn't be fair to drag children from house to house …'

Work it out if you can. There's enough of them; house owners without a home. The nomadic albions making five hundred pounds profit every twelve months. They are the kind of people who stagger home from abroad with every allowable tax-free item to save a few shillings.

'They're cunts, both of them,' the man said.

I hadn't noticed him come up. He was holding two drinks in his hands and I looked for the girl; but one was for me.

'They can't think any higher than their step-ladder, but don't let that worry you. I'm running this series, not Joany Scattercrap.' He shook my hands with the Spanish burgundy slopping. 'Mac Gordon McKilvey—Mac.'

'No,' I said. 'I'm Horace Fenton. Horace Spurgeon Fenton.'

He laughed. 'I know who you are, Horace. We worked together on *Escapers' Club*. I was an actor in those days. '56, '57? I was just watching you sliding towards the door. You've changed your mind about working on the series. I admire that but somehow I've got to keep you. I'm script editing. Bring your drink, sit down. What do you think of the idea like the baby's real father is like a Roman Catholic priest and that's why she can't tell anybody?'

Mac is a toughie, full of bitter humour. He looks and sounds like James Cagney. His disdain and hate for everybody sometimes embarrassed me, but only because of its honesty. He didn't wait for people to go out of range before giving his opinion. And he knew the inside dirt better than the dustbins.

'What we've got here is a gallows,' he told me later in the evening; he seemed to be concentrating on me rather than the other writers who were busy idolising Dinah Thing. 'It was dreamed up by Ian Barker and pushed through while Robbins is in the States.' He was talking real company and corporation names big in the TV world and I have to change them if I want to work again. Apparently the UM series, far from being the fulfilment of a long-needed want, was no more than a way of getting a disliked executive to waste a hundred thousand of the corporation's money and get himself the chop.

'Won't it get on the screen, then?' I asked.

'Now that's where you and I come in, Horace,' Mac said and he lowered his face to his wine with his Guy Fawkes expression. 'We're going to make this thing so fucking good they'll scream for thirty-nine episodes and then another thirty-nine—' he detected that he was depressing me with this awful prospect and swerved quickly: 'We'll have a short ride on the wagon and pull in top rates—how much has Joan offered you? Six twenty? Give me a first-rate pilot for that and I'll double you on the rest . . .'

In case you think I was being given the privilege as the eldest and best writer in the room of writing the pilot script I have to confess that sitting in the loo with a sack hanging in front of my nose because something was happening to the door I heard Mac talking to Pee-Wee Hunt in the kitchen:

'Give me a first-rate pilot at that price and I'll push you up to a thousand pounds a go...'

This is the script editor's job. Lying.

'Horace. Come and meet Dinah,' Joan called in a gym mistress voice.

Dinah looked at me and so the other writers looked at me. They were all children. Isn't it funny the way professionals used to be middle-aged and now they're not? Half of them were wearing their hirsute masks.

'Don't tell me Horace is writing this series?' Dinah Thing said. She was half-gone on laced cider and was being funny. 'That's the kiss of death.' And having delivered this blow she cocked her mini-skirted thigh a bit higher. She told the now listening room: 'I once had a film career until Horace wrote me a script.'

'You didn't do me any good either,' I said.

'Horace has got some marvellous ideas for the UM,' Joan said. And to me she said, slightly desperate in case Dinah was being serious: 'Did you hear Dinah's new line for the show? "What's an UM? It's a MUM without a wedding ring." Get it? Unmarried Mother?'

'Will somebody get me a glass of orange juice for Ariadne?' Dinah asked.

Everybody went for orange juice and we were left alone for a moment. She flicked my balls with her cherry and spoke sub-rosa. We had worked together for one movie at the old Walton Studios just over a hundred years ago and we really felt like old comrades.

She said: 'How come you're slumming with these BBC amateurs?'

'What about you?'

'Darling, I need the loot.'

'Snap!' I said.

By which time the children were back with fifty glasses of orange juice for Dinah's child.

'Where is she?' I asked. The chicks around the room all seemed too old to be illegitimate.

'She's in bed,' Dinah said.

'We put her to bed at nine o'clock,' Joan said. 'Perhaps you'll see her when she goes. I wanted everybody to see her.' And intensely to Dinah as if paying her a parental compliment: 'The casting for the Ariadne part is going to be terribly interesting.'

'I think my child in the series should be a boy,' Dinah said. 'Make it a girl and ugh! Icky! For me, I mean.' She meant it would revive all the old gossip and conjecture. The scandals from the Dennis Dova era lay across our faces like dead leaves; the secrets of the Cookham bungalow that leaked to the world through an efficient publicity agent; the death of Myra Simpson and Dennis's suicide in a police station cell. The police raids had made double-page spreads and the revelations about see-through mirrors, corrupted shop-girls, drugs, wine sipped from pelvic cavities had carried something of the shock and revulsion to a thrilled public as the liberation of the Nazi concentration camps. 'And besides,' Dinah said, 'I don't want anything I do on television to touch my little girl.'

'You have nothing to worry about,' Joan Scattergood said. 'You are going to be the most loved young mother in the world.'

And to prove it she called: 'Mac! Come and talk to Dinah.' To Dinah she said: 'Mac's got a truly brilliant and inspired idea for the identity of the child's father.'

'I know,' Dinah said. 'He always had.'

Mac McKilvey came across the room, uncertain about the loud laughter getting funnelled his way. He was trailing a girl scriptwriter named Joanna Browne whom he had obviously been clueing up about Dinah and the series. The girl was staring at Dinah with real fear, rubbing her chin hard, swallowing.

'What's Mac the Knife been telling you about me?' Dinah asked.

'How do you do,' Joanna Browne said, shaking the star's hand. Joanna had made a quick name for herself with a debbie book about show-jumping; on the strength of this she had done eight TV shows, cut a record and got signed up for three series. Her parents were titled, her father a member of the House of Lords, her mother a lady novelist. Until tonight, Joanna told me afterwards, she had always thought Dinah Thing was a character in a Hank Janson paperback.

Mac said: 'Joanna's writing a brilliant episode for you, Dinah. Upper crust stuff. You go as housekeeper to this earl in this great mansion in Suffolk —'

'It begins to sound like — you know this is the third companion-stroke-housekeeper-stroke-stroke plot I've been given tonight?' Dinah told Joan. 'It begins to sound like that agony column for homeless kinks in *The Lady*. Why not call it "Live in — anything considered"? Couldn't I just be a typist? Most unmarried mothers are typists.'

'Listen,' Mac said, 'it's not like that. This is a deep psychological story. You barricade your bedroom door only to discover, dot dot dot, that the old earl has a crush on the child. The first curtain you're pulling the barricade down again to get to the screaming child.'

'Oh my God' Dinah said. 'Who's writing this — Horace?'

'So you see it has to be a little girl,' Joan informed her, opportunely.

'I don't see anything of the kind,' Dinah Thing told her producer. 'Frankly this old man young girl think revolts me.'

In some odd way the revulsion seemed connected with me at that moment. It made me angry.

'Oh come on, now, Dinah,' I said. 'You were a young girl once.'

Joan Scattergood said, brightly: 'How's everybody's glasses?'

We drank our Spanish burgundy and ate our cubes of mild English cheddar on cocktail sticks and I tried to get mixed up with Joanna Browne by talking about publishers and agents, royalties and debts. She didn't know what execution warrants were. Isn't it marvellous. What do those kind of people have to worry about?

'So what happens if the bailiff comes and you haven't got the money to pay him?'

There was a lot of banging going on upstairs and some shrieking; this seemed out of place at a BBC party but I didn't know what it was until somebody said quite close to the back of my neck (I was sitting on the floor almost between Joanna's knees):

'She's locked herself in. She won't open the door to anybody.'

As I turned round to see who was talking I managed to slide my hand up Joanna's thigh. She didn't move it and I had that glow you get when nothing seems quite so bad any more — even the wine was heady. It was Wilfred Oundle (Prowl Car) talking; for some reason or other his hair was wet and he was wiping his beard with a napkin.

'That's the third glass she's poured over people,' Dinah was saying. 'Now she can go without.'

'I'll go,' Doctor Scattergood said. 'She'll open the door to me. I've got the bedside manner.'

Everybody was laughing as he went out of the room and I thought this was good: it was more like an ITV party. In a strange and yet understandable way the extra prudishness you meet in writing for the commercial channels, because of the authority censorship, gets reversed in their private off-screen happenings. One company in Golden Square had a back lift permanently labelled 'Out of Order' for use as a staff love-in. With the BBC it's the other way round; anything goes on the screen but the corridors are like monastic cloisters. I had now extended my little finger and it just reached; she still hadn't moved and I still hadn't turned back to her. Then I noticed Joan Scattergood staring over my head and I turned round. Joanna Browne's face was so terrified it was attracting attention; her eyes were riveted on my hand as though it was a large spider. I took it away and lit a cigarette with it.

'The one thing I like about this UM series is there's a chance to work a message into it,' I said.

'Yes,' she said.

'Now come on, Horace,' Joan said. 'Other people want to meet you too.'

And as I went across the room I heard her say to you-know-who: 'Sorry about that, darling . . .'

It makes you fume. It makes me fume. This hypocrisy you get from girls who go around showing their crutches and wearing religious attitudes. It's like those Victorian nudes; fat tits and arses and spreadeagled limbs but faces that look as if they're in another room doing the cooking. All I did was extend my little finger. I didn't even have to push her skirt up.

I went up to the loo again which was on the bedroom floor (I never know whether that's 1st or 2nd) and passed Doctor Scattergood tapping and talking to a door. There were about six glasses of drink and a plate of pastries on the floor.

'Let me in and I'll tell you a story,' he was saying.

'Hah hah hah,' I said. 'It might work at that. Fight 'em with their own weapons.'

He turned scarlet and hurried downstairs, falling the last three.

'Who's that?' said a girl's voice through the door.

'I'm the police,' I said. 'Open up.'

Ariadne opened the door and looked at me. She was beautiful, delicately featured, fully-fashioned, wearing very long black hair scattered willow-fashion over a man's nylon shirt.

'I'm Ariadne,' she said.

It didn't seem possible. She was twelve!

'Thanks for treating me like a woman instead of a child,' she said. 'Did you know you've got a lovely dark brown treacly voice?'

'Yes,' I said.

She said: 'Come in.'

I went into the bedroom and she locked the door behind us. 'No, don't do that for God' sake. I'll get your orange juice.'

'I don't want any fucking orange juice,' Ariadne said.

I got out of the bedroom just before the party came rushing up the stairs and was able to empty the contents of a glass of orange juice over my head and say that she had locked the door again.

'God be praised,' said Dinah Thing.

But in that small interim her daughter had got my name and decided to get my number. I didn't know that she had. But she had.

Two

Inside every man there is a boy and sometimes the boy wants a girl. I've fallen in love desperately and forever with a high-school girl in the short bus ride between Jack Straw's Castle and Highgate High Street.

The straight, unfussed hair, the clear brow, the fearless thrust of eye, woman-curious, the merest dust of a smile. She gets off at the church but the dream and the fantasy go on; sexless, romantic, Arthurean. She is in a garden picking flowers, now punting on a summer river, now her parents have died leaving her penniless and frightened; no, better perhaps to upset the punt, rescue her. 'Change your wet things. I won't look.' And not looking; not even peeping; that's important. 'I trust you,' she says, I trust you, I trust you, I trust you.' And she can. That is important too. Almost time to have the parents die again. 'Couldn't I come and stay with you?' It wouldn't be right, you tell her. It's most important that it wouldn't be right. 'But I love you. I do, I do. Age doesn't make any difference. I could look after the garden.' She is in the garden again wearing a simple short white dress of Grecian simplicity, nothing on her legs and feet, a white ribbon tying her hair at the back. Others tying her arms. A gag in her mouth—

'Tickets please!'

After all, what's forty years' difference in ages when you're in love. What I'm trying to say is that Ariadne didn't see me as an older man. Young girls often don't. I think it's my conversation. It doesn't impress grown-ups the same way. They tried to kick me off the series.

'Did you enjoy the party?' Ruth Baxter asked me.

She's my agent now. She's not beautiful but she's the most attractive agent in London. Feminine rather than smart with a fetching little habit of adjusting things below desk level; sometimes she just briefly touches her fingers into her bra and a moment later secretly sniffs them as if for reassurance. She knew as much about the party as a ten minute high-pitched phone conversation from SHE 8000 could tell her.

'Now listen, Horace,' she said then. It meant that what she had to tell me shouldn't reduce my ego or lower my confidence but it would be better if I submitted a three-page synopsis of my first UM story before asking for a contract.

'I'm not working on spec. They know what I can do. Free samples is for beginners. Ruth, it would diminish me if I did that. I shouldn't be writing for TV at all now—'

'Horace, listen—'

'Seven novels, five A-feature movies, two hundred short stories—'

'They're frightened of your ideas, Horace.' Hm? 'The ones you gave them—for the pilot. A ten-years-old child having an affair with a Roman Catholic priest—'

'That's not mine! One half's Joanna Browne's and the RC bit is Mac McKilvey's—not her lover, her father. I gave them some of my Caxton Drakes. They were published for children—frightened of what ideas? I'm going to write a tender, moving, poignant tale about a persecuted young girl who runs away when she discovers the true facts of her birth—'

'Write it in three pages and send it to Joan Scattergood,' Ruth Baxter urged. 'You'll have a two-fifty advance very quickly.'

'Two-fifty? They were paying—'

'They have to be cautious about the budget till they know how the series goes.'

'By that time all the scripts are written at cut-price.'

'Horace, there's nothing else on the books at the moment.'

I shouldn't need anything. I should be writing my next novel. ''What happened to my first-day-of-shooting payment from Hollywood—ten thousand dollars?'

'I've written to you about that,' my agent said. 'They paid last week—the film is on location now.'

'Bugger the film, Ruth—where's the money?'

'That's what I've listed—I'll get you a copy. You know there's nothing to actually come. Well, we knew that, didn't we?' Did we? 'American tax, our tax, my commission; the rest the Official Receiver directed us to pay to your trustee in bankruptcy. Your creditors have been paid more than two thousand pounds. You should be happy about that.'

My creditors are inland revenue. They tax it and then they take what they haven't already.

'How many pages of synopsis?'

'Three—double-spaced. It won't take you a minute.'

That's not the point. All the construction and logistic faults show up in a synopsis and you can only work them out at full length when the characters are working for you.

'Synopses are a waste of time. Nobody sticks to them.'

'It gives them a bit of paper and a title to pay you on— that's all it is. Oh, and, Horace—we've had some mysterious telephone calls for you. He wants your present address, won't give a name.

You haven't been getting credit, have you? Bankrupts can go to prison for that.'

'What does he sound like?'

'I don't know. Every time he phones he uses a different voice—rather badly disguised.'

I had goose pimples.

It could only be Albert Harris and he was dead.

She must have run her fingers under her breast in the fractional time I was turning to go because when I said goodbye to her from the door Ruth was sniffing her fingertips and finding the result pleasant and satisfying.

I'm bankrupt. I meant to tell you that. It doesn't change anything. When I was a boy I thought bankrupts wore black suits and went about setting fire to shops. Nothing like that at all. You're not allowed a bank account, that's all. One day instead of the usual judgement summons you find notice of a receiving order being made against you by some creditor without a reasonable amount of faith. I posted it on to Charles Fenton, another writer, but it didn't work. The next thing you know an examiner has been appointed and in my case I was closeted in a small office in Kingsway with him for days on end, answering intimate questions about my life from when I used to clean chitterlings in a Cambridge slaughter house to the Royal Film Première of *The Cast Iron Shore*. His name was Smithers and he was dead tired all the time.

'Now what schools did you go to?'

There were thirteen schools and it took a week. Then we started on jobs. If anybody's interested in my biography they should go to Victory House and talk to the Board of Trade Inspectors in Bankruptcy.

Mr Christian the Official Receiver was a jolly man full of enthusiasm for bankruptcy itself. 'It's really wonderful,' he said. 'Sit down, Mr Fenton, let me tell you the advantages . . .' It was as though he was running a holiday camp. He mentioned a number of famous people in show-business he had made bankrupt and who were still grateful to him. 'It was the best thing he ever did,' he kept saying.

Well, it was nice to know that I'd pleased everybody and it was nice to have the wolves away from the door. When I had my last meeting with him he asked me if I had any friends in similar trouble; it was rather touching and I felt sorry to leave him all alone.

The telephone rang in the hall and Wendy's voice called through the door it was for me. When I went out her bare bottom was vanishing back into the bathroom. I share this fiat with five nurses now in Hampstead.

It was Mac McKilvey. He sounded very American after a recent two months in Australia.

'Horace?'

'Yes. Who's that?'

'Mac—who was that?'

'Horace Spurgeon Fenton.'

'No, no. That dame. Who was it? She sounded something, man! Are you shacked up with somebody now?'

'No, that was Nurse Thompson. Mac who?'

Apparently he had been fighting Joan Scattergood on my behalf.

'You know what killed it for you?'

I thought I knew but I was wrong.

'It was your cufflinks.'

'What?' For a crazy moment I thought maybe I had laddered Joanna Browne's tights when I ran my hand on them.

'Were you wearing paper clips?'

'Yes, of course.' I always wear paper clips. I lose cufflinks every time I have a shirt washed. Mostly I use buttoned cuffs, but for a party I've got this special pale blue number which is part of a little symphony (as Neville Freville used to call it) harmonising with a blue blazer, blue top hankie and blue socks; and I have a very tight pair of blue pants (trousers) but they have a nature stain on the front at the moment. I'll try to remember to recap on this later. Wendy went back from the bathroom to her room holding a towel around her.

'She couldn't believe Horace Spurgeon Fenton would have bits of wire twisted in his shirt cuffs,' Mac said.

'I'm writing a synopsis for her,' I told him.

'Balls to that. You're not an amateur. You just get some like suede shoes and tuck a hankie in your sleeve—no bits of wire. This is the BBC, man. Have you got a story worked out?'

'I'm just working on it now.' When a writer says that you know he's watching television.

'Forget it. I've got something quicker you can knock off in two days—four hundred pounds. Okay? How would you like to collaborate with Joanna?'

'Joanna Browne?'

'She's got a peach of a story but she can't do the scripting till you show her. She likes you, Horace. She jumped at the idea.'

'Are you sure?'

'I don't know what your secret is but you've got the right touch.' I thought for a moment she'd told him about my little finger but no; I mean he wasn't laughing. 'I can't get anywhere with these mummy and daddy types. I had a sixty-minute conference with her this afternoon without like swearing or being foul. When she went I'm not kidding I was sweating under the strain. Who's Nurse Thompson then?'

'What do you want me to do then, Mac? Will you post her story on?' I didn't want to get involved mentioning names; the girls can hear every word you say on the phone. When I'm working in my room sometimes I have to put up with half-hour telephone conversations. Specially you get them on the subject of clothes.

'You're kidding. Joanna's got a car and a chauffeur if she wants him. I'll get her to drop by. Did she mention the story-line to you …?'

While he was talking I heard giggles coming from the girls' room. They have two bedrooms across the landing from mine and we share bathroom, toilet and kitchen. Mac went waffling on about Joanna's storyline and Wendy came out again dressed just in black nurse's tights with panties underneath and a bra. She was holding a kitten of all things.

'Just a minute, Wendy,' I said to her.

'What?' Mac said at the other end; he was in Wimbledon—isn't that amazing? I always think that's amazing.

'It's all right,' I told him, 'go on. The old earl starts eyeing the kid. Yes, Mac?' I'd heard this before, been blamed for it. From Joanna it was all right.

Wendy said: 'Can I just whisper, Horace? Will you come and play with my pussy while I'm on days?'

'What?' Mac said, at the other end.

I know it sounds like corny comic dialogue, but the girls had planned it that way. A shriek of mice-laughter went up as Wendy took the kitten back to their room. They had heard me mention Wendy's name, she had probably exchanged a few sexy words with Mac and this was their idea of a joke.

Mac was saying: 'What kind of a situation have you got there, Horace? Couldn't we discuss the whole thing at your place tonight? Like now?' He called to his wife: 'I may have to go out to a script conference with Horace Spurgeon Fenton ...'

Do you ever get the feeling you're being used?

When the blackcurrants are ripe for picking I have to take Edna to Ipswich to see her decrepit old mother. It's funny, they have all the spring and the summer to get ripe yet they always get ripe the day I'm doing something important.

'You don't like doing important things,' my friend Albert Harris used to say, bitterly, in the days when he was trying to push me and my career and make me famous. 'It's eleven o'clock and you've got an important date with Harry Smeltzmann at half-past and here you are walking the poodle and after that you have to get some potatoes for the old lady next door—and it takes an hour to get there.'

This was an exaggeration, of course. I prefer not to make appointments at all, especially with people like Harry and Chubby who have telephones instead of ears, but when I do I'm not the kind to plan my day round them, that's all. Here was Joanna Browne in a leather mini-skirt with her own tame Bentley following her up and down Squires Mount looking for me, and here was old Edna on the phone could I get to Ipswich today before the currants fell off.

'I woulda thought you coulda come straight away. We didn't see her last year.'

That wasn't my fault, there was a currant blight.

'She'll think there's something wrong.'

'It's time we told her. Why don't you tell her? Take Mr Fortin with you—'

'I couldn't tell her I'm married again at her age!'

'With her eyesight she won't notice the difference.'

This may all sound obscure but it's simple really. Edna's family in Ipswich don't know we've been apart for twenty-three years; don't know that I've raised another family with Tres since then, parted from them, lived in the caravan with Diana for three years and am now a bachelor in Hampstead; don't know that Edna is married to a Mr Fortin who was our next-door neighbour. This annual blackcurrant and blessing of the fruit ceremony is the only duty I have to perform these days. I visit the children in their various marriages and ruts but not as a duty. If I'm lonely in the middle of the night I drive up to Dunstable or down to Redhill or into Welwyn Garden City and throw a stone at a window. Big families are nice; there's always somebody to have a cup of tea with.

'Is that you, Dad?' they call out.

They know it's me. 'Mr Spurgeon Fenton?'

Joanna's mouth was calling to me through the letter box as I stood telephoning in the hall. Through the dirty muslin curtain on the door I could see her stooping to it.

'Just a minute,' I called. Then to Edna: 'All right—but don't expect me any particular time.'

'Will it be before lunch? Dinner, I mean. No, lunch. Mr Fortin comes home for lunch at one.'

Now I have to fit in with Mr Fortin?
I don't know. Just get ready.'
'All right then, ta. Before three?'
'I don't *know*. I've got a script conference—yes, before three.'
'All right then. Ta ta.'
'Ta ta.'
This is what a marriage comes to after thirty years.
'Have you got a basin?'
'What?'
'Or a plastic bag or something? For the currants.'
I hung up on her.
'Who was that?' Joanna Browne asked when I let her in.
'My wife. My ex-wife.'
'Which one—Edna or Tres?'
'Edna.'

You write about your life and soon complete strangers have a disconcerting knowledge about you. And more disconcerting since they're inclined to prefer the bits you made up for dramatic effect. When my mother read that passage in *My Mother's Second Husband* where she finally pushed him off the ferry-boat and walked home singing *Beulah Land* at the top of her voice, she said : 'Fancy you remembering that!' I made it up.

'Phew!' Joanna said when I took her into my room.
'You like it?'
It was the smell. I hadn't noticed it.
'How could you stand it? It's obscene!'
I love this, don't you? Somebody comes into your home and goes prying around through the crap looking for the smell. She was on her knees already showing her crutch and I didn't even look.

'Can we open a window?'

She destroyed the whole thing. Quickly, I mean, before she'd taken anything off or even put her umbrella down. The windows were shut, the curtain drawn together, the wooden shutters bolted and barred and the soft light over the bed was on, shining on the bottles of drink that Mac had over from the nurses last night. It was one of those tacit barter arrangements. I mean Joanna Browne didn't have to drag all the way up from Hampstead Heath to have a script conference with me. Nobody ever comes to me.

'I've managed to get you an appointment with Peregrine Danvers Farquuson,' my agent says. And I drive through Hampstead, West Hampstead, Willesden, sit in Scrubs Lane for two hours, walk up twenty-two flights of stairs and spend five fatuous minutes with one of the BBC's freckled youths saying something that could've been said in ten seconds over the telephone. They never come to the author. Nobody ever comes to the author.

'I think I've found it,' Joanna Browne said.

She had wriggled backwards from under the bed and was looking round so that her face and arse were visible together. The unspoken arrangement was that Mac would send Joanna to me if I would let him take a bottle along to Wendy last night—which I did. We had nurses and kittens and bottles and glasses and nighties coming and going all night practically.

'You've got it made!' Mac said at the quiet intervals.

I haven't got anything made. Nobody who reads me could say that I've got it made. I've never taken advantage of the fact that five nurses are trapped in a flat with me at night. It would be so easy it's corny. I treat them very circumspectly, respect their privacy, join in their little jokes, listen to their love problems, empty the dustbins, do their washing up, scrub the bathroom and toilet and hoover the landing and corridors for them. I've got it made? My visitors and chums have got it made.

'Give her Campari and Pernod mixed,' Mac had instructed me about Joanna Browne.

She seemed more at home sitting there with a dog's dish full of forgotten, mildewed Kennomeat in her hand.

My crippled girl-friend Diana took B... the poodle, with her when she ran off with Trotsky. I shall tell you about this later.

I must have brought the meat from the caravan when I moved. What I do is, to save a lot of sorting things out, pile

25

everything into a blanket and tie it up at the corners, put it in the boot of the car. Then I transfer it under the bed.

And: 'How can a famous author like you live in a tatty old bed-sitter?' Joanna Browne said.

People always call me famous when they're trying to criticise me on the way I live. It's a beautiful room. It measures around twenty-five feet each way and has a lovely marble fireplace and picture windows that look directly across the Vale of Heath, the Leg O' Mutton Pond, the grassy hills and trees and shrubbery that landscape away over to Highgate.

'Before we start work,' Joanna Browne said, 'I'll muck you out.'

This is the show-jumping fraternity, you know. I think now with her literary debut she was only just beginning to meet people on foot. While I was in the bog with the Daily Mail I heard her banging back the shutters like stable doors and when I came in I caught her waving to the chauffeur out in the Bentley. Waving? It was a prearranged signal: I...AM...ALL...RIGHT...SO...FAR...

She blushed and so she bloody should.

'That's George. Daddy's chauffeur. I got him to pick me up at my place. He waits at The House all day for Daddy. Tell me about your lovely young nurses,' she said while she was swilling disinfectant over the lino.

I'm very slow.

I knew why I'd got her up here but not why she had chosen to come. She was after material for another of her debby memoirs. I got angry. Kneeling there in her antique leathers I felt like giving her something she couldn't talk about at a Foyles' lit lunch. You know what I'm like when I get sexually angry.

'Here, have a drink,' I said.

She wouldn't drink. She wouldn't drink. It's not fair. Roll up, this is the world, folks. Knock every girl you meet, have it off with your neighbours' wives, forget their names before they've found their own way home and nobody thinks the worse of you. But live a good clean life and record it accurately without trimmings and you get a great horny reputation.

'Can I throw this away?' she was saying.

She was holding up a used contraceptive she had found under the bed to see if there was anything in it. I don't know whether she was that innocent or just naturally mean. It wasn't mine. It wasn't even mine. It was Lang's. You remember Lang, my eldest son? He came in one night recently with a dolly and whispered to me in the kitchen. Was I thinking of going for a drive for an hour or so? It was one o'clock in the morning. I gave them my bed and slept on the floor on the other side of the screen—I've made this screen out of rose-trellis and coloured corrugated plastic sheets. They were as quiet as they could be, I suppose, but it drove me mad. Hot whispers, bumping, squeaks.

'You don't kiss like that! That's not the way to kiss!'

He's only twenty, for God's sake. He was doing his best. I was so frustrated. I've never had a girl in this room. I haven't had anybody since Diana went. She was paralysed but she liked it. She would sometimes nip underneath me when I was doing my press-ups on the caravan floor. Mostly it was for laughs but sometimes it worked.

'Don't! No! Careful!' the dolly was whispering. I'm sure she knew I was listening although occasionally for their peace of mind I snored. Girls are strangely addicted to that kind of safe voyeurism. Diana would squeal and laugh louder than was warranted sometimes so that the men in the other vans would know that she enjoyed it if only they could get there. It's not 'voyeurism'; but I know what I mean. I ought to get some new words, I'm running out of words.

Anyway, it worked on me. I got my climax before Lang did. In the morning while he was shaving in the bathroom I got the dolly's name and telephone number but never followed it up. I felt that I'd had her already.

'Couldn't you be reading my story while I finish tidying — oh, I'm sorry!' Joanna Browne had come round the screen just as I dropped my pyjama trousers. She turned as white as a sheet and went back to the cleaning.

'I tell you what I think, Joanna,' I said.

What I thought was I'd get shot of her and go to Ipswich. What with the bodyguard outside and her not drinking I preferred Edna. I didn't put it in so many words and I had to explain what it was about. She was instantly interested and avid for the small details.

'I think that's fantastic,' she said. She almost came back behind the screen but then sat on the end of the bed with her back to me. 'But surely her family — (Edna's, she meant) — must have seen the divorce in the papers. 'Oh no!' she exclaimed. 'There wasn't any divorce — you weren't actually married, were you? You missed the service and got there in time for the reception. Didn't everybody know?'

Why should they? You get enough ribbon on the car and you're married. You don't even have to go to church.

Joanna laughed. You won't believe this but she was peeking at me in the mirror. 'You're always late for everything, aren't you, Horace?'

I think that was the first time she used my name. Drink or no she was getting friendly.

'It saved my life,' I told her.

And I told, her how I'd missed the second world war through getting to the labour exchange ten seconds too late to register. I don't know whether you know this. The D's, E's and F's had to register between nine and six and I got there just as the man was locking the door.

'Can I come back tomorrow?' I asked him. I'd ridden two miles on a bicycle.

'No,' he said. 'It's G's and H's tomorrow — I's and J's the day after. No more F's, sir.'

And I never heard any more about it. All the chaps from the radio factory who'd got there on time were killed.

'Do you mind if I make a note of that,' she said, when she'd stopped laughing. And then I saw the reason she'd been sitting on the bed with her back to me was that she was making notes in a little red book. Writers who have to make notes will never be writers. They'll be just writers in little red notebooks.

Then she suggested that I let George drive us all to Ipswich in the Bentley; she was angling to meet Edna and her brother and the blackcurrants. She was after material.

'We could work on the way,' she said, unconvincingly.

A number of unnerving things began to happen on this day. I didn't recognise them for what they were, part of a sinister pattern, until several had happened and I saw the earlier ones in retrospect — and remembered what Ruth Baxter had said about the mysterious telephone calls. I had one then, while I was putting on my wine shirt with the knitted gold tie (incidentally, I have to use a good deal more of this detail, my publisher says; and connoisseur things about drink and so forth — for instance we had been drinking *Typhoo* tea).

'It's for you, Horace,' Joanna Browne said, handing me the phone. We were on our way out.

When I put the receiver to my ear there was just the dialling tone.

'He must have hung up,' she said.

I didn't get goose pimples till we were out in Squires Mount getting into the Bentley. Then I saw this man sitting on the edge of a manhole, his feet dangling inside, wearing large black sunglasses and holding a telephone in his hand; the cable came from inside the manhole.

When we drove away I was still looking back at him from the rear window and he was staring after the car. I often see things like this in the third person.

'What did he say?' I asked her.

'Who?'

'The man on the phone?'

'He said is Mr Horace Spurgeon Fenton there, please.'

'Did he have a foreign accent?'

'Yes.'

'Sort of Mexican? 'Ees mistair Horass Spurgeeon Fenton —' sort of thing?'

'Yes. Why? Do you know him?'

It had to be Albert Harris. But Albert Harris was dead.
'No,' I told her.
A Boeing 707 flew over my grave.

Three

Albert was killed in an air crash. The AK-Edgar disaster. There were three millionaires aboard. It was a Global Films flight to Venice film festival. The headlines said:

ALBERT HARRIS DEAD

He would have liked that.

I wrote an obit for the *Sunday Times* (From Milkman to Millionaire) and as a result got commissioned for a full biography. His mother stopped it going through. Does anybody remember Albert's mother?

'Ah don't think you're the right person to do it, Horace,' she told me, after the butler had taken the whisky away. She had married Sir Ambrose Argyle the chairman of Albert's film company who also died in the crash. Then she told me something I'd only suspected before. 'Ah don't like your writing. Ah never did so. It's too personal.' She rushed on, getting angry the way Cedric does (Cedric's shacked up with Tres!): 'You don't write proper books with heroes and heroines. Just a lot of gabbling gossip about your friends.'

I don't know who wrote it in the end but reading it you'd think that Albert Harris was one of the world's great benefactors. One line I remember and prize:

'Wherever Albert saw evil, he stamped on it.'

He rolled in it.

The last thing Albert had done for me was get me crucified on a tree overlooking the Stevenage by-pass.

It had been a rotten day altogether. Everything had gone wrong on the milk round, dropped bottles, broken eggs and the float battery going flat halfway up Mardley Hill. It was because of this that I had cut through the woods to the caravan site and found Diana naked on her back on the caravan floor with Trotsky kneeling over her. You would swear that he was rapidly doing up his trousers but in fact he was transferring *plana* from his hands into her nervous system. Trotsky (Gordon, not Leon) made a living — and, I believe, made several of the caravan wives—by curing their complaints with his faith-healing. He was a short, strong man, with scrubbing brush hair and a black moustache like a lion tamer.

I moved my leg!' Diana cried. 'Horace: I moved my leg!'

'I thought you were coming at two o'clock this afternoon?' I said to Trotsky.

'That's typical of you,' Diana said. 'I move my right leg two inches off the ground and you worry about the time.'

It wasn't the time I was worried about. You think you know your friends, but *do* you?

Albert came in that same night.

We, Diana and myself and the neighbours, were sitting staring at each other across the rain-sodden site. There's nowhere else to stare. When you sit down with your back against one wall your feet are pressing against the other. Wherever you look you're looking outside. There is no inside.

When Albert banged the window my head was resting against I nearly shot through the roof.

'What are you up to?' he said when he came in.

You may as well ask a rabbit in a hutch what it's up to. He didn't want to know, anyway.

'D'you mind if I have a slash?' he asked as I was putting the kettle on the calor-gas ring.

It was just about dark enough to piss on the tow-bar of the van without being seen. It was nice standing there doing it together; it was like old times. Except in those days, you remember, the caravan had belonged to him and he was the milkman, living there with his mother. Now when his fly zipped there was the flash of gold cuff links.

31

'This is great, Horace,' he said, comfortably. And: 'I see you've given the old van a coat of paint,' he said, as his water washed away the dirt. And then he said — and it was the first thing he'd said that he'd come here to say: 'Have you heard anything from Norman Freville?'

'I thought he was still in prison?'

'No, he's not,' Albert said grimly.

The point being that he had not driven thirty miles from London and walked up through the wet wood just to pee with me on the tow-bar. What he said next confirmed this and frightened me.

'Have you noticed any strangers around here lately?'

I told him everybody is strangers. I'm nearly a hundred years old now and I don't know more than three people by sight.

'Now I'll tell you why I left my car with Buggsy on the by-pass — I was followed.'

I caught my foreskin in my zip and cursed.

Albert held me back from the van for a moment. 'You don't have to tell Diana this, but Freville says he is going to nail you to a tree when he finds you.'

'Oh?'

He reached deep into his inside pocket and brought out some visiting cards. Most people have just one.

'Now look. You can get me at any of these numbers night or day. Especially this one in Ireland — I'm having a yacht built at Belfast.'

That was going to be a great help in an emergency.

He said, and it cost him blood: 'You see I feel it's partly my fault. I let him read the typescript of your last novel.'

I know what it means now when your spine freezes. I'd lent Albert a copy before changing all the names and bending facts so people wouldn't recognise themselves.

'Well, it slipped my mind,' Albert admitted. 'There he was in Parkhurst prison with nothing to read. I was the only one visiting him.'

'You were the only one who put him there,' I said.

He'd fed Norman, knowing how hot-blooded he was, false information about me and Norman's girl friend Countess Jane Chapell. It was the shooting that followed that put Norman's business into Albert's hands (Sir Ambrose into his mother's hands and ad inf). It had all been carefully calculated.

'Well, don't worry,' Albert said. 'If he does anything like that to you, he'll go into an asylum this time.'

Once again it was part of a business schedule.

Norman's Wardour Street boxers came up through the woods a few hours later and took me away, nailed me to a sycamore. You notice this verbal style I've developed? It's because I'm dictating into a machine. I can't type yet; I've got holes in my hands. Hanging there, I counted one hundred and twenty-three cars pass before one had the decency to stop. It was in all the papers and I daresay you saw it. I sometimes suspect it was Albert's way of publicising his latest film and getting Norman out of the way again — this time for good.

Norman was lying on a purple couch in his padded cell when I visited him, taking him a ripe honeydew melon and some peppermint creams.

'I've got a great idea for a movie,' he said. He told me I could write the treatment and script if I would help him to escape. He didn't seem to remember anything about having me crucified on the by-pass but had some kind of time-slip and kept asking after the Countess Jane and asking me to pass information to her and get her to do things in the way of setting up the new production.

'Tell her to try for offices in Berkeley Square,' he said. 'The dustbins all stink in Soho.'

The hilarious thing about this was that he got the great idea for the movie from me. You know that thing that film people do, listening deadpan to your ideas, ignoring them or dismissing them, then unashamedly trotting them out as their own five minutes later? Well, insanity seems to make it worse. Even when he said 'Good morning' he said it as though he'd said it first.

I'd said it first.

You will have realised by this time that this is not a novel — it's my second nonfiction. I'd been looking hard for an idea after getting my freedom; that is after Diana had got hers and gone off with Trotsky and the dog. The little legacy we received on Albert's death enabled me to get this room in East Heath Road and would have covered my writing a book — if only I could get the right idea. Then, visiting Norman and Cell Barnes, I got the idea and the title in one go. *One Last Mad Embrace*—how do you like it? It's about this lunatic who escapes and remains free for the required six months necessary to prove his sanity. Then at the very end just as everybody's breathing a sigh of relief because he's free and hasn't broken any laws — he commits the nastiest sex murder.

'That's a great theme,' my agent said. 'We'll sell the film rights for a bomb.'

And I told it to four hundred people at the *Yorkshire Post* literary luncheon at Harrogate Arts Festival and they all thought it was terrific. But of course you can't write the things that everybody thinks are terrific.

Anyway I trotted out this idea to Norman on an early visit and he ignored it; then a couple of Sundays later he trotted it back to me.

'You realise that if I can get out of here and stay out for six months without blotting my copy-book,' he told me, 'then I'll be a free man. I should have to be re-certified. That wouldn't happen if I lead a responsible life.'

'Oh?' I said; as though it was news. Frank Mitchell the mad axeman (later murdered) tried to do it when he first escaped from Rampton — remember his letters to the papers? Then driving past Fulbourn asylum with Diana one afternoon we saw a middle-aged mum in a nightie and carrying a shopping basket racing along the grass verge followed by twenty or thirty doctors and nurses and staff — I saw her face as she passed quite closely and it upset me. It was as if she had got fed up with all the white coats and restrictions and drugs and visits and had suddenly decided to buzz off to Tesco's for some shopping. Well, this and my sister Christine who kept kidnapping my autistic daughter Diana (the other Diana) from a mental home and now Norman's predicament had all at last clicked into a book in my head — which really is the way books happen. If you only knew it you'd find that some of the world's most famous books had to knock at the writer's head for years before he got the message.

'If I could get out of here,' Norman said then, 'you could hide me out up at the caravan. We could spend the six months writing the movie.'

His purple couch was bigger than our caravan. He had no idea how little we possessed at that time. I was driving the milk float to the hospital to save bus fare, hiding my white coat before I went in, giving him the week's special offer as though it was a thoughtful present. This week it was melon and peppermints — another week it was a chocolate swiss roll and a give-away pastry board.

'Where's Albert now?' Norman asked me as if the thought of freedom had reminded him of the thought of opportunity; I think he had quickly realised that he had had the wrong man nailed to the tree.

'Doing the film festivals,' I told him. It had been in the papers; the Global board with their new aircraft AK-Edgar buzzing off with a bunch of pretty starlets all over the world — Rio, Belgrade, Acapulco, Rome. I didn't say too much about it because I didn't want to rub it in; they got what was rightfully his. Nothing unusual about that in the film world; some go up and some like Norman and poor Arturo Conti fall by the wayside.

'One of these days,' Norman Freville now said, 'it would be nice to see them off, old boy.'

Remember that, will you? I always shall; Norman lying there on his back on the purple couch, his hands clasped on his belly, his face filled with plans.

Because a few months later Norman was free and Global were in the drink. But was Albert in the drink? I realised more and more — before the messages and phoney voices — that I had never deeply believed in Albert's death; that Albert, being

Albert, was unlikely to catch a plane that was going to blow up or crash.

It's a peaceful thing, looking at a garden, hoeing the soil between the beets and the spinach, breaking off the asparagus fern and smelling your fingers; undraping the butter-muslin from the currant bushes and nipping off the little fruity sprays.

'You'm got a nice old lot of berries there, mother-in-law.' That was me. That was me talking! That accent is not difficult: losing it is difficult.

We see so little of her that she thought Joanna Browne was our eldest daughter Lang and when she'd finished hugging her and kissing her and telling her off about her disgusting skirt, she said:

'My goodness how youm growed, m'dear. An't she growed, 'Orry? Time you was wedded with childer. Make your ol' dad a granpa — tame 'im down a morsel!'

Joanna took it all in good part, promised to write more often and lengthen her skirts. Edna struck a sour note by admitting to her mother that she was pregnant again.

'How disgusting,' I said. 'You're fifty-one!'

'I'm not fifty-one,' she said. 'You're fifty-one. I'm only in my forties.'

'That's a lie. You went to the Wembley exhibition when you were nine years old in 1926.'

'No no, that were her sister Katie,' said her mother.

I didn't know Edna had a sister Katie. Anyway it was splitting hairs. The idea of old people making love is sickening. You wouldn't think Mr Fortin could produce enough semen to stick a stamp on a letter.

'You've got a thing about your age, haven't you?' Joanna asked me on the way home. We had dropped Edna off in Welwyn Garden City.

I haven't got a thing about age. When you're dead, that's as old as you get. I am now twenty-two years older than my father. The Get-Ready man is calling me, this I know; and old

Sloughfoot has picked up my scent. A small wind is rustling the snottygobble tree that grows in my graveyard.

And when I got back to my pad I found that somebody had put the black spot on me.

Joanna had gone straight home, no doubt to get her notes woven into the next chapter while they were still hot. Wendy was flapping around the flat in her blue afternoon nightie and I called her in.

'Did you do this?'

It was a black ink spot about as big as a halfpenny on a clean sheet of paper turned well up for easy viewing in the typewriter roller.

'I wouldn't come into your room,' she said.

I didn't know quite which way to take that.

'Have you got any friends in?' I asked her.

Friends? Freaks, layabouts and *yeti* masquerading under human names like John and Ronald would turn up to sponge on or impregnate these provincial girls at rituals called parties. I would find bodies in sleeping bags outside my door in the hall and strange bearded dwarfs padding around the kitchen sneaking bacon in the mornings.

The Hampstead police were always dashing in and whipping them off. We had two dragged out of a locked bathroom during the Regent's Park Hippy Murder Hunt, three drug raids, several arrested for house-breaking (also sometimes called *parties*) and one for bigamy.

'Fancy Percy married!' Patricia, the junior nurse, said. 'Rotten bloody shitting swine!'

The neighbours once got up a petition to have us evicted. That's nice, isn't it, when your name is cropping up in the *Radio* and *TV Times* every other week and there's three of your books in the local public library.

The trouble is we are the only tenement-type house in this little area; the other houses have whole families living in them which is a little old-fashioned perhaps but nice. Nice to look in the windows when the lights are on.

A lot of 'old Hampstead' and 'preservation' type thinking goes on and there are blue and white and brown dead-celebrity plaques stuck up everywhere. Keats, Sir Gerald Du Maurier, Constable, Kathleen Mansfield and Others lived here during, I am sure, their more riotous years; in that respect our house is closer in spirit to the rollicking roots of the place than is the family ménage: Hampstead has always belonged to the people who are still kicking it around.

Nearly everybody I meet in television has lived in Hampstead, but never when they were fifty-one. Walking to and from my car in Squires Mount I feel like a suspect. Some of the Hampstead wives give me little half-smiles of the guarded kind they can withdraw or re-direct at a puppy if I take it up; this is very twitchy because you find yourself doing the same thing back at them. Some play it really safe and ignore me, even when we are struggling back up Christ Church Hill with similar loads of shopping. And some, which is worst of all, talk to me with an air of bravado, hoping the neighbours are watching and marking their liberality (I know what it's like to be black).

'You live in the brothel, don't you?' Mrs Martin once told me. She's the pretty one next door.

'There's been a man here,' Wendy told me now. 'I think he's a detective.'

'Did he come in here?'

'Nobody's been in here,' she said. 'Only that girl.'

I detected at this stage, this late stage, that Wendy was in a mood because I had a girl in. The nurses had never shown the slightest interest in me; not girl interest

'He's coming back tonight,' Wendy said.

'You look sexy,' I told her, to try and lighten the mood.

'Oh yes!' she said.

She went out like a bitchy wife. Apparently, and this was news to me, I belonged to the nurses; or at least to the flat.

I didn't see the detective that night, but I think I might have heard him; if they were his footsteps padding me down to The Wells and back. By day they call it Happy Hampstead but at night it's not safe to walk the dog. In the four years I've been here there've been murder, ritual suicide, black mass and folk music. In the warm afternoons a lot of exposure goes on in front of young mothers and children who come long distances and there are borderline perverts torn between being sex and chess maniacs, very often of respectable age and appearance. At one time there was a Dormobile full of peeping toms organised as a kind of tourist facility by men who knew all the right windows and times. I once found ten cigarette butts on my front windowsill, several of them stained with lipstick. I didn't know until he suddenly came in that Norman Freville was watching the house for a long period and living rough over by Kenwood—this is while he was working at the zoo in Regent's Park.

Live accurately, William Saroyan says. By this he means write accurately, too; because with good luck and hard work it becomes the same thing. Correcting your mistakes is not accuracy; preserving them is. In fiction there is a tendency to make everything happen quite quickly and to follow a dramatically interesting shape, perhaps towards a climax. Real life doesn't have any kind of shape or if it has you forget what it was. I'm trying to confess that I've forgotten what happens next: Detective-Superintendent Jamie Kinnear, Norman Freville or Ariadne.

Lucky associations jog the memory better than anything else and I remember that the discovery that I was being investigated as part of the AK-Edgar crash inquiry came on another wet Sunday. Flood reports were coming in like news of an invasion. In the middle of it my sister Christine telephoned to tell me that she had kidnapped my daughter—remember Diana the monster?—from a lunatic asylum and was stuck in the heart of Essex with no transport and the police after her.

'Where are you?'

'I think the sixpence is going.'

The pips went, there was a background of swishing rain and a child's voice, oddly harsh and a little common, shouting something. I heard the word 'bugger' repeated. Just before we were cut off by the machine I got her location; a telephone box in the High Street of Marks Tey. It was a fifty or sixty miles drive eastwards along Eastern Avenue and the A12 which in one way I welcomed and in another I didn't. Anything was better than struggling to bring Joanna's Unmarried Mother story to life—she had left it with me and I was battling with the first act.

But I didn't relish meeting Diana.

'Are you my daddy?' she asked me when I picked them up in the Capri. There's little room in the rear seat and she was squashed against the gear lever between me and Christine.

'She's so much better,' my sister was saying. 'I couldn't leave her in that place.'

'They pull my hair,' Diana said.

It was a sort of dry-mouthed shout. She couldn't stop shouting. Shouting and being obsessive and repetitious.

'Are you my daddy?'

'Yes,' I said.

'Are you my daddy?'

'Yes, this is your daddy,' Christine said.

'Don't *you* answer !' Diana snapped. 'You're a fucking bleeder.' She turned to me: 'Are you my daddy?'

'Yes,' I said.

'You don't look like my daddy,' she said. 'Where do you live?'

'London,' I told her.

'My daddy lives at the seaside,' she shouted.

I told her that I'd moved.

'Are you really my daddy?' she shouted.

'Yes,' I said.

She said: 'You've been altered.'

You can't improve on that kind of dialogue—children or lunatics. The police were waiting at Christine's house.

'Hello, Diana love,' the sergeant said. 'Coming for a nice ride?'

'Are you my daddy?' Diana asked him as he carried her out to the car.

Christine made me some tea without crying. 'She sang "Lily the Pink" all the way on the bus.'

I said: 'She didn't know me.'

Christine said: 'How many times has she seen you?'

Then she said what she's been saying for years; Diana has never been certified. A letter from me or from Tres, and Christine could have her.

Diana is a full time job for three women working eight-hour shifts. My sister is five feet one and weighs seven and a half stone. And although she looks young and pretty, still climbs trees after stuck kites, she is fifty-five years old.

'I'll tell you what I'll do,' I said. 'I'll think about it.'

Jamie was waiting in my room when I got back. Detective Superintendent Jamie Kinnear; he told me his first name in the hope that I might use it. He called me Mr Spurrajon, having somehow lost my surname as some people do.

'Ye'll not mind me making meself at hame?' he said, and things like that.

I don't propose to go into a long question and answer thing here. After all these months the Air Ministry official inquiry into the AK-Edgar disaster had just reached the stage where they knew it had been sabotaged. Everybody connected with the list of victims, as beneficiary or not, was therefore under surveillance. It explained some of the creepy feelings I had had lately. Including the one that Albert may still be alive.

'Tell me, Mr Spurrajon, ye're a personal friend of Lady Argyle, are ye not?'

I told him I was not and explained why; the obituary unpleasantness, her general antagonism. She had always blamed me for the way Albert had turned out at the beginning and took credit for the success he'd made in the end.

'She doesn't like me,' I summed it up.

'I find that verra verra difficult to accept,' he said.

I began to like him. I'm not much good at describing people but if we ever make the movie the part should go to Fyfe Robertson, the popular TV Scot. Twenty years ago Alastair Sim would have got it.

'Would it surprise you to know that Lady Argyle has been receiving mysterious telephone calls?' he now asked.

Why shouldn't it surprise me?

'Ye've been having the same trouble yourself, I understand?' he then said.

'Yes. How do you know?'

He smiled a slow, Scots smile and said: 'Wee dugs hae big lugs!'

It was his belief that all the calls were being made by one and the same person, that the person was named on the list of victims of the air disaster, that the death of the directors of Global had enabled a fraud involving several million pounds to be perpetrated, that all the evidence pointed to one man and that that man was now trying to establish contact with a friend or relation as discreetly as possible in order to cash in on his crimes.

'Can you guess who that person might be, Mr Spurrajon?'

I had no idea.

Jamie said: 'The documentary evidence proves beyond all doubt that it is Sir Ambrose Argyle himself!'

This proved beyond all doubt to me that it was Albert. If there's one thing Albert's good at it's documentary evidence.

'Now I would like you to tell me who sent these,' Jamie said.

They had been interfering with my mail, hoping to find a letter in code from Sir Ambrose Argyle; as I'd never met him it was most unlikely. There was a coloured postcard from Paris showing the Eiffel Tower; and on the reverse side, scrawled in pencil: 'What an erection!' It was signed 'Arthur' and had come from the chap in the flat above who was now on holiday.

'And this one?'

This one was more obscure and less obscene. It was also a postcard, a grey-looking view of a graveyard with a stone monument in foreground. 'The monument to Flora MacDonald at Kilmuir on the Isle of Skye,' said the inscription. On the message side was: 'See you soon. Don't be late. Love: Angela.'

Jamie said: 'Who's Angela?'

I didn't know.

'But it sounds as if you've got a date?' he said.

'It does, doesn't it.'

I still didn't know. There's old Angie, of course, but that was years ago and she's married. I had visited her once since but got no farther than the kitchen table—this is the nature stain on my blue trousers. Could be one of the girls downstairs—there are six more girls downstairs on Mrs Bracknell's floor. But I hadn't got a date with anybody.

So far as I knew.

'Think about it,' Jamie urged. 'Ask around, as a favour to me. You're a writer—use your imagination. Study the card, think of the implications—Flora MacDonald was Bonnie Prince Charlie's mistress. Does that mean anything?'

I concentrated on the postcard in a hopeless kind of way.

'There is one remarkable thing about this card,' the Superintendent said then. 'Of all the people who must have handled it since it was printed, there's not one fingerprint on it. Not even the postman's.'

'I see,' I said.

I wonder if you can work that out?

Ariadne did, and she's only twelve.

The dream and the substance begin to overlap a little now.

The telephone rings at four o'clock in the morning and nobody answers it. It rings any reasonable hour and everybody rushes into the hall no matter what they're doing or how they're dressed. 'Are you Miss Baker?' you ask the girl you've been calling 'darling' or 'love' for the past six months. You seldom get to know surnames in a shared flat.

'Swiss Cottage double-six-o-six?'

It was a beautiful girl's voice. I don't know how you can tell but you always can.

'Yes. Horace Spurgeon Fenton. Who's that?'

'I knew you'd say that,' she said; there was a chuckle in her voice. Then: 'I'm glad you're awake, Horace. I couldn't sleep, either.'

This slightly insane assumption should have given me a clue, but it didn't.

'Horace, I've got to apologise to you,' she said then.

'You don't have to do that.' I thought she was apologising for ringing me at four o'clock in the morning; but it was something in our past. This made it too late to ask who she was.

'I'm sorry I swore at you,' she said, softly.

This means it could be one or two million people. Let's try to narrow it down a little.

'It was my fault, darling.'

There was a pause, then she said, rather breathlessly: 'Oh no. You were really sweet. That's really why I had to ring you. I've been thinking about you. Ever since. I nearly rang you last night.'

A soft, intimate thing had come into her voice since I called her darling. It had suddenly become like a four o'clock in the morning conspiracy. There was love, tenderness, excitement there; and trust and friendship, too. She could have been curled up inside my ear.

'Are you in bed?' I told her where I was and she said in a tiny, fading voice: 'I'm in bed . . .'

She said something else which I didn't catch. 'I can't hear you,' I said.

And she said a rather horrifying thing then; she said: 'I can't speak very loudly, Horace. 'I've got the receiver under the blankets with me...'

Jesus. Couldn't you just see her husband jerking out of his sleep at that point; listening without letting her know?

'Horace?' she said.

It wasn't romantic any more.

'Have you been thinking about me?' she whispered.

'You know I have.'

There was a long moment before she said: 'I'm glad. I think I can sleep now.'

'Goodnight, then.'

'Horace?' I was just too late hanging up. She said: 'Can I telephone you again?'

'Do you think it's wise?' I can't stand the way some people stand marriage. This casual infidelity.

She said, softly, sadly: 'Do we always have to be wise, Horace?'

Just from that I could tell: if it wasn't me it would be somebody else. And at least I have some respect for marriage. This girl needed guidance. The way she was she could fall into anybody's hands. There are two things I like to know before embarking on that kind of desperate adventure. Is her husband jealous and has he got a gun. Remember Norman Freville?

'I don't want to get shot,' I told her.

'They're too busy with rehearsals to worry what I'm doing,' she said, bitterly.

This was a clue. 'What rehearsals?'

'The UM-pilot,' she said. 'What else?'

And then the penny dropped. This has happened to me before. I don't know whether I mislead people, sometimes. There was this electro-chemical engineer who came to work for me during the war when I was in charge of the industrial automation department. He was a BA and God knows what, but I just used him for blowing glass-electrode membranes. Then one day his wife turned up at the laboratory and was introduced all round. All I did was shake her hand, like everybody else, yet after she'd gone I found a note pinned to my bicycle saddle out in the rack.

'Gorgeous,' it said. 'Isn't it thrilling how we know right from the first meeting that nothing will ever be the same again. Will you meet me out of flower-arrangement classes at the tech, eight o'clock Tuesday night? Love: Margaret.'

I was astonished.

I don't remember even meeting her eyes when she was in the laboratory. I might just possibly have kept hold of her hand fractionally longer than the polite period; this is the norm for all women under twenty-four who are reasonable. She took me on the golf course and she brought a basket as though for a picnic; it contained two bottles of Guinness, ham sandwiches and a packet of contraceptives.

The whole thing sickened me with its lack of romance. Nothing the same again? I should think it was the same every time. She had been working at an American Air Force base while her husband took his finals and it must have coarsened her.

'Don't keep taking it out,' she said. 'Let it pickle.'

In the same way this familiar, tempting, intimate voice on the telephone at four o'clock in the morning was obviously one of the wives I met at Joan Scattergood's UM party. I still couldn't place her but did it matter? Her husband lying there in the same bed? Very poetic. Working all day on rehearsals, tired out—what rehearsals? It suddenly struck me they hadn't got a script yet.

'Whose script are they rehearsing?' I asked her.

'Oh!' she said. 'You made me jump!'

'They haven't got a pilot script yet,' I said.

'Yes they have. It's crap. Mac McKilvey wrote it months ago—do you think he's a good writer?'

'He's a bloody con man,' I said.

'Ssssh!' somebody said near at hand. The door across the landing was partly open and three of the nurses were grouped there. 'Who's that?' Wendy whispered.

I don't know,' I said. I was so angry. The first episode in the series scoops all the press reviews. Those BBC rats; I should worry about her husband. 'Why don't you drop by sometime?' I asked her.

'Can I? Can I really, Horace?' she said. 'Like tomorrow?'

It was tomorrow today.

'Like Thursday,' I said.

'Is it all right in the morning?' she said.

'With you,' I said, 'it's all right anytime, baby.'

'What?' she said. Then she said: 'Horace—are you drunk?'

'Can you make it?' I said. 'Or are you backing out?'

'I'll make it,' she said. 'I'll tell Mummy I'm going to school.'

Four

I got a message from beyond the grave. I'm not a Christian but what the hell; you don't have to belong to the AA to use their road services.

The message came from a dead dog and was given to me by Mrs Bracknell, our landlady here. She came in to empty the telephone box while I was making some black coffee for Wendy. It was about eleven o'clock and I had just got up to find Wendy crying over the gas stove; she had a cushion in position to kill herself but hadn't the courage to turn it on. She was pregnant again. Women and pregnancy is like the municipal services and the floods; it's always happening yet they're always taken by surprise.

'Have you had a communication from a foreign place?' Mrs Bracknell asked me. I remembered the two postcards and she said: 'Well, one of them bears a message of great significance. Make the right decision about it because it may be a matter of life and death.'

'There could be something in it, Horace,' Wendy said when the old girl had gone. 'You'd better look at them again.'

'I don't know any dead dogs,' I told her.

The 'What An Erection' card made Wendy laugh, which was something; the other one of the Flora MacDonald monument on Skye had her puzzled. She didn't know any Angelas and neither, to her knowledge, did the other nurses.

'We had a girl named Angela on the kidney machine— you met her. But she wouldn't go to a place like Skye. She has to have her blood scrubbed three times a week.'

They had a party here one night and the guests were all kidney machine patients. Can you imagine that? They were all dying and yet from the merriment, noise, dancing and snogging on the stairs that went on you would think they were hippies. Three times a week they go along and have their wrists opened up, by-pass their blood through some kind of dry-cleaning process. And Wendy gets suicidal about having too much life inside her? If only I could write drama. Put a party like that on the West-end stage and it would run for yonks.

A number of things happened while I was waiting for my young visitor on Thursday morning. The most important came out of the fact that I decided to cover the bed in sheets of manuscript, make the place look as much like an office and little like a bedroom as possible.

To do this I ransacked drawers that had not been ransacked before; tipped out boxes and untied blankets which had been filled even before the caravan days. And there in front of me on the bed I came across a batch of tear-sheets of old short stories I had published in everything from *Britannia and Eve* to *John Bull*. I should worry about cooking up new plots for UM? I got on the phone to Mac McKilvey and he asked me to take them to the rehearsals at St. Luke's School, North Finchley, which I did.

The little old Victorian school was in a side-street off Finchley High Road. According to the plaque it was built in 1850 roughly eighty years before Baird transmitted his first radio picture. It always strikes me as odd to find all the rehearsal paraphernalia of television in these croft-like ancient places built before *Gone With The Wind* source material had started happening, before Bertrand Russell was born. It is always raining on these places.

'Leave them with me. I'll read them. You want to watch the rehearsal?' Mac said.

Shabby men and women in raincoats, reach-me-downs, sports coats, hair-scarves sit around the room, bored, hard-up, worrying about their laundry; this is the cast, these are the actors and actresses whose names will roll up on your screen, who will become policemen, lovers, gangsters, magistrates, according to their part in the script. The director is doing something called 'blocking out'; this chalk line is a door, this one a desk, this one the front entrance of the Hilton Hotel. They are murmuring together, the two or three cast involved in the first bit of action. There is a terrible Monday morning type boredom and ennui and angst in the room. You would never know their agents have fought for these parts.

'Is this a joke?' an actor says.

'I think so,' the director says. 'I'm not sure. Say it with a sort of half-smile …'

'Horace!' a voice whispered; it was Joanna Browne. She sat beside me in the child's desk, her big knees and thighs practically in my mouth. She grimaced a smile; I don't know why people think this quieter than an ordinary smile. 'Have you done it?' she hissed.

'Sssh!' I said. If you haven't done something always say 'Sssh!'

Nearby Joan Scattergood was instructing the art director about one of the sets though her mind was on the bathroom that was going to be turned into a kitchen (this furniture was her perks).

'Big white cupboard, terribly terribly modern, roughly five feet eight and a half inches long,' she said.

'Don't forget the camera has to come through in one shot,' he said.

'Oh God!' she said. 'That'll ruin it! Can't we change the scene?'

'Can we have some bloody hush?' the director shouted.

Everybody froze; Joan Scattergood bit her tongue and then held it. It was bleeding.

'Now watch him go into his prima-donna act for the brass,' somebody whispered. It was Mac and he indicated who had just come in. Don't ask me who it was; probably the Director General. 'Now find a hole in the script,' Mac McKilvey urged.

'Mac!' the play director shouted. Then, seeing him: 'Mac— have a look at this line, for God's sake.'

Mac went over with knives in his smile.

'Couldn't we adjust it later?' Joan called, nervously; then smiling at the executive: 'It's going beautifully. There's some beautiful white furniture going into this set, isn't there, Archy? Archy's doing a wonderful—'

'Shut up a minute!' shouted the play director.

He was normally a very mild little man who probably got hung up on Orson Welles while he was still at art school.

'Now this line on page twelve, act two,' he was saying to Mac. 'Georgina doesn't know how to treat it. Is this boy's mother heartbroken or isn't she? Her son has just been picked up for stealing a car—right? Then why when she gets the news does she say: "One son and he has to be a lunatic!"?'

The actress, who like the others in the scene had dropped back, deferentially, as they do when the script is being discussed, now summoned the personality to say: 'I wouldn't say that about him if I were heartbroken, would I?'

Mac said: 'What do you usually say when you're heartbroken then?'

The director detected Mac's mood a shade too late: 'I tell you what—get the writer in tomorrow and—'

'I wrote it,' Mac said.

The whole room was listening breathlessly now. With any luck there was going to be a row to jolly things up.

Mac said: 'What's wrong with that line?'

The director said: 'It's probably just the emphasis—'

'Don't talk like a fart,' Mac said. 'This woman thinks her son is a fucking lunatic for stealing that car.' And to the shocked actress he said: 'Listen, Gina, I don't know why they cast you but I don't want another of your broken-hearted house-flannels wrung out all over my play.' And to the director: 'Does that answer it?'

'That's fine,' the director said. 'That's marvellous. Okay, Gina?'

Mac came back and the rehearsal murmured on. I asked him what the play had to do with the unmarried mother and he said the woman's son had stolen the car to impress Dinah whom he had fallen in love with. Then the mother finds out about the illegitimate child and puts a stop to it.

'It's not as good as yours, Horace,' he conceded. 'Yours will be the first on the screen,' he added, pulling our relationship out of the grave as an afterthought.

'Dinah!' the director called.

'That's better,' Mac said. 'He should have tackled a woman the first time.'

'Not here yet, Walter,' Joan Scattergood called, anxiously.

There followed an embarrassing exhibition. The fight for status and esteem, the struggle to get noticed by the critics or given a film to direct, takes this backstage form simply because there is no other way. The chance of turning a brilliant script into a brilliant play is practically nil except by accident. A film director works on the floor, interprets the script to the actors, the actors to the camera-lighting man and the negative to the editor. The TV director is only concerned ultimately with split second timing; a good play often gets in the way of this. On the night of the recording he sits in front of a hundred knobs, six clocks, a dozen monitor screens with his crew around him, the inter-com crackling as though about to drop a bomb from twenty-thousand feet onto a Nissen hut.

'Somebody laughed,' one of them said to me one night in a panic. 'Is this supposed to be funny, Horace?'

'Yes, it's all right,' I said.

'You've over-shot on Camera 3!' a girl screamed.

'Oh Christ! Run it again. No laughing! Watch it!'

Up comes the clock again: Five, four, three, two, one—

It's all technique and no talent. Armed with the same book of instructions as everybody else the only thing they can do to compete is this:

'Not here?' the director said, gently, to Joan. 'Do you mean Miss Thing has not honoured us with an appearance yet, Joan?'

'She rang through, Walter. She's got some domestic trouble…'

'And *yesterday* when she was a half-hour late and then forgot her script and at the *read*-through when she didn't turn up till lunch-time and we had to do it again—' And then he did this very neat thing which he must have practised of turning scarlet and throwing a piece of chalk at the blackboard and screaming: '*Bloody film stars*! Why can't we have an ordinary hard-working actress? What am I supposed to do without the leading character?' And he stood and trembled.

It was quite good, I give him that.

Even Mac was impressed and I heard the executive say to Joan: 'What's his name?'

'Walter Mayhew,' Joan said, not without pride.

You see, it works. Ten top-of-the-charts Wednesday plays wouldn't have got his name across to the Director General with quite the same lasting effect. This is not his real name, of course. At least, I hope it's not; I've forgotten what it was.

I've been sued twice and cautioned several times for using names I didn't remember were real; but christen everybody Smith, Brown or Jones and you are heading for stereotypes. Even car numbers can get you into serious trouble—

'What sort of domestic trouble?' I asked Joan.

I had forgotten all about Ariadne until that moment. I had come out and locked up my room so that she couldn't get in even if she arrived. When the realities start impinging on your dreams and fantasies, when you know your own weaknesses, then you can't afford to take chances. I didn't want Dinah Thing ever to accuse me of enticement.

'Her daughter's run away from home,' Joanna Browne replied instead of Joan who was trying to shut her up. 'Oh, I forgot,' Joanna said then. And to me: 'She doesn't want anybody to know, not even the police. Not after what happened before—'

'Joanna!' Joan said.

'We'll go to the beginning of Act 3!' the director was calling.

'Are you all right, Horace?' Joanna asked me.

I go weak and pale quickly; I don't know whether it's artistic nerves or asthma or just that I have more reason.

'There's some coffee in the girls' lavatory,' she said.

I remember staring at the blackboard for what seemed like a very long time. There was the white splodge mark where Walter

Mayhew's histrionic chalk had struck and there was a little children's play rhyme:

> *'I am a pirate, brave and bold,*
> *I'm out for a fight and I'm out for gold!'*

Kids are nice, aren't they? This is the mood I was falling into now. For instance on the girls' lavatory wall when Joanna was making the coffee I saw more wit than you'd ever find in a TV script, even one of mine.

'Marjorie: I am going to murder you—Janie'

And underneath:

'Janie: I am going to murder you back—Marjorie.'

'Drink this,' Joanna Browne said.

I didn't have to ask her about Ariadne; she was dying to tell somebody.

'Promise not to use it because I want it,' Joanna said, which is the typical attitude of a writer to his friend's tragedies. She was more professional than I thought and rose in my estimation.

'Ariadne has popped off before. I can't say I blame her. She rebels against this professional bastard image. She was picked up in a Soho drug raid once and came up at Bow Street in need of care. It didn't hit the papers because she used another name.'

'Ariadne? She's twelve years old. A baby. She drinks orange juice.'

'Rubbish,' Joanna said. 'As long as Ariadne stays twelve years old her mother can stay twenty-nine.'

It's enough to make any child run away.

'The authorities wanted to take her away from Dinah. Don't you remember? The Cookham orgies, that girl's death, Dennis going to prison for procuring—he was Dinah's current boy friend. They only let her keep Ariadne on condition Dinah stayed put in London. That's why she went into *The Rat Trap*—you can't stay more put than that.'

I remembered vaguely; a few custody headlines came floating back, misty now as the Rector of Stiffkey and the chorus girls or the hanging of Ruth Ellis.

'How old d'you think she is, then?' I asked Joanna.

'Thirty-five. That's my guess.'

Good heavens. No wonder she gets cheesed off at being treated like a baby.'

We both thought about this for a little while, then we spoke together. People think I'm trying to be funny but I'm not. I wouldn't waste the number of gags it takes me to get through the day. She was talking about Dinah. She thought Ariadne was fourteen or fifteen.

'Not sixteen?' Sixteen would be better, the way she was talking last night. Or was it me talking that way? Come to think of it, she didn't say anything a child wouldn't say. On the other hand, I did and it didn't frighten her off. I don't know whether I was frightened or hopeful. I'm a funny age, apparently.

'Then of course there was that VNI that my play's based on,' Joanna Browne said.

'VNI?'

'Very Nasty Incident. (Keep your eye on this VNI because it's right on plot and to do with Sir Ambrose.) With that dirty old man in Canvey Island. Do you want some more sugar?'

'What kind of sugar? I mean what play?'

'The one you're writing for me. Can I come home with you and see what you've done so far?'

'Sure. What dirty old man?'

'Didn't Mac tell you?'

This was Mac. Of course it was Mac. He knew enough dirty anecdotes about people in the business to furnish storylines for a five-year series. But was he reliable?

'What happened?' I asked her.

'Ssssh!' she said as Joan Scattergood came in; creeping practically and suspicious.

'And when am I going to see your first draft?' she asked me.

'I'm just researching it,' I told her.

'Joanna, can I talk about something else?' Joan said, sitting down rather rudely with her back to me.

I went for a pee and made my last mistake on that series. The boys' lavatory wall graffiti was even funnier than the girls'. Amongst a lot of other neo-filth was something that had been either badly or reluctantly rubbed out by a master:

'Re-arrange the following well-known phrase or expression: OFF FUCK.'

I couldn't resist writing alongside it with my blue ballpoint the words: 'Full marks—10/10.' And as I was doing it the Director General or whoever he was came in. He just looked at the whole wall of filth and then at me—he thought I'd done the lot. I can't tell you what was there or how much worse it was going to sound when he'd related it a few times in the executive restaurant at The Centre and how much trouble it got me into later.

'And who's that?' I heard him ask Mac a moment later in the rehearsal room.

'Horace—come and meet Sir Edgar,' Mac called. 'Horace is one of our best writers. You may remember *The Cast Iron Shore*—it had a Royal Film Première.'

'Ah,' said the mighty one, shaking my hand and raking his distant memories of the silent film era. 'So now you're writing for the little box, eh?'

This meant now you're a has-been, on the skids, getting your kicks from scribbling on lavatory walls (did you ever read Fitzgerald's Pat Hobby stories?). Then he was turning to greet a rainbow that had just blown into the scruffy little school; Dinah Thing in all her platinum glory; you could suddenly see dust-motes churning the air like the sun beamed in.

'Hi everybody! Walter, Mac, Joan—and oh hello, Sir Edgar!'

'Did you get home all right last night?' he asked her.

Whatever the play director was going to shout at her he didn't shout it.

'We had a little dinner at the Savoy,' Sir Edgar was explaining, 'to celebrate Dinah's new series for the Corporation.' He waved in the air and snapped his fingers and a crate of champagne appeared. I wish I could do that.

'And now a little drink all round before I let you carry on with the good work …'

As he organised it Joan whispered to Dinah: 'Everything all right now?'

'Ah, shit,' Dinah said.

'Don't worry, she'll turn up, darling.'

Dinah prayed: 'Not in one of my friends' juicy divorces, I hope. I'm not kidding. She's the sexiest twelve years old monster in the world.' The telephone rang in the headmaster's office and she said: 'That's probably for me. I've rung all my friends to ring me here if she turns up anywhere.'

'It's for you, Horace,' an Asst. Stag girl said.

'Hello, Horace,' Dinah said. As I went away I heard her say: 'Was he listening?'

'Horace?' Ariadne's sweet voice on the telephone in the headmaster's office.

'Yes.'

In my back, near the open door, Mac, Joan, Joanna, Walter, the blonde assistant stage-manager, a dribble of actors and actresses, Dinah and Sir Edgar, the clink of glasses.

'Can you talk?' she said.

'No.'

Mac said: 'What's this "yes" and "no" stuff, Horace? Is this Wendy? Or Mary? He's got a fucking harem up there in Hampstead. Can I talk to her?' He came and took the receiver from me. 'Hello, chick—this is Mac. Remember?' And to me: 'She's not answering. Is it Claire?'

'It's my daughter,' I said.

'Oh,' he said. 'Sorry about that! She's hung up.'

Five

It was a long drive home. Finchley to Hampstead is not far but multiplied by two thousand times round my head and two cigarettes parked in Hampstead Way makes it far. There was a lot of thinking to do. I had to persuade Ariadne to go home and not to mention where she'd been and all without sounding too pompous. She didn't need a probation officer; I knew what she needed.

I called in the off-licence at Temple Fortune and bought a bottle of Pernod for me (for her) and lemonade for her (for me). Then I went to one of those tatty little wog-shops, the only one open, for some groceries. The black man running it frightened me to death. It always seems to me they're wearing one of those black Guy Fawkes masks with their eyes shining through at you. I want to walk round the back of it to see who's there. You feel embarrassed for them. Besides all the curry-smelling rubbish and tins of chopped fingers and Caribbean debris and rotting prawns they have these shelves of real food, though it all looks as if it's been dried out after being ruined by flood-water.

'No corn flowers, sir, only corn pads,' he said.

'Cornflour. It's a kind of powder,' I explained for ten minutes.

Do you think sometimes they're taking the mickey?

There was a police patrol car outside my pad and guess who was hovering around the entrance hall examining all the names on the bits of cardboard.

'Helloo, Mr Spurrajon!' he cried, merrily. 'By jiminy ye look like Teeny frae th' neeps!'

I told him I'd had a hard afternoon at rehearsals and I wanted my dinner.

'By the smell of it it's ready and waiting the noo,' he said, following me inside with: 'D'you mind if I come in a wee while…'

He'd been in. He'd already been in. Ariadne came breezing through from the kitchen, dressed (thank God) in tight blue levis and a long chunky sweater, her hair and the steam from the dish she was carrying spiriting together around her happy smiling face. She greeted Superintendent Kinnear like an old friend and permitted him to hold open the door to my room.

'Thank you, Jamie,' she said; and to me she said as we followed her in: 'You've had some anonymous phone calls — isn't it exciting! He's got a telegram for you.'

The superintendent was decent enough to be embarrassed as he handed me the telegram; it had been sent priority but was date-stamped several days ago.

'It's been with de-coding,' he apologised.

It looked like a code, I grant him that: REGRET TO INFORM YOU B— (my dash) PASSED AWAY LAST WEEK STOP BURIED UNDER RHUBARB STOP LOVE DIANA.

They were both waiting for an exposition, the detective's face shadowed with suspicion. I just said 'Thank you' and tucked it behind the clock; I didn't feel like discussing anything so painful as my dog's death with strangers. But then suddenly it hit me, what Mrs Bracknell had told me about the message from beyond the grave. I had to sit down and Ariadne (and I shall never forget this for it showed her real concern) quickly gave me a glass of water.

Is it bad?' she asked.

'My dog's dead,' I told her.

Her face crumpled into tears. She was twelve, there was no doubt about that; more than twelve and they don't cry over dogs. I didn't know then, but anything other than a dog dying would have left her unmoved (me dying, for instance).

'And who sent the cable?' Jamie asked me, narrowly.

Ariadne blazed round at him: 'You can't ask him questions now!' And to me she said: 'I've got some brandy in my bag.'

'I'm sorry to hear the news, of course,' Jamie said.

'Couldn't you come back tomorrow?' Ariadne asked and it wasn't a request, it was a command. This is what I've always needed, a woman to protect and cosset me; I could have kissed her in sheer gratitude. However much he had heard on our early-hours telephone line and whatever he thought our relationship was, I could see that he was beginning to respect it.

'We'll leave it th' noo. I'll be seeing myself out, dinna fass y'selves.' All that Harry Lauder stuff.

I heard the police car start up, went to the window and watched it drive away; noticed the tramp sitting on the seat on the heath across the road, one eye on the house. It was Norman Freville, the escaped film producer.

'How old was your doggy?' Ariadne was asking me.

'Just a minute, Ariadne.'

I got the Flora MacDonald postcard and sat down to examine it. That dog hadn't spoken one word to me all the five years we were together; what it had said now, through the medium, had to be important. I was aware of the girl telling me not to let the food get cold, that she was pulling the small table over to me, setting out food and serviettes, pouring wine.

'Now come on, Horace, you must eat something if I'm going to look after you,' she said. 'Tell me if you like it.'

How far could I trust her? I felt that I had to tell somebody.

As we ate I told her about the plane disaster, the suspicions of sabotage, its connection with Albert Harris and Sir Ambrose.

'I hope he's not still alive,' she said. 'He's horrible. Try the ravioli and then I'll bring the chicken in—I've fricasseed it. I think.'

I told her about the mysterious telephone calls and about the black spot and the secret intruder. She shivered:

'It's better than going to school!' she said.

'I think Albert's still alive,' I told her.

'I hope so,' she said. 'He sounds nice.'

I paid more attention to the meal and the wine while she studied the card; I was sitting in the only armchair on one side of the mock-marble table, she was on her knees on the other. It was one of the nicest, tastiest meals I've had. Where she had got the ingredients I didn't know until later.

'It's got the wrong date on it,' she said. 'Look.'

She showed me. The post-office franking across the Queen's head was dated '13th August'—it was now only the third.

'It must be a post-office mistake,' I said.

'Don't be stupid,' she said. 'Haven't you ever been round a sorting office?' Who wants to go round a sorting office? 'The date stamp for franking letters is locked and sealed into the machine. It's one of the most vital things. Otherwise all the bookies would be swindled. Dennis used to do it, I know.'

Dennis was the one who hanged himself in a Police Station cell.

Then she said: 'This date stamp has been forged. It hasn't been through the post at all. It must have been delivered by hand. Gloved hand. No fingerprints.'

'Listen!' I told her.

Somebody had come into the hall; they were listening too.

'Wendy!' I called.

'Wendy?' Ariadne exclaimed. 'Is that one of your nurses. That was the name written on the paper the chicken was wrapped in.'

'Whereabouts?'

'In the fridge with the rest of the stuff,' she said.

Now I examined the menu properly for the first time.

'This is only part of it,' Ariadne said, beginning to catch my alarm. 'The rest of it's keeping hot. I've been cooking all day. Mummy never lets me cook.'

I now began to recognise odd things and put a name to them: Mary's prawns, Wendy's shoulder of lamb and chicken, Claire's gammon of bacon, seven different kinds of frozen vegetables.

'I've done thirteen courses,' she said, proudly. 'Are you ready for the duck? I've glazed it.'

We both listened without mentioning it this time; there were sounds in the kitchen.

'I thought everything was yours,' she said. 'What was yours?'

'Only the rolled and stuffed breast of mutton.'

'I didn't bother about that,' she said. 'We give that to the animals.'

The outer door slammed. Footsteps went past the window. It was probably Mrs Bracknell checking the gas meter. I went to the window and she followed me, looking down to The Vale.

The tramp had left the seat. I saw him scurrying across East Heath Road away from the house.

He had two heavy carrier bags in one hand, bumping together; in the other hand he was carrying something that looked like a meat dish.

On inspection I found that the tramp had cleared the kitchen of all our portable food, blown his nose in the sink and stolen— it later transpired—half a horse-ful of the nurses' undies. As handkerchiefs, it later transpired when I taxed him about it. Funny way to prove your sanity.

'Whatever are we going to tell the nurses?' Ariadne said.

'We'll say a tramp broke in and stole all the food.'

'But that's what happened!'

'I know,' I said. 'That's what gave me the idea.'

She laughed at me in an objective way as though she were in the audience. 'I knew you were good news, Horace,' she said, 'right from the moment I heard you say you were the police.'

I went to hold her arm and then didn't; went to hold her hand and then didn't; wanted to tell her to go home but fluffed it. She looked concerned.

'What's the matter?' she said.

I said: 'Ariadne, you're illegal.'

'I'll go home,' she said, brightly. She took my hand and led me back to my room. She sat me down in the big chair, pulled the table away for my comfort, switched on the television. 'When I've made you some coffee.'

I don't drink coffee but I let her make it just for the sake of having those long legs, that woollen breast, that dusty high-school smile in the pad for a little longer.

While the coffee was boiling in the kitchen she slipped back and stood looking at me gravely from the doorway for a moment.

'May I ask you one thing and will you tell me the God's honour truth?'

'Yes.'

'Yes, I swear it.'

'Yes, I swear it.'

'Are you my real daddy?'

It shocked me and then it didn't; we were all in the B-picture game around Walton around twelve years ago.

'No, I'm not,' I told her.

She pretended to cross another one off her list and then smiled at me, mock-provocative. 'Good,' she said.

And she went back to the coffee. Behind the home-made coloured perspex screen and through the leaves of the tall philodendron plant I noticed the new blue leather suit-case between the bed and the open wardrobe; for a girl who proposed staying another ten minutes she had brought a lot of clothes.

What could I do? I had very mixed feelings about her. On the one hand as a responsible adult member of society and, worse than that, a novelist with social pretensions it was my duty to safeguard the morals of the young; but on the other hand I wanted to fuck her. I also wanted a mansion in the country, a motor yacht and a Silver Phantom Rolls Royce with just about a similar chance of achieving them. Sexually aware young women are protected in this country more effectively than close-season wild life; which at least doesn't jump at your rod with provocative thigh-exposing micro-skirts and a *cri de coeur* to get hooked and stuffed as quickly as possible.

'Do you mind if I get into something comfortable?' Ariadne said when she brought in the coffee.

You see what I mean?

When you switch on the bed-light behind the coloured perspex screens and undress by the wardrobes you project: the kind of shadow-show they use to sell soap. I watched everything come off and everything go on during the following exchange:

'Now may I ask you one thing and will you tell me the God's honour truth?' This is me.

'Mm.'

'Mm, I swear it.'

'Mm, I swear it.'

'Are you really twelve years old?'

She laughed and dropped something, started putting on something filmy over her head.

'Well,' she said, chattily. 'I thought you were going to ask me if I've started menstruation. That's what men usually ask you first.'

She came back round the screen.

'How do I look?'

She didn't look any different. Blue levis, jumper.

'I've put a bra on,' she explained, cupping it in her hands. 'It gets all prickly against the wool.'

To do this she had to strip and dress again in shadowette?

'This is a lovely bed,' she went on, in that airy, 'I am not aware that you can't stand up because you have an erection' tone of voice. 'Do you use it?'

'I don't sleep in a tree.'

She giggled a giggle as fresh as a green salad. 'You know what I mean, Horace Spurgeon Fenton!'

'Writer, artist and year book,' I said.

'What does that mean?'

'I always say that. What do you always say?'

She sat down at my feet with her coffee and rested her head back against my knee. 'Take people as you find them, that's what I always say,' she said.

'That means you've been hearing things about me.'

'A few.'

'You've been asking things about me.

'A few.'

I didn't have to ask her who she'd been talking to. She was running her right hand idly up my leg.

'Like what?'

'You're impulsive. Impetuous. You take terrible risks— that's Pisces, isn't it?'

She looked round and up at me, a little coffee dribbling from her lips: 'I'm like that.' And she straightened her little finger and touched me on the scrotum just one definite time. 'You'll have to help me fight it.'

I started to say something but my voice cracked. 'You'd better go, Ariadne,' I told her. 'Dinah will be worried sick.'

'Let her. She won't anyway. I never go back the same night.'

'You can't sleep here.'

'Why not?'

'I could go to prison.'

It was really the only reason. This is the only reason. And the publicity, *The News Of The World*, the country's greatest non-nuclear deterrent.

Author Denies Schoolgirl's Allegations.

Everybody reading it: Tres, Edna, her old mum, Lang male and female, Mr Fortin, Cedric, Ruth Baxter, Albert's mother—mind you, it wouldn't surprise her. It wouldn't surprise anybody. It's always harder to fight the things people know you want to do.

'I could go to prison now—just sitting here with you like that, your hand on my leg. Technically it's indecent assault.'

'What, doing this?'

'Don't!'

'Well, I'm doing it, you're not doing it.'

'They don't look at it like that. I'm fifty-one and you're .twelve.'

'But you don't know that, do you?'

'You're the most well-known twelve-year-old in the country.'

'That's only my professional age,' she said, and she leaned her head right back into my crutch and yawned.

If I sniffed around that little scene any longer it would become pornography and also it would lose its accuracy; the things that happened to stop me penetrating Ariadne's body would click into place just in the nick of time like a Whitehall farce and give you entertainment instead of truth. This is the truth—just that yawn.

All this poor little showbiz kid's troubles were in that yawn. Don't get the idea this is a story of a nymphet and an ageing author; innocence in peril and a beast at large. Lolita's been done eight times to my certain knowledge and never as perfect as the original. This is not a novel; nothing that happens to me is as convenient as that. This is the story of two people with one problem: age. She stuck at twelve, me stuck at fifty-one.

'I'm sick of it, Horace,' she said. 'Every year I have to move school so as to keep in the same form. It's like running on the spot. It wasn't so back before I got this great booz.'

I wanted to slide my hand round to check it out, but somehow it wasn't that kind of mood any more. It was a tragedy in a way; she was caught like the perennial juvenile in a long-running TV serial.

'Instead of a drink men offer me a glass of water,' she said, bitterly, 'then roll their genitals against me while reaching for the tumbler.' She looked round at me again and I had to pull myself back slightly to miss her ear: 'It puts me in a false position, Horace.'

I understood this and she knew it and this is why she was here.

'You talked to me like a man and you treated me like a woman,' she said. 'There was no orange juice and early to bed about your attitude. You desired me, loopy-loos and all.' I was getting really roused now and she could feel it. She said: 'The only thing that stops you putting me on that bed is the thought of going to prison—isn't that true?'

I had to admit it. And suddenly she was crying and I was holding her.

'What are we going to do, Horace?' she whispered.

'We'll think of something,' I told her. It was nice, suddenly having this mutual problem thrust upon us.

Dear Evelyn Home:
I am twenty-two years older than my girl friend's mother, do you think this matters? I would be glad of an early reply in your column as I have one hand

on her breast and the other between her legs and she's panting for it.
Frustrated, Hampstead.

Funny how just writing a letter like that in your head makes you feel better. I had not actually touched her anywhere important nor kissed her on the mouth. Had I done so everything would be lost. Just in time I had brought the outside world to bear.

'What's the matter?' she said, conscious of nothing except that the rush to disaster had stopped.

'Get dressed.'

'I *am* dressed!'

'Isn't that odd? I could've sworn she was naked from the moment she went behind that screen. I got up, lifting her under the armpits and to her feet. 'I'm going to drive you home.'

'Why?'

'Because you're a child and I'm a well-known writer.'

'I'm not a child, Horace. You know I'm not. You're betraying me. Look, I'll show you something.'

She stood and stripped naked and I stood and watched her. It took about fifty seconds and she had nothing on. Her breasts were about seventeen and between the legs she was older than Wendy.

'Okay,' I said. 'But you'll still have to go home.'

Naked, she didn't tempt me any more; naked they're all the same. She could see that my interest had gone and she didn't protest any more; gave me a sad, disgusted let-down look and took her clothes behind the screen. I went to the kitchen to wash up the shambles of the dinner and her marathon cooking.

Kitchen work absorbs the mind and then releases it for higher things. What I used to do when I first discovered I was living with five nurses and was anxious to please them was pile all the dirty things into one of the twin stainless steel sinks and cover them with water; then wash them and put them into the other sink for rinsing. This is not the best way to do it. For one thing the hot water releases the grease and muck and you are finally washing up in a kind of syrupy mixture. I now recommend washing everything individually in a sink of nice soapy water (and *Fairy Liquid* is no better than anything else whatever they say) and occasionally renewing this. Then rinse under running water and stack for drying. Never leave the drying; that's messy and slovenly and nothing shines any more.

It took nearly an hour. I did the crocks, cutlery, saucepans, frying pans, baking tins, getting all the best of the meat and chicken dripping into a Scott Fitzgerald type cracked bowl; then I did the gas stove, surfaces and sinks, tidied the fridge, emptied the dustbins and washed the floor over with *Flash*. This was my daily task. Once a week I cleaned the bathroom, the toilet and the hall and once a month I did the outer hall and bottom of the stairs which was a communal thoroughfare and was shared by others.

'You make me feel awful,' the nurses were always saying when they came home and found everywhere nice.

Their combined female presence in the flat I found sufficiently rewarding; the odours and perfumes and bits of crazy clothing, the never-ending problem of their fingernails which seems to concern women more than anything else in life; their late-night sex talk which gave us a mutual vicarious satisfaction.

I learned things about women of which I'd been ignorant all my life; silly, useless things sometimes but things which somebody who had not got married at nineteen to someone he never saw undressed would have picked up in his first brief encounters. For instance I'd never been able to unfasten a girl's bra and one night Claire was ironing one and showed me how they worked.

'You can do it with one hand behind your back,' she said.

And one more serious night when the talk got round to their lectures and exams they became astonished and alarmed to find that I knew so little about the female sex organ. Apparently the water and the womb cavities are quite separate. I had always thought a woman had to remove her sanitary pad during a period to pass water— this is not so. Mary had a diagram in her exercise book and she showed me the cross-section.

'No wonder you had all those kids!' Wendy said.

It never interested me. That sort of thing has never interested me. I mean it can get in the way of what you want to do; if I'd known all this before I would never have had a woman in my life. Even as it was it took me and Edna nearly a year to make love although I'd already given her a baby. We didn't know it had happened; it was unbelievable.

'But you didn't do anything to me!' she kept saying when she was worried sick about the pregnancy.

'I must've done, mustn't I?'

And there was a dismal Sunday afternoon with the rain beating across the heath and the sixth showing of the same old movie on television when they were waiting outside the bathroom door after I'd just had a good old soak and asked me if I would mind letting them examine me. Patricia, who was a young probationer nurse, very thin and shy and with a slight cast in her eye who came from Leeds, said she'd never seen a 'whole man'. I lay on my bed naked and they wore their whites just to lessen the embarrassment. They looked at my rupture scars and passed professional opinions, criticised my foreskin.

'That should've come off,' Wendy said.

My mother used to say that. She used to say I'd have difficulty when I got married. She used to say that my father had terrible trouble.

'What's that?' Mary exclaimed at one stage of the examination. It was my bump. I've got this big bump on my chest.

'Breathe in,' Wendy said. 'Let your diaphragm go slack and sink in.'

When I do this the bump stands up about as big as a golf ball where my bottom ribs meet in the middle at the front. Claire squealed with horror and covered her face.

'It's a carcinoma!' she exclaimed.

'Stop it!' Patricia said. 'You're frightening him.' And to me she said: 'Don't worry, she's hopeless.'

In these and other ways we became related as you do in a shared flat; I worried about their troubles, they worried about mine. However, I was never jealous about their boy friends—well, not really jealous. Wendy's sulky possessiveness at the appearance of Joanna had astonished me. What would they say to Ariadne; especially when they knew that she'd used all their food and the tramp had stolen their clothes.

I was doing that last kitchen job, putting out the washed-up milk bottles when I heard the girls coming.

I don't want to sound like an old woman but I always know my own girls right from the bottom of Cannon Place. The mouse-squeaks were much more agitated tonight as though their cheese had suddenly turned mouldy.

I intended to get in and hide before they got home; I often did this if I didn't feel like clashing my day with theirs in interminable recaps. I would put out my light and lie quietly on my bed—perhaps with Ariadne. Perhaps with Ariadne! What a marvellous good moral reason for getting her on the bed in the dark—

'Horace!'

Fuck.

Claire had sneaked on ahead and was coming up the steps; I could still hear Patricia's voice trying to calm what sounded like Wendy crying.

'Have you got any money, Horace?' Claire asked me; as she would say: 'Have you got a glass of water?'

With all their medical contacts—and I mean this in the foulest possible way—they had been unable to con any of their doctors into giving Wendy an abortion; that is without paying for it. They now brought Wendy in and sat her in a kitchen chair; I couldn't very well not follow them into the kitchen.

'What about that Robin Hood record?' Claire now asked.

I wasn't going to mention that; well, writing scripts for Stanley Black's kiddy-albums is hardly good for my image. Anyway, I turned it down.

'Oh, marvellous!' Patricia said. 'It's all right for you!'

'What about the Unmarried Mother series?' Claire now asked, determined to remind me that I'd got some money.

'I haven't had a story accepted yet.'

'How long will it take to get the first payment once you do?' she asked me. 'Do you get it in cash?'

I told her it would take a fortnight and Wendy gave a harsh kind of laugh, as though she would be dead by then. I left them and heard Claire say: 'Men!' as I closed the door. What were they going to say when they opened the fridge?

Ariadne had gone. Home? No. Her blue levis and the Arran jumper were still lying on the floor, the bra and panties and tights on the back of the old shell-armchair, her flip-flop Dr Scholl sandals also on the floor. To commit suicide? Yes. At some point in the last sixty minutes while I had been whistling, dreaming, thinking and banging about in the kitchen hoping fruitlessly I'd change my mind about her staying the night she had gone tearing out of the house and across Squires Mount and East Heath Road and across the heath and down through the bushes and thrown herself naked into slimy, muddy, tench-ridden Leg O' Mutton pond.

I have to admit it, I wasn't seeing poor Ariadne's dead body covered in frogs' spawn, I was seeing the headlines that would follow: *'Dead Girl's Clothes Found in Author's Bedroom..'*

This thought hit me when I was halfway across the road; I ran back and got her clothes with some half-formed idea that I could throw them in the water or leave them under some bushes and later on burn her suitcase and belongings. Luckily nobody knew she had come to my place—what am I talking about? Detective Chief Superintendent Jamie Kinnear had almost had dinner with us! 'Oh Christ!'

He answered almost immediately: 'Horace!'

I stopped my mad charge through the wet grass and looked up at the sky; it was dark now and through a ragged hole in the low cloud I saw the bright red and white light-cluster of an airliner trapped on its glide path and descending with that muffled terrified scream at the hazards of the landing ahead.

'Horace!'

She was all right. She was sitting on the bench seat donated by W. R. Keeble in 1927 and she was not naked.

'Sit down,' she said. 'It's nice here after the rain. Look at the lights down there on the pond. Is that somebody fishing?' And she said: 'What are you doing with my clothes—' Then she gasped: 'Oh no! You weren't going to dress up in them, were you?' Fortunately I didn't have to deny this because she got there on her own: 'Oh Horace, you thought I was naked! You thought I'd drowned myself!' She stood up (I wasn't going to sit on a wet seat) and flung her arms around me: 'You're wonderful! You were coming to rescue me! Fancy remembering the clothes!'

I don't know whether you know what happens to a school duffle-coat when a girl raises her arms around your neck and hugs you; to find out just slide your hands around her arse. Ariadne's was perfectly innocent and bare to the cold night air.

'Oo!' she said. 'Naughty!'

I let go of the cheeks of her arse and held her face sideways and kissed her on the mouth. She parted her lips; I just briefly had my first taste of her. She was just faintly peppermint.

'Good evening,' somebody said.

I tried to release Ariadne but she wouldn't let go; women are right about this: men are too inclined to drop what they're doing no matter how important it is for something unimportant in the way of a stranger. It's bad manners for one thing. This was a family I knew by sight from the Vale of Health; mummy, daddy and a couple of school-age girls. They were walking their Afghan and politely averting their eyes until Ariadne shrieked at them:

'Daffers!' She was still in my arms, still showing her arse; her clothes were still in my hands, my pockets, trailing from under my arm.

Daffers shouted back, though they were only three yards along the path: 'Ariadne! What are you doing here?'

'Oh, you know,' Ariadne told her old school chum.

'Miss Arrowsmith got the push!' Daffers called.

'It was true then,' Ariadne said. 'Who've you got now?'

'We've got a man. Oh boy! He's really good news!'

'Come along, Daphne,' her mother called.

'Give me a ring,' Ariadne called as they were departing. And to me she said: 'What's your number?' I told her and she called it out. The family departed. 'Miss Arrowsmith was having it away with the Judo master,' Ariadne mentioned in total explanation of the exchange. And as a sort of final punctuation just in case anything had been missed the Afghan came trotting back and licked Ariadne's underclothes the way dogs do; Daffers' father had to return and drag the animal away.

'Goodnight,' he said.

'Goodnight,' we said.

'He's a barrister,' Ariadne chatted as he walked away. 'But he had a stoppage of the bowels and had to have an operation.' And she said: 'Do you mind if I slip these on?'

She was twelve years old again as she donned the levis and jumper and sandals, holding my arm to prevent from falling over; I felt by turns a monster and a father: it would be interesting to see who won.

'Coming walkies?' she said.

It was our first walk together, pilot and trailer of the adventures ahead. Even the contours of the heath were a taster of the remote wildnesses waiting for us now in the Scotch mists between the Kyles of Tongue and Ben Loyal; the landscaped Hampstead hillocks like a planners' miniature of some outward-bound course in hardihood.

'Stop!' I whispered.

We stopped walking; the footsteps I had heard behind us also stopped. We walked on; again they padded at the same pace. We stopped; they stopped. We walked on; they followed. Pat pat pat pat.

'Run for the light by the pond!' I told her.

We ran holding hands, Ariadne laughing though I couldn't see why. She hadn't had the black spot put on her.

'Stay here a minute,' I told her.

We stood by the railings under the lamp and watched the ducks and the moorhens cruising like ships in and out of the darkness and mist.

'Now walk on and if he passes the lamp we shall see him,' I told her.

Pat pat pat pat sounded behind us; I looked back to the lighted bit of the path; nobody. Footsteps sounding close behind us and nobody in sight. We stopped. They stopped. Ariadne was killing herself.

'Are you serious?' she said.

'Didn't you hear him?'

'It's not a him, it's a her,' she said.

'Your mother?'

'No—me!' She lifted her foot up to show me: 'My sandals. They flip flop against my heels as I walk. Listen...'

Pat pat pat pat. She was right.

'You've turned as white as a ghost, Horace!'

Why do people always assume that ghosts are white? Ghosts are red. Old Slough-foot is green with age and decay and slaver. Only the tiger is white and he is life; he is lagging farther and farther behind. He is going to let them get me.

We walked through the dark stilled entertainments of the resident fairground below the Spaniards Road; Ariadne sprang onto the switchback and I had to follow her round, still holding her hand; when she jumped down I held her again, though not sexually. She smiled up over my shoulder as though to someone standing behind.

'Excitement, Fun and Laughter,' she said.

The words jumped in phosphorous colours across the side of a yellow pantechnicon. We walked on through the miniature village of the Vale, music from beyond drawn curtains here, the sound of a typewriter from some high attic, the blue blur of television in a basement. We walked on up the winding miniature lane between the trees and the pat pat pat pat of Ariadne was beside me and behind me and inside me.

When we entered the hall Claire was trying to open my door; not very hard because she was the ladylike one. From behind the closed kitchen door I could hear some sort of emotional mouse-squabble going on.

'I did knock,' Claire said. 'I thought you said come in. Can you help us?'

The kitchen door flew open and banged against the fridge, several glassy things fell down inside; Patricia was looking out with a red face and holding something between finger and thumb.

'Is he there? Oh, Horace, hurry up! I can't do it!'

We all went into the kitchen; nobody was acknowledging Ariadne, the situation was obviously too fraught.

'I'm sorry about the food—' I thought that's what it was but no; Wendy was stretched out on the kitchen table with her blouse half-off, one arm dangling down, weeping and moaning. 'What's the matter?' I asked them.

'She wants me to cut her wrist!' Patricia said; the thing she was holding was a razor blade. 'I can't do it!'

'Cut her wrist?' It was one of those stupid repeat everything situations.

'The ambulance will be here any minute!' Wendy sobbed.

'The ambulance will be here? What for?'

We heard the bell coming in the same moment.

'Oh my God! Horace, you do it!' Claire said.

I forget the precise order of babbling hysteria that at last informed me and Ariadne that they had just telephoned emergency services that there had been a suicide attempt; it was Wendy's last desperate plan to procure a National Health abortion.

'We want to do it just as they get here,' Patricia explained, 'then there's no danger of her bleeding to death.'

'Only she's funked it,' Claire added.

I can't do it either,' Patricia said. I might cut an artery.'

'No, you won't,' Ariadne said. 'I'll show you where to cut.' She rolled up her jumper sleeve and twisted her arm to show long raking scars on her forearm and wrist. 'That's an old one,' she said. 'This is newer—do one like this. You do it, Horace—'

The bell clanged and stopped and suddenly there was a blue light beaming and pulsing on the ceiling from the ambulance outside; doors slammed, voices shouted, footsteps ran.

'Quick, somebody!' Wendy said.

I took the razor blade from Patricia, studied Ariadne's pattern for a moment, then cut. Wendy screamed and the blood spurted. I gave the blade to Patricia who handed it to Claire who gave it to Wendy who dropped it on the floor and then the ambulance men were pounding on the door. I tried to take Ariadne into my room before they came in but my door was locked. How could my door be locked? The key was on the inside.

'Has she taken any drugs?' I heard one of the men ask from inside the kitchen.

Next moment they were carrying Wendy out on a stretcher; her arm, resting over the blanket, had some kind of instant tourniquet clamp on it. I suddenly knew that I had cut too deeply and that Wendy was going to die; I knew too that because she was pregnant and we slept in the same flat, I had a motive. On top of this I was an undischarged bankrupt...

'We're going with her,' Claire said. I was standing there like an idiot trying to open my own door without a key. 'Don't worry, Horace, she'll be all right.' Notice this gradual shift of responsibility towards me. 'Mary's at the hospital waiting. She'll fix the entrance docket—self-administered wounds.'

They should let women like this go to work on the economy.

'Who's in there? Somebody's moving!' Ariadne was on her knees at the keyhole.

A man's voice inside my room said: 'Horace?'

'Yes?' I answered.

The key turned. Ariadne stood back and motioned me to go in. I declined and motioned her to go on. You never know what's waiting for you behind a closed door. Ariadne went in.

'You're not Horace,' I heard him say. It took me two seconds to place that Woolwich Tech High drawl.

It was Norman Freville. 'Where's Horace?' he said.

I went in. It was the tramp. Norman Freville. He was half-stripped, had a towel round his shoulders and was holding my Gillette safety razor and Boots' Aerosol Shaving Cream.

'Where's the bathroom?' he asked me, and went out

'Who's that?' Ariadne whispered.

I told her.

'The film producer? I thought he was locked up?'

'I thought he was.'

Norman Freville looked back into the room, his mad face already half-covered in foam. 'Oh, and Horace—' he pointed to a big scruffy hold-all. 'Be going through these toilet rolls—we've got a lot of work in front of us.' He looked at Ariadne: 'Make some coffee, love. Lots of coffee —we're going to be working all night.'

She watched me unroll the first of the Izal toilet rolls; they were the non-functional hotel and institution kind, treacherously slippery on one side. The other side was covered in small ballpoint hand-writing. It was the lunatic story *One Last Mad Embrace*.

'It sounds terrific!' She was reading it over my shoulder. 'I'll put the coffee on.' She also went out and came in again with a new, bright smile: 'This is more what I expected. I've been waiting for you to start working like crazy so I could look after you.'

It was like old times. The worst part of the old times. The slave-driving part. He came back across the hall already issuing orders, exchanged some boisterous conversation with Ariadne in the kitchen and I heard her squeal with laughter; he came in wearing the bath towel around his middle, all pink and shaved and smelling like my *Old Spice*.

'First of all get that typed up on double-spaced quarto,' he said. 'Then we'll work on a draft treatment with indicative dialogue. Paramount are waiting to back it.'

'I'm up to my eyes in television work,' I said.

His face filled with compassion: 'That's terrible. I'm really sorry. I heard you were slipping. Did you know they've taken your name out of the *Writers' Who's Who?*'

I didn't know that. He'd been looking for my new address. 'Never mind. I'll soon have you out of television, away from those B-picture cunts and documentary bastards. This is going to be a grand re-entry for both of us, Horace.'

He lay flat on my bed in the damp towel and clasped his hands across his stomach in the old familiar dictatorial tycoon manner. 'You can add your name to mine on the title page,' he told me, generously. Then he called: 'Honey —hurry up!' And to me: 'Nice little thing. How long have you had her? What about the wives and the kids? That crippled girl and the little librarian? You're keeping them all, I suppose. That's where you go wrong, Horace.'

What people don't realise is that they keep me as much as I keep them. Ariadne came in with a tray of coffee, efficiently.

'And when you've done that,' Norman Freville said, 'get rid of my old clothes where the police can't find them.'

'Are you on the run?' she said, giving him his coffee. 'I'm on the run.'

'And pull those shutters right across,' he went on. 'You can see right into this room if you stand on the window-sill outside.' I looked up from the toilet roll I was reading and he was just about sensitive enough to know why. 'I've been trying to get you on your own,' he explained. 'You're never here to answer the telephone or if you are here you're surrounded by a lot of dollies. You haven't worked for weeks.'

Ariadne took his old tramp clothes out to the dustbins and then he set her to work massaging him with my *Algipan* embrocation. He had been living rough on the heath for the past six weeks, he told us (it explained why he had lost weight and could now get into one of my suits). He had done casual work at the Regent's Park zoo, tramped from London to Cardiff and back and spent several weeks working on the Manchester Ship Canal. He'd also done other things which I didn't discover till much later.

'It's all there on those rolls,' he kept saying as he recounted it. 'You won't have to make anything up. Now my buttocks . . .'

I couldn't concentrate on the tiny scribble with all that fleshy slap and tickle going on behind the screen. Very worrying to have young people in your care. Somehow I felt responsible for her.

'I haven't seen you in here before, have I?' I heard him say. 'Where do you sleep?'

I wondered if I could slip out to the lavatory and quietly dial 999, get old Jamie round. As I thought about it the telephone rang.

'Be careful what you say!' Norman Freville instructed me as I went out to answer it.

It was Claire phoning from the hospital. Wendy was all right, the plan had succeeded, the psychiatrist had recommended the termination of her pregnancy and she was to have a National Health Service abortion which is generally reckoned to be the safest and best.

'Is she staying in?' I asked her. Yes, she was. 'Can my guest have her bed tonight?' Yes, she could.

'But you're slipping, aren't you, Horace?'

'What's she saying?' I jumped. Norman Freville was behind me with a gun in his hand.

'Nothing. It's Claire. It's all right. Put that gun away. Don't you trust me, or something?'

'I'm on the last lap, Horace,' he said, taking me back into the room. 'I can't afford to take risks.'

I was glad to see that Ariadne was sitting down and looking white at last; it had just got through to her that we had a lunatic on our hands. An escaped lunatic bent on carrying out my plot.

'Another six weeks,' he said, putting the gun back into the hold-all, 'and I'm officially a sane man. That's more than most people can say.'

Ariadne looked at me as if she was expecting me to take some sort of heroic action. 'That's excellent,' I said.

'Now this is what we do,' Norman Freville said: 'I keep the girl here with me—I shall need a hostage.'

I could no longer avoid Ariadne's eyes. I said: 'You can't do that, Norman. She's only twelve.'

Ariadne said, anxious to be twelve again: 'I'm Ariadne Thing!'

'I know your mother well,' Norman Freville said. 'I gave Dinah Thing her first part in movies and changed her name. Her real name was Cox.'

'Dix,' Ariadne said.

'And you sleep in Wendy's bed,' Norman Freville told me. Instructing the girl again: 'Let me sleep for a few hours and don't wake me up unless you really must, darling. I shan't want to make love till I've rested.'

'Righto,' the poor child said, wildly.

'If you want to do wee-wees go and do it now,' he told her, 'then come back and lock the door,' He dropped the towel and stood there scratching his balls. 'You take the toilet rolls with you, Horace. Try to get them read by the morning and early tomorrow we can talk about construction.' He lay flat on my bed. 'Cover me up, honey.'

Ariadne drew the covers over him as over a bad accident, her face averted.

'Now hurry up and get the light out.'

I went out carrying the five toilet rolls, left Ariadne undressing; we were not looking at each other now.

It was the same Norman Freville; the same megalomania, the same gun, probably. The only frightening difference was that he had now been certified.

Part Two

Six

I am a lunatic, was written on the toilet roll labelled *Volume 1.* The second paragraph starting :

If I can escape from this asylum and avoid recapture for six months then I am not a lunatic.

Notice how, in spite of what he says about not intending this writing for publication or commercial purposes, he has in fact neatly put the premise of the forthcoming movie into the first two lines—the only two lines distributors read. It is typical of the fiction mind which suddenly sees its own misfortune as a saleable scoop; condemned to death your fiction man will be working on the angles and assessing the value of the free publicity if only the gallows fails to function or a pardon arrives in the nick of time.

This is the law, he went on, the ball-point breaking through the paper occasionally. *My fifth application for my case to be reviewed has just been turned down. Guess what I am therefore going to do. This chronicle is not intended for publication; it is an additional proof of my sanity.*

There followed the perforations and then on to the next square :

I am in the lavatory of the Red House—reserved for semi-violent patients—writing on toilet paper with a ballpoint pen which I keep at present in my anus (there is a strip search every night).

Tell me what's semi-violent about nailing somebody to a tree on Stevenage by-pass.

Of course I need not begin writing this until I am out of this place; but to do so, to escape observation, to write and carry and hide the plan of my escape under their noses seems to me to be the epitome of ingenuity; the certain indisputable proof of my sanity and rational state of mind.

Rational state of mind? *I shan't want to make love till I've rested ...* Oh boy—I should try that sometime. The terrible thing is it seems to work. I've been sitting reading in the kitchen for half an hour without hearing a single scream. The nurses are not back yet; I go on:

ITEM	CONDITION
Two tennis rackets (racquets?)	Almost new
Four tennis racquets	Reasonable
Sundry balls	Useable.

What's this? Where are we now?

Eleven of those feathered squash things.   Useable.

I think that's probably enough. You probably wonder what's happening. I've got myself appointed secretary of the sports club. I can sit and write all the afternoon and I don't have to show any of it to Doctor Thatterday. Otherwise everything you write is examined for diagnosis. There is something unpleasant about this I think. Perhaps not if you are really insane like Colonel Crowther—

Oh my God he's found an enemy. I bet he's dead by the third roll.

They caught him writing ways to kill Doctor Thatterday. 'This shows a big improvement, Colonel,' Thatterday old him. He got his case reviewed!

And on and on and on. It began to hold me. I've got to admit it—it began to hold my interest. The trouble was the kitchen was filling up with unrolled toilet paper.

'Whatever are you doing, Horace?' Patricia asked when she came in. Helen, that was the other nurse's name—have I been calling her Mary? Doesn't matter; I'll have to change them anyway.

Helen said: 'It's toilet paper!'

'Just a minute,' I told them.

'She's going to be all right,' Claire said.

'Shut up a minute then,' I told them. I'd just found a bit about me:

Horace came in this afternoon with his usual idiot chatter . . .

That meant surely that he was already planning his escape while I was visiting him. He'd been very clever about not mentioning it; or had he? He asked me to help him once—this must have been the project.

He dropped one or two good titles which he'll never use. Odd fellow. Brought me fruit. He seems completely to have forgotten that I had him crucified. I can see how Albert and that tilted bastard used him to steal my business and get me certified—

I say—this is new!

'What is it?' Helen asked.

For a writer, it continued, Horace doesn't seem to know what's going on.

'Do you mind if we make some coffee?' Patricia said, sarcastically.

I asked them to make me some. 'I'm in terrible trouble — there's a madman in my room with a twelve-year-old girl.'

'I see,' Helen said. 'And you're sitting in here reading toilet paper. Oh yes. Now pull the other one.'

'All these things are sent to try us,' Claire said.

'Instant or proper coffee?' Patricia asked.

I let them see the epic written on the bumf; they were nurses, Helen had been in Colney Hatch, they recognised the situation. They told me not to worry, either ring the police or the nearest hospital and they'd bring a strait-jacket for him.

'He's got a loaded gun and a hostage.' It wasn't that so much. I didn't like turning him in. Especially if Paramount were really interested in the story.

'We'll get her out,' Helen said. 'Good God, I got a naked woman off the end of a flagpole on the Queen's birthday.'

She turned to Claire: 'Just tap the door and ask them if they want some coffee.'

They're very efficient. You think they're just bits of girls — Patricia with her squint, horsey Claire, sexy Helen in her little dress, showing her crutch every time she raised her arms to touch her hair—yet they took charge of a situation like this as if they were a commando team. I still felt they were doing the wrong thing, mind you.

'Why don't you lock yourself in our room till it's all over?' Patricia asked me, kindly. 'You've had a tough night, what with

85

cutting Wendy's wrist and everything.'

I said: 'You'd better let me talk to him through the door.'

Helen said: 'You sit there and roll up your bum paper.'

They were enjoying it. First of all Wendy's abortion, now a lunatic with a gun; this is why they left Barrow-in-Furness.

I heard them knock on my door.

'Horace! Would you like some coffee?'

'Who's that?' came Ariadne's voice from inside.

'Ask Horace if he'd like some coffee,' Helen called.

Patricia came back into the kitchen. 'Who is she?'

I told her and she laughed. 'She's more than twelve! She looked eighteen.'

Suddenly there was a crash and shout from my room. 'Hah!' like that in Ariadne's voice. 'Hah' again and 'Hah' again.

'Oh my God!' Claire said.

Helen said: 'We've got to break the door down— Horace!'

I went out to the hall and was about to crash my foot on the door when Helen stopped me.

'Listen,' she said.

It was quiet inside now. Then the key sounded in the lock and the door opened. Ariadne, out of breath, looked at us. She was fully dressed in her school uniform; green gymslip, white blouse, black shoes and green beret with the Highgate badge.

'I think I've killed him,' she said. 'I gave him an *O-Goshi*.'

We went into my room. Helen made a brief examination of Norman Freville who was now lying naked stretched out on the floor by the door. She stood up, shook her head.

Ariadne said: 'I used the wrong throw—it was Karate.'

What had happened was that she had dressed herself in her school uniform as a sort of self-protection after I'd gone out of the room. Freville had slept right through. Then when the girls knocked he had woken up, seen Ariadne dressed and assumed she was about to escape and bring the police in. He had gone for her and Ariadne had defended herself in the well-known Highgate tradition— but with the wrong throw. That's what all the 'Hah!' business had been about.

Now Norman Freville was dead.

'And now we can phone the police,' Patricia said.

'Oh crikey!' Ariadne said.

She really looked twelve now; all she needed was a hockey stick. The girls appreciated this and looked at me.

Claire said: 'What a night!'

'I don't understand it,' Ariadne said. She was looking at her hands, the fingers clawed inwards like a murderess; 'I could swear I used the *O-Goshi*.' Then with some pride, pointing: 'I threw him from there to there.'

The nurses were doing that thing that groups of listeners do; they were almost saying little things but not quite: bird nods from Claire, eyebrows shooting up and down from Helen and Patricia, shocked by the dead body, kept making funny little throat-clearing noises. Mary was squatting by the body trying fruitlessly for reflexes and I could see up her thighs.

'Susan Wentworth-Sawston did it to Mr Latimer—that was our Judo master—and he gave her a yellow mark,' Ariadne was going on. 'I must have chopped him first.'

Make no mistake, it's men they're training these girls to fight; another generation and they'll be issuing them rifles. 'He wasn't trying to rape me,' she added. 'He just tried to stop me getting to the door.'

Mary noticed where I was looking and closed her knees.

'I'll telephone the police,' Patricia said again.

'Don't keep saying that!' Ariadne snapped. And when they looked at her, she nearly sobbed: 'Well it's all right for you. You didn't do it.'

I said: 'You won't be blamed. It was self-defence. He's a certified lunatic. They're looking for him.'

'Do you think that makes it better?' she said.

She was right, of course. The more lurid the circumstances the bigger the headlines.

'She's a real little bastard, they'll say,' Ariadne said. 'It'll kill the series stone dead. They'll cancel mummy's contract. She needs this job, Horace. She's on the skids.'

'Oh!' Patricia said. 'Are you Elizabeth Garner's daughter?'

'Dinah Thing,' Ariadne said.

'I've read about you no end of times,' Claire said.

And Helen said: 'Is it true you're only twelve?'

Ariadne said, grimly: 'I am from now on…'

I put up the dots because the conversation took a few tortuous female turns after that. While Norman Freville grew cold for the last time we had coffee and discussed what to do. It was a creepy situation for me because one plot I've always got myself hung-up on is the disposal of bodies—now I had one in my lap. I've often been criticised for not taking death seriously in my writing and perhaps this is true; and perhaps the reason lies no deeper than that I am terrified of it. When death, particularly a violent death, touches your own life then it is ugly and tainting. You remember in *Hitler Needs You* where my step-father tied up a negro and threw him into a river on the fairground and again how the pilot of the Blackburn Bluebird aerobating at Sir Alan Cobham's circus hit the ground at two hundred miles an hour and got the joystick through him. They were not funny incidents and if they sounded hilarious then it's my deficient writing.

'Couldn't you say you did it?' Helen suggested at one stage.

I don't know any Judo. That would be the first thing they'd check on. And if they find a lie mixed up with a death like this it no longer looks accidental.

Claire said: 'Supposing we just dressed him in his tramp clothes and put him back on the heath?'

The trouble with Norman!

'That's a good idea,' Patricia said. 'They're always finding corpses on Hampstead Heath. They use a rake, practically.'

'It's where our last H & L transplant came from,' Mary remembered. 'Only it didn't take.'

'They're the ones that don't get into the papers,' Claire told Ariadne, pushing her less-publicised profession in a competitive way as people do.

'Which dustbin did you put his clothes in?' Mary had finished her second cup of coffee and was standing near the door, yawning. They had to be on duty at eight-o'clock in the morning and it was now three am; nothing unusual for them. You see the nurses climbing Haverstock Hill any morning as the rush-hour cars stream down to the city, the drivers peeping and whistling at them; they never get any response. The girls are hanging onto each other just to stay upright; zombies in dresses, capes and caps ready for a quick six-hour shift against dirt and disease and then back to the Witch's Cauldron.

'Spare yourselves the trouble,' I said. 'You go to bed and I'll phone Superintendent Kinnear—'

'Now what's wrong?' Ariadne said. 'You don't have to go waking the police up. He'll be found tomorrow over near Kenwood or somewhere.'

I explained to them why it wouldn't work. As soon as Norman Freville was identified there would be a connection with me—and a motive. I recapped on the circumstances that led him to believe that I'd run off to Italy with all his money and his girl friend, the Countess; how he had followed and shot her and gone to prison and how Albert had taken over his flat and moved into his movie territory and how Freville had come out of prison and had me nailed to a tree—

'And you gave him your bed!' Claire exclaimed.

'Then what happened?' Patricia asked, avidly. 'I mean after you were crucified? Didn't you tell him it was Albert all the time?'

'Albert's dead,' I said.

'You don't know that,' Ariadne said; then gushing on to the nurses: 'You see Horace keeps getting these telephone calls and now Scotland Yard are working on the theory that the airliner was sabotaged—'

'That's not Albert,' I told her. 'They're looking for Sir Ambrose Argyle.'

'Honest to God!' Helen said, 'can I tell my mum when I write or is it *sub judice*?'

'Wendy would know what to do,' Claire told me. 'Why don't we ring Wendy? She's good at this sort of thing.'

'Who's on Nightingale Ward tonight?' somebody said.

It was taken out of my hands for a time; the girls crowded out into the hall and got on the telephone, I was left with the body of Freville. I felt sorry for him. There was a look of utter surprise in his dead face. All his life adored by everybody and then suddenly thrown across the room by a schoolgirl. Another bit of colour had gone out of the movie business; first Arturo Conti, now Norman Freville; he lay there redundant as a silent movie. Never again would he storm out of the middle of an expensive production, bankrupting his sponsors and driving everybody mad with fury.

'A bit of a fight in Horace's pad,' I heard voices from the hall.

'Don't say too much!' I called. Nobody heard. Patricia popped her head in:

'Is he Catholic or Protestant or don't you know?'

I didn't know. She went back and the chatter reached a higher pitch of excitement.

'And this girl's run away from home and she's shacked up with Horace—she's only twelve! You saw her. Dinah Thing's daughter. Dinah Thing—her boy friend hanged himself in prison—that's right! Is he? Is he? Here, what d'you think? That West-Indian porter's on duty tonight, you know, the one who— what? Your knitting? All right, I'll bring it in tomorrow . . .'

The caravan was lonely at times, but I got more work done. Still, isolate yourself and soon there's no work to do, nothing to write about. I wish I could characterise them more distinctly for you; it's like trying to characterise a nest of mice. I'll try to get their measurements later on, Incidentally the coffee was *Lyons Blue Tin*.

'She doesn't know,' Claire said, leading the procession back into the room half an hour later.

'Now perhaps I can ring the police,' I said.

Ariadne followed me into the hall. The poor kid looked worried. 'Couldn't you say he tripped?' she said, as I dialled a number from one of Jamie's cards.

'*You* say he tripped—'

'What's that, sir?' said a voice at the other end.

'Stop! Hang up!' Patricia screamed as she came running out of my room.

'Sorry — wrong number,' I said, and hung up. 'Oh Christ! ' I said, clapping my hand to my mouth in the B-picture tradition. 'They're recording my line at Scotland Yard. The Superintendent'll be round here like a shot— he's waiting for something to happen to me to help him with his case.'

The rest of the girls were out in time to hear this and Claire clapped her hands, decisively: 'That means we've got to work fast. Listen, Horace, I don't know why I didn't think of this before. Are his kidneys all right?'

'What?'

Helen said: 'Your friend Norman. Was he a heavy drinker?'

'Aubrey's doing his nut for a fresh pair of kidneys — Doctor Parsons. He's with the transplant unit. You be ringing him,' she detailed Mary. 'You'll find his number in my dates book —'

'I thought you said you'd never been out with him?' Helen squealed.

'We didn't *go out*! Now you know. Bloody nosey parker. There is such a thing as medical ethics, you know.'

And to Ariadne: 'Can you tell me exactly what time he died, dear?' To Patricia: 'Oh, and they'll want his blood group.'

And to me: 'What about his next-of-kin?'

'She's in the Bahamas,' I said.

How did I know this right off without thinking?

I don't often know things like that, do I? Marjorie Freville moved to Nassau soon after she had Norman certified; besides what he had done to me and the Countess in public there were all kinds of private things went on on the rare occasions he spent weekends with his family. One thing that sticks in my mind is that he used to go out into the garden naked on rough nights and conduct the storm with a baton. And then the horror of what they were suggesting came home to me. You can't just have somebody chopped up, can you?'

'If it means saving somebody's life,' she said. It seems to me it depends who's saving whom.

'We've got five patients waiting for kidneys at the moment.'

'But what about — the rest of him?'

Helen said: 'Don't worry, they'll use him up.'

Use him up? They're talking about our loved ones. The day before you're taking them flowers and grapes.

'Now ring the ambulance unit,' Claire was telling Mary, 'and ask for Sid and Charlie again…'

The white, Martin-Walter-conversion Ford Thames ambulance shot away up Squires Mount and vanished into Cannon Place as a black Rover 3.5 police car and a 12-cwt Austin prison van came blah-blah-blahing up the hill and squealed to a stop at the foot of our steps.

'Is that you, Mr Spurrajon?' Kinnear's voice came from the blue darkness of the car: 'Are you all right, man?'

I knew it was me and I knew I was all right and I told him so. He came in anyway, peering at the nurses and at Ariadne in her school uniform. We had got our story fixed just in time, keeping almost to the truth and shifting the time factors and forgetting the advent and death of Norman Freville. One of the nurses had attempted suicide and though I had started ringing the police I realised that with the passing of the act it was no longer police business.

'Lucky you were all up and dressed and ready for it at four o'clock in the morning,' he remarked. I was stumped and so were the girls so after a minute's wait he decided to let us off the hook with: 'No doot they'll allow the poor lassie a surgical intervention.' And to me: 'Are you the proud father, Mr Spurrajon?'

'It's Doctor Parsons,' Helen said, angrily.

'How do you know?' Claire told her. 'You don't know.'

'I've been counting up,' Helen said. 'Since she said that.'

By some nimble means probably connected with his Scottish sheep dog ancestry these few lines of dialogue had enabled Jamie and a coloured detective-sergeant to round us all up and back into my room.

'Are these your boots?' he now asked.

We had hidden everything except the boots.

'Yes,' I said.

'Now that's strange,' he said. 'They're the same size—' that was lucky, '— but the laces are tied in a different manner'. He pointed to my Hush-Puppies. 'You'll notice that you tie your shoes as your mother taught you, Mr Spurrajon —like a child. Your ringer through to form the bow and the laces coming up the simple way in diagonals. Then when you've tied the bow you tie it again in a knot.'

'Sometimes,' I said.

'Those sort of things never vary,' he said, sternly; then picking up a discarded cellophane cigarette wrapper: 'Nor does this—not many people bother to twist it into a butterfly and spread out the wings.'

'What are you trying to say?'

He now picked up another cellophane from Norman's scruffy ash-tray by the bed — it was screwed into a ball. Then as if starting on a different subject having finished with those, he said: 'Have you had any visitors, Mr Spurrajon?'

'No,' I said.

My eyes and the girls' eyes went round the room with the two detectives' eyes in a sort of mad race; everything else including the toilet rolls had been hidden away. We were all of us surprised to discover this; we relieved, they irritable, like two opposing teams in a panel game.

'No more telephone calls, postcards, telegrams, letters?' Jamie asked, staring me in the eye. 'Nobody trying to contact you at all?'

'Nobody,' I said.

The girls went to bed and I showed the police out. I was worried and unhappy about Freville's death and Kinnear could detect this; he seemed to sympathise with what was going on even though he didn't know what it was. He shook hands with me outside on the terrace which was quite unnecessary. He wanted me to know that I was not being watched and my phone was not being tapped except in my own interest.

'I would have known it was you,' he said, in a jolly voice. 'Even had ye not spoken a wurrrd. I could hear the arsthmar. If I were you I'd get to ye bed. Tis a dricht night.'

'Aye, it tis,' I said.

There was something going on around the police van and car which I didn't at first get into focus. The rain had started again. Several houses along Squires Mount had their lights on at the commotion; some that hadn't were nevertheless awake and white blob-faces peered from windows and doors. Tonight's activities hadn't done us any good at all with the Hampstead Preservation Society. And then too I noticed two police handlers coming back across the heath with their dogs and somebody they had caught. It would be almost impossible to go onto the heath at this hour with dogs and not catch somebody. When they came up to Kinnear I found it was an elderly woman wearing an ankle-length coat over her night attire. She pointed at me.

'That's him,' she said, accusingly. And she came closer, glaring at me — I had noticed her going backwards and forwards down the Vale pulling her little shopping basket. Fred the milkman reckoned she used to be a famous star in the Rank charm school days. 'Have you got my tramp?' she said.

'She leaves stuff out for this tramp,' one of the young policemen explained to Kinnear. 'Last night he didn't collect it. She's been looking for him all night.'

'He comes here, you know he does,' she said to me. And to Kinnear: 'They were once in business together but now he won't help him.' Then angrily to me: 'Have you been feeding him? I found lots of empty dishes and nasty frozen food under his tree.' And then, more specifically to the coloured detective as though expecting to get something written down: 'His name's Norman. He sometimes wears a sack over his shoulders.'

'We'll find him, madam,' Kinnear told her.

'Oh, will you really? Thank you, Inspector.' And finally to me she said: 'You ought to give him a partnership!'

She said goodnight and toddled off down the Vale, peering into the bushes and making cat-calling noises. The police were looking at me as if for an explanation. I was forced to tell them that somebody had broken in and stolen some food.

Jamie looked hurt. 'You didn't mention that before.'

'Is it important?'

One of the dogs was playing up and barking and didn't want to get back in the van; you can't blame them it's not much of a life, always being bundled into vans and having bits of material rubbed on their noses and told to smell somebody out. It's nice to know at least that there is a life-after-death for them and a few Mrs Bracknells in the world.

'Try to keep those double-doors locked,' Jamie Kinnear told me, earnestly. 'Anyone can come and go all night.'

'That reminds me,' one of the young bobbies said, 'I owe you a pint of milk.'

No wonder our lavatory cistern's singing all night. The nurses always accusing me of trying their doors. And not opening them.

All at once a black killer Alsatian who wouldn't know which fork to use at the Savoy suddenly broke away from its handler and leapt at my throat. Jamie and his man Friday had to hold onto its collar while others bundled me into the police car and locked the door. It was the door-locking that showed the real respect the force has for these animals. The dog had been trying to get at me ever since it came back from the heath and the reason was not difficult to divine — it had been scented with one of my old socks before they left Hampstead police station. I worked this out while they were subduing the beast and then taxed Jamie with it. They didn't come up here looking for any intruders — they were looking for me; thought I had gone on the run and were prepared to hound me across the heath. He shook his head. This meant I was wrong.

'Nearly, but not quite,' Jamie said.

I brought my fiction mind to bear and came up with the answer: 'Looking for my body?'

He laughed, admiringly: 'Aye, laddie. Full marks.'

At what he said next I was thankful to be sitting down in the car; it made me feel quite ill.

95

'There's five million pounds sterling missing from the company assets of Global Films,' he said, steadily, 'and it's my belief, Mr Spurrajon, that you know where it is.'

I swore that I knew nothing whatever about it.

'I believe that too' he said. 'But to certain persons involved you are just as much a danger. In fact I might say that if you have the information without knowing it then you're more of a danger.'

This was ridiculous; I know nothing whatever about Albert's and Sir Ambrose's company business beyond what I read in their press-handouts.

'And yet,' the superintendent said when I told him this, 'according to my sources you were instrumental in bringing the company into being in the first instance.'

This is a laugh unless there's someone waiting for you on the heath with a knife. If the man who's just been bludgeoned is responsible for the hold-up then what he said is true. Albert picked my brains, stole secret documents from my car and blackmailed his way into the film business; only his mother could view it any other way. News of the sabotage must have come as a shock to her and she was fighting back; white-washing Albert and Sir Ambrose, safeguarding her fortune and to hell with Horace.

'Take great care, Mr Spurrajon,' were Jamie's parting words. 'You're playing a dangerous game. . .'

That's what he said. It's ridiculous but that's what he said. He was talking about the five million pounds. He was so concerned with fantasies he hadn't found out that Norman Freville the escaped lunatic had been running around with a gun for the past four months. Talking to the girls about this later on they told me this is not unusual; that unless the escape is from somewhere like Broadmoor then it's not publicised that much.

'They're always popping off home or somewhere and getting brought back,' Helen said. 'We just notify the local police if they're not considered dangerous.'

Norman had been in a normal kind of mental hospital, if

that's the word (normal, I mean); he hadn't actually killed anybody. He wasn't a bad chap, really.

I stood outside on the terrace looking at the heath and my stars (Orion, The Plough, Seven Sisters and Venus) and feeling galactic about Freville's death. And quite suddenly for no reason except her name had come up during the night, I wondered how Marjorie Freville ever got the money to move to the Bahama Islands. And it doesn't take my kind of mind long to plot out the fact that in his toilet roll chronicles Norman had accused Albert and Sir Ambrose of having him put away. By using me? How? By leaking the information to Freville of where I could be found for crucifixion? Or by paying Marjorie enough to get him certified and take her to New Providence Island?

It begins to sound like a detective story, doesn't it? And then worse: from across the heath in the dark gorse bushes there came this ghastly cackle of noise. It could have been a tropical bird escaped from Tony Armstrong Jones' aviary at Regents' Park — or a small child drawing a stick along the wooden pailings of a fence.

I ran into the house.

Seven

I don't know about you, but I can't get really interested in this plane crash. I go through the motions, I built up a lot of false drama in the last chapter, but it's not the kind of writing that survives. Yes, I miss Albert, I'm sure you do too. He was the best thing in the last book, apparently, nobody liked me; I hope the critics realise that this is honesty at least. I don't care who blew the plane up or who's got the five million pounds but I do miss the odd natter with Albert. I infuriated him but he liked me; he was the only person who had found out that I haven't grown up yet. Other people are inclined to pull me down.

'Another nine years,' his mother told me last time I saw her, 'and you'll be sixty, Horace.'

What do you do with people like that? What I think is they're people who know that they're past it and can't bear to see other people still alive as though nothing's happened.

'You don't remember me, do you?' That was one of those ex-sergeant-major door porters at Granada. What I don't usually do is I'd managed to get one of the waitresses away from the canteen. I had half-promised her a part in one of my plays. 'You used to be our milkman,' he said. Then at the time of the bankruptcy hearing, Leonard Wray the solicitor—you remember Albert had this solicitor on the milk round: 'You must set something aside in future. Make provision. Think seriously about your declining years.'

I tell you something. Shall I tell you something? This is the kind of advice, these are the kind of well-meaning people who drive you to shacking up with a twelve-years-old.

So I had that dream where you've almost got it in but she keeps moving away, hour after hour, it seems. I woke up with an erection like a barber pole under the candle-wick bedspread. Ariadne stood looking at it.

'There's been a call from New York for you,' she said, as soon as my eyes opened.

I defy anybody to answer that with a quick command to jump into bed. New York? Film rights? American publication rights? Dollars?

'Do you know somebody called Jane Chapell?'

Don't we all? Ariadne was looking at the bump under the quilt which was slowly subsiding; I think it had impressed her. Up until now she had been a bit reckless with me, but after this she started playing her cards. Young girls have a terrific instinct about a man's potential; a kind of shrewdness cloaked in innocence. The nearest she had come to a man's prime until now was in biology with old Daffers giggling in her ear.

'What did she want?'

'She didn't say. She kept laughing. It was two o'clock in the morning in New York. She was in a night club called Framis's. There was some very good modern jazz going on. I love New York.'

'Why didn't you wake me up?'

'We couldn't. The girls were all in here naked practically. You kept groaning.'

No wonder.

'They told me to lock the door on the outside then bang it. Is that what they do?' She could see it wasn't and she laughed. 'They were afraid you might attack me.'

I said: 'If you want me you will have to attack me.'

She lost her smile.

'I'm joking, Ariadne.'

She nodded, very soberly. ' I know. I came to you because I knew I could trust you.'

This is one of the nastiest weapons a girl has at close quarters. I sidestepped it: 'Didn't she leave a message?'

Ariadne gave me a piece of paper. 'That's the international operator's number. Call him and he'll re-connect at her expense. Only I think she'll be gone home—it's ten o'clock now. Four o'clock their time.'

She was very knowledgeable for twelve. I've had secretaries who couldn't have told me any of that.

'Dial one-o-eight,' she added. 'There's a sixpence on your desk. I'll be getting your breakfast then I'm going home.'

'No!'

'To get my cello.' You could see she had theatrical blood. One precisely accurate bit of timing and delivery and she had tricked me into betraying everything I hoped for and committing myself into asking her to stay. 'If I get my cello Mummy knows I'm all right and I'm not coming home yet.'

'She won't let you come back.'

'She'll be at rehearsals. Have you got a priest?'

'What?'

'I feel awful.'

'You're not going to die. You're only twelve!'

'Chicken shit,' she said. 'I feel awful about your friend Norman. It's going to prey on my mind.'

'I'll get you a priest.' Where do you get priests? 'See Mrs Bracknell—she's religious. I'll get her up here.' Mrs Bracknell sees the ghost of this old lady who died in the back room; she sits on the end of one of the nurses' beds. 'She's there again,' she says, when she's doing her rounds. And she describes everything the ghost is wearing. Nobody else ever sees her except Mrs Bracknell and sometimes her dog.

'Did he have any family?' Ariadne asked then.

I told her about Marjorie in the Bahamas who, by the way, divorced Norman when the new insanity laws were passed. And I told her again how Jane Chapell used to be Norman's mistress until she ran off with his end money and he shot her in Italy. I was using a different emphasis this time.

'Then why has she phoned from New York? That's funny, isn't it? Do you think she knows anything?'

I told her to stop worrying but she wouldn't; she wanted to go to the authorities and make a clean breast of it, get it off her mind; apparently she hadn't slept very well. She certainly wasn't thinking straight this morning. What about my mind and the nurses' and the doctors' minds?

'What about the poor chap who finds out he's wearing a murdered lunatic's kidneys?'

This quietened her down a little and she went to get the breakfast while I tried to get through to New York and failed. I could see it was going to be a long time before we even ran the risk of breaking the law together. She was wearing—did I tell you what she was wearing? One of the nurse's blue tunics which should have had a skirt below it. From the telephone in the hall I could see her bending over the electric stove in the kitchen, the one that doesn't work. Had she been at the gas stove I shouldn't be able to see her. She was titillating me.

'Your party is no longer there, Mr Fenton...'

Why was the Countess ringing me? How had she got my number? I had seen and heard nothing of her since Albert had transplanted her from Freville's car into his own with a neat bit of grafting. There had been an occasional mention of her in the odd show business page and the last I had heard was that she was running Global Films Hollywood office. Little did I know then, as the novelists say, that she and I were already the nominal partners in one of the biggest business deals ever carried out; between us we were worth five million pounds not dollars.

'Have you got any eggs?'
'I don't think I paid the milkman.'
'When I get my cello I'll bring my money box …'
God is all.

Soon after Ariadne had gone home a boy of about thirteen wearing long trousers came scrabbling at the windows of the double doors of the flat. People often do this and scratch with their two hands on either side in the hope they'll see something going on inside before anybody hears them and answers. I'm talking about people who know our place by hearsay or live nearby. We are going to be a legend in our own time. When you first move in here and become aware of what you've done it's like you've walked into the wrong door at the zoo and found yourself in the lions' dining-room. You immediately start looking for another flat but somehow or other you don't find one; you get caught up in it all or you get used to it. Chakravarti, the architect on the top floor, was all set to go the first murder hunt we had but he didn't; first he was going to buy a place then build one and then design one.

'He keeps rubbing it out,' his wife, Sue, says, hopelessly.

You finally get so that you can't sleep unless somebody's screaming or the police are pounding in.

The boy said something about having a message from Doctor Parsons.

'What does he say?' I asked him.
'What does who say?' said the boy.
'What's the message from Doctor Parsons?'
'I *am* Doctor Parsons,' he said.

Never trust me on ages.

Later I'll give you a list of things not to trust me on. Maybe you've already got your own.

'I want to thank you for those kidneys, Mr Fenton. I felt I ought to tell you personally that the operation has been a success as far as I can judge. The graft has taken. The patient will live.'

'Good,' I said.

Then he became strangely secretive and said: 'You are probably anxious to know the patient's name. I think that you should and I'm going to take the responsibility of telling you.'

To tell you the truth he really embarrassed me. He thought it was all so vital that everybody was on tenterhooks. Are we all like this about our jobs? You would think he was going to say the most famous name in the world, but no:

'Barry Smith,' he said.

'Really,' I said, 'Barry Smith. Well well. Thank you.'

Curiously enough, and quite by the way, it was a name that cropped up again later after he had died (well, success only means a few weeks) and his wife came to me. She had got some garbled story and thought that I personally had donated one of my own living kidneys to prolong her husband's life. She was twenty-six and pretty and grateful (she worked at Marks and Spencers) and we had quite a time for a few weeks. She couldn't do enough for me.

'It's funny,' she said, 'but I feel I know you already.'

That's always a head start. Or a kidney start.

'If there's anything I can do, Mr Fenton,' Doctor Parsons said, 'I mean anything—let me know.'

You can never think of anything when people say that. The rupture's been taken care of as you know but I've still got this bump in the middle of my chest yet my thought is for other people.

'Could you give a prescription for a good supply of the oral contraceptive to a young friend of mine?'

'What's wrong with her own doctor?'

He doesn't want to get struck off the medical register.

'She's very young and very shy and doesn't want her family to know.'

'Is she pretty,' he asked.

'Oh yes. And I think she's a virgin. But she's just about to start living with her boy friend. Disgusting, but what can you do these days?'

His manner toward me had changed and not very subtly.

'Good-o,' he said. 'Send her along. I shall have to make a few tests.' So young, and yet he could already say this without the slightest sign of guilt. And then he said, as if we were now on the same side: 'What did you think of Wendy?'

What did I *think* of her?

'Do you know what,' he said, 'she's got the tiniest vagina in the hospital.'

'Oh?'

'They couldn't fit her for a cap—she was too tiny.'

'Ah,' I said. I always say 'Ah' when I'm refusing to involve absent friends in personal reminiscence. Still, I must admit it intrigued me.

'We may be able to do something about that,' he said, 'when she has her "d" and "c".'

He made it sound like the planning of a new by-pass for the benefit of the community.

'Yoo hoo! I'm home! Horace!'

I knew she was home; I had sat at the side window watching Squires Mount for the past hour and it was now three o'clock in the afternoon. I had seen her come round from Cannon Place carrying the big cello in its brown case in one hand and a small hold-all in the other; even thus burdened she was jumping up onto the Martins' front garden wall and jumping down again, then skipping hopscotch on the last paving stones before our front terrace. Mrs Martin looked round from her back garden when Ariadne called and I called back. I was pleased to hear her call my pad 'home'.

'I've got you some tea ready,' I told her from the window. 'Crumpets and honey.'

103

'Oh, yummy!' Ariadne said, running into the house.

Mrs Martin was getting interested and I gave her a little wave; she had a girl about the same age as Ariadne and I was glad of the opportunity to show that I could be trusted with schoolgirls; that they liked me. People you go to live amongst when you're fifty have no idea of the family life behind you and the number of people who look up to you and respect you. You have to start trying to prove yourself and sometimes fifty is too late. Besides, Mrs Martin was one of the wives who didn't quite smile at me in the street; or to be accurate who smiled not quite at me. I was hoping to improve on this; she was getting quite close to my right ear now. She gave a little wave back but I was experienced enough to know that it could have been to the window above mine; sure enough when I looked up Arthur's wife in the flat above was just withdrawing her duster.

Isn't it fantastic the life that goes on in these seemingly deserted residential areas on a quiet afternoon; they are as secretly teeming as one of Henry Williamson's otter ponds.

We drank tea (*PG Tips*), ate hot crumpets with some of Edna's runny blackcurrant jam, listened to the Eddie Lang/Lonnie Johnson plectrum guitar duets on the Parlophone LP.

'Wum wum fum,' Ariadne said with a mouth bulging with food and her eyes towards the cello, 'ah tah mah chalah—' She gave a big gulp. 'Sorry. And you count my money in the piggy bank.'

'I don't want to touch your savings.'

'Oh don't be so touchy. I don't want to be a kept woman.'

Laughing, joking, her tuning her cello (ah tah mah chalah) while I held the pig upside down and poked a knife blade into the slot, shaking it.

'There's nothing in it,' I told her.

'Yes there is.'

I shook it. 'No there's not.'

'It's not *pennies*' she said, exasperated. 'I don't save pennies.'

'What's in here if not pennies?'

'Fivers.'

What?

'Pound notes. Presents from men. Mummy's friends.'

A picture grew in my mind which I didn't like. 'Do they ever—are they ever unpleasant?'

'They're always unpleasant. Popping up to kiss me goodnight. Especially Dennis. Dennis was the worst. That's why Mummy shopped him. After that we got Bruto. He was a floor-sweeper at Cinnecitta. That's when we lived in Rome. Bruto looks after me but I don't like him. He would kill you if he knew I was here.'

'I've been thinking,' I said. 'Your mother's going to be worried to death when she finds you've collected your things.'

'Let her suffer,' Ariadne said.

She plucked some harmonics to check the octaves. 'I want her to suffer. She once did something unforgivable.' This sounded interesting. 'What was it?'

'I'd rather not talk about it.' She looked down at the carpet. 'It's to do with my puberty.'

I leaned over and rested my fingers lightly on her bent head. 'I'm sorry.'

She shook me off and bent closer to the carpet. 'Move out the light. I've dropped my resin.'

I had mistaken it for an emotional moment. This often happens with me where I find I'm the only one getting worked up.

I told Ariadne that she was going to have to ring her mother and tell her where she was.

She said: 'Then I'm going to tell her who brought me here and what we did in bed last night.'

'We didn't go to bed!'

She just gave me one rather pitying glance and went on tuning her top string.

'A medical examination would soon prove that,' I said.

You know what? That plang plang plang about a half-atone down seemed to comment that I was about a half-atone too late and she knew it. There was so much sophistication in her face

105

when she glanced at me, as though accidentally, that I felt I had insulted her. I didn't know what pit of dejection my face revealed to her but she suddenly put the bloody cello on the floor and wriggled back to get her head between my knees again, curled her hand up and round my neck, pulling my head down and kissing me briefly.

'I'm sorry, Horace. I didn't mean that. I would never get you into trouble, I promise you.'

She had played a wrong card and was blatantly reshuffling the desk but what the hell; I liked it.

She leaned forward and took another crumpet (Lyons) from the marble table and that's when I saw the marks on her throat. The top button of her gym tunic had come undone and there was an angry scarlet weal across her jugular vein. I would swear it wasn't there when she stripped off last night.

'What's this?' I put my finger on it.

'What is it?'

'These red marks.'

She laughed: 'Well what do they look like?'

'They look like the marks of a rope.'

'Oh, do they?' she said, as though I had paid her a compliment. She took out a vanity mirror and studied herself, craning her head to one side. 'Well that's what they are,' she said. 'Bruto tried to strangle me with a rope.'

'When?'

'This afternoon. He caught me coming out of my room with my money box. I managed to throw him.'

'He tried to strangle you?'

'Yes,' she said. 'You see—I know too much.'

'What about?'

This time when she looked down it wasn't to find the resin. 'I'd rather not say...'

It sounded ugly. It sounded very ugly for Bruto; it sounded like ten years inside followed by deportation for life.

'You poor kid,' I said. I ran my fingers down her poor slashed wrists, glad I hadn't questioned her about them. The whole squalid, sad picture was in my head as she clung to me, her teeth gently biting me in the thigh to stop herself from crying. Puberty coming up fast and Dinah, too busy living her life to care, appointing this Italian animal as watch-dog. I saw the big shambling figure against the dim light of the window, the girl screaming with no one to hear. And afterwards the rush to the bathroom and the razor, the futile attempt to end the shame and the horror; and the life of fear ever since—

Why am I holding up the action with this prize-winning crap. The first intimations of mortality, the first bump on your chest and you start trying to make your mark.

'Do you like this?' Ariadne was biting a little fiercer now.

'For God's sake, girl!'

'This is the first thing I remember doing,' Ariadne said. 'It's the only memory that I've got of my father. I was three years old. Do you think that's possible?'

I don't know whether it's possible, it's certainly more decent at three.

'That was in Durban,' she said. 'What's your first memory, Horace?'

'The Town Crier in his three-cornered hat shouting O-Yez! O-Yez! O-Yez!'

She sat right round and looked at me, her elbow now lightly resting in my groin. 'You have to be joking!'

I told her about dancing round the maypole, Jack-in-the-Green, decking out the farm wagons and the horses; about the model-T Ford vans used by Somerlite Oil; about people like Ronnie Footer and the first girl I ever kissed, Nina Vaughn; I told her about 1921 and Hertford Castle and the *Four Horsemen* with Rudolph Valentino.

'Oh boy!' she kept saying. 'And here you still are.'

The telephone rang and I beat Ariadne to it.

'Never answer the phone!' I hissed at her.

She grinned, punched her forehead for being stupid.

'Is Ariadne there?' Joanna Browne asked.

'Just a minute I'll get her,' I said.

It came out automatically; I had heard the question as if she was asking to speak to Ariadne, not is she there. Too late now—a squeal of delight at the other end.

'Really! I thought she might be. It was sheer inspiration the way you ran home from rehearsal last night.'

'I was joking,' I said. 'You know I was joking, Joanna. She's not here.'

'You're lying. I know you're lying. I took you off guard. Don't worry, Horace—I won't tell anybody, promise. I'm coming straight round. They've scrubbed the play. Has Mac phoned you? They're full up. They've got the first thirteen.'

I had that feeling of vast relief you get when you haven't got to do something after all; it is closely followed by the financial panic which made you take the job in the first place. I telephoned my agent but got put off for ten minutes; Ruth wasn't available could she ring me back and she didn't. Then could it wait till Monday she was off to her cottage at Thetford.

'What's the panic?' Ariadne asked me, standing at my elbow with her piggy bank. 'I've got some money.'

'You get ready to go, I'll drive you home,' I told her.

My name was mud already without messing around with precocious schoolgirls.

'I'm not fucking going,' she said—

'Ssssh!' Ruth was on the line at last

'I don't care about "sh"—I'm staying with the nurses across the landing. It's nothing to do with you. I'll be moving my things—'

She had stalked off and I was talking to Ruth who was being so evasive we might have been strangers. No, she hadn't heard the UM slot was full up (liar) and yes she would speak to Wednesday Play about me—

'But, Horace, listen,' she said. 'I hate to lose you but I'm having to cut down my list or expand and I want to stay small...' I've got good news for her.

'You cunt!' said Mac the Knife over the line. 'When did you start drawing on lavatory walls?'

Within half-an-hour of toasting the crumpets I was finished with the BBC for life.

'Don't cry,' Ariadne said.

I wasn't crying I was sitting with my head in my hands on the beer case which we use for a hall chair for the phone. The girl was wandering backwards and forwards transferring her things from my room to the nurses'.

'I don't know why you're doing that. Wendy's coming home tonight. There's no spare bed.'

She said: 'Can I use my sleeping bag on your floor, then?'

I told her again that Joanna was on her way over; that everybody in the business was going to know where she was by this time; that the lines were probably already growing hot.

'Joanna won't tell anybody. It would spoil her scoop.' Then she screamed the way Diana used to scream with sharp, self-inspired pleasure: 'Oh God! I know what! Yes, why don't we? Oh Horace, please—she's such a snoop— why don't we be having an orgy when she arrives? I'll strip off and you dress up in chains and be my slave— that one.'

That one. Twelve years old? Whose side are you on now? My daughters at her age were knitting for the Girls' Friendly Society. Anyway, we hadn't got any chains.

We took the quieter course of being out when Joanna arrived. I'm sorry—but this is not a novel.

Eight

Friday is laundry day. I've got eighteen shirts now. Up until I was thirty-three I had four; I suppose that's some sort of achievement. When I don't like shirts I change as much as three times a day, but when I do I'll make one last three days. By Friday I've usually got an enormous polythene bag stuffed with sheets, pillowcases, pants, shirts, hankies, tea-towels and bath-towels (2).

'I could do some of these,' Ariadne suggested.

I slapped her hand away from them. Stir shit, snot and sweat into romance and you might as well be married, then what have you got? At twenty-one you can preserve the dream maybe but at fifty-one you've got to work at it.

'Your father was a real gentleman,' my mother used to tell us kids when it seemed necessary. 'He used to go right to the end of our long garden if he wanted to pomp.'

It never struck her as funny that everybody in the street knew what he was going to do. It seems to give it an importance it just doesn't have. Even so I like the principle. I never knew him. He was killed fighting for you.

'Laundry must cost you a fortune,' Ariadne said, when we were ready to go.

It doesn't cost me anything more than a little humbled pride, which comes cheap.

I take it all to Tres.

'Why didn't you go to the police?'

On the way to Wimbledon I was quizzing Ariadne about Bruto.

'I couldn't. He's got a hold over Mummy. Or rather he's got a hold over Lenny Price—you know the boxer? —who's got a hold over Marie Annike—that's the model—who's got a hold over—well anyway, they've all got holds over each other.'

'They sound like a bunch of crooks.'

'Well they are. Some of our house guests were ex-cons. Once the police found our house full of stolen property— only they were in with Dennis. He had a hold over the police. Dennis used to make Mummy strip at the point of a gun in front of everybody. At parties and so on.'

There's no business like show business.

'And they used to throw people in the river with bricks tied on them.'

'How did they get them out?'

'They didn't bother.'

There was a time I thought London a great sprawling mess of dirty streets; now I know it as a number of villages strung together. Hampstead, Swiss Cottage, St John's Wood, Marylebone, Marble Arch, Hyde Park, Kensington, Fulham, Putney and pretty soon you're running south into Wimbledon. I don't know why I said all that, you can get a map for sixpence.

If Hampstead is London's flaming youth, Wimbledon is its dotage; a place for rich retirement. Just off the timbered High Street are the timbered houses with their timbered garages and Cedric lived in one of these.

'You get your laundry done here?' Ariadne exclaimed.

'Stay there and try to keep out of sight,' I told her.

But Tres had already seen her from the top window.

'Who's that child in your car?' she asked me as she emptied the washing into her Ali Baba basket (they've got all these twee luxuries). 'For God's sake don't hit the papers now, Horace. Fiona's engaged to a nice boy at the London School of Economics and Cedric is on the local council.'

'Where's Lewis?'

'He's in prison in Sweden. Cedric's just had to send twenty pounds to Gothenburg—you ought to pay that.'

You would think seeing her nearly every Friday I would know all this, but I swear it's a different pattern every week. Fiona in

Sweden, Lewis engaged, Tres on the council, Cedric having a gallstone out; family news gets like that and sometimes gets mixed up with friends' news or bits in the paper.

'Did you start your driving lessons?' I asked her. I never like to just go in and come out as though I'm using her.

'What are you talking about? I passed my test years ago.'

Somebody had told me recently they were starting driving lessons. I couldn't think of anything else.

It was a funny set-up, really. Cedric's wife was killed in a car crash about the same time Tres and the children left me. You remember Sheila who used to count Cedric's french letters? Well he was a pulp editor in those days but with the money from her life insurance he took a chance and started to freelance in the publishing line. Do you read *Movie Comics*? They're Cedric's. He steals picturisation rights in stories and then has them illustrated in colour with balloonage and dramatic narrative — WHAM! and KRRKKKKK! and stuff like that. It's hardly literature but it sells.

'I suppose you haven't got any spare cash?' I asked Tres. She hadn't got any cash but she gave me a brown paper carrier bag filled with potatoes, parsnips, onions, some stale streaky rashers, half a black pudding, part of a knuckle end of leg of lamb, three eggs and part of a bottle of Spanish burgundy wine.

'What the hell's this?'

I was looking at a garish poster advertising one of Cedric's forthcoming *Movie Comics*. 'Don the Con' was the title.

Read how Supercon Don Cons the Bon Movie Megaton of Crackling £Tons—by Horace Spurgeon Fenton (sales 10,000,000! ! !).

'Who gave Cedric permission to use my name on his crap?'

'It's not his crap it's your crap,' Tres said. 'One of your old *Caxton Drakes*.'

He can't use my old Caxton Drakes, they belong to me. Nobody can use my old Caxton Drakes. Slowly I'm turning them into bound novels and creating new potentials for them. Besides, he hasn't bought them.

'He doesn't have to buy them,' Tres said. 'Picturisation rights are not mentioned in your contract with Fleet Periodicals.'

How clever. How bloody clever. You buy First British Serial Rights, allow the author bound rights and soft-cover over three shillings, together with film and dramatic rights and you carefully reserve picturisation rights for yourself; then you give up your job and go into business with a great steaming pile of stolen stories. Tres, my ex-wife and Fiona and Lewis, my ex-children, were not only condoning this smash-and-grab but carrying the bricks.

'Oh my God!' I suddenly remembered: 'That story comes out in bound next month!'

'It's *Grownups Only*,' she said.

'I've rehashed it, taken out *Caxton Drake*—retitled it *Unfit for Babies*. The film rights are sold. The film rights are sold! He can't bring that out as a comic! Besides, what's it going to do to my reviews? The critics will never take me seriously again!'

'Oh Horace,' she said.

Those two words written like that do not really say what she said. Oh Horace, who does take you seriously, who ever did, what is there to take seriously, why don't you get rid of those illusions of literary grandeur.

I think I get it from my mother. Every November 11th toddling up to Westminster Abbey with poppies for the Unknown Warrior. He wasn't unknown to my mother (buy *Hitler Needs You* now)—she swore it was my dad. I mean she really believed this.

'There's you still cadging onions, still trailing round with a schoolgirl hiding on your back seat—and do you know where Cedric is? Lunching at the Press Club.'

Oh? Everybody raise your eyebrows.

'And do you know who with?'

Don't stop now, give yourself a treat.

'Arnold Petts!'

Not *the* Arnold Petts? Not at the Press Club? Not with Cedric?

113

'He's programme director at the BBC. They're putting *Caxton Drake* on television. Cedric will be in charge of the whole series—he may give you some scripting work.'

That's nice of him. 'Who's going to write his stories?'

Tres pointed to the poster: 'He's got them all—over a hundred already written. Yours might be the first to go on if you write a good script.'

'Can I use your phone?' I was using it anyway.

'Who are you phoning?'

'Lassiter Arkwright and Frobisher,' I said. 'Can I speak to Mr Wray please? My solicitor,' I told her.

'He's not your solicitor,' Tres said. 'He's Albert's solicitor. All those stories he conned out of you and never paid you a penny for them.'

'They were not set up,' I told her. And to Leonard: 'Leonard—this is Horace. Horace Spurgeon Fenton.' Even their mothers have to give their full name, solicitors have such a busy time. 'Can you get a list of the books I optioned to Global Films? Send it to a company I'll tell you who, warn them that if they use these stories in any shape or form—Leonard? Miss Who?' It was a crossed line.

Tres cut me off, then took the receiver from me: 'All right, I'll tell Cedric. But you're cutting off your nose to spite your face.' Only a western writer could use a ready-made slogan like that; but then she was living a ready-made life these days: comfortable, happy, secure. QED: 'You just hate it that the children have got a proper father at last.'

What with her critical attitude and Cedric's critical attitude it beats me the laundry ever got done at all. Without my knowing it she had worked herself into an emotional state.

'I baked a cake yesterday,' she said. This couldn't be true. I looked at her. She was trembling. I should think so, too. This wild kind of bragging only betrayed that yearning for normality which had undermined our whole relationship. Baked a cake! She wanted to show it to me but I wouldn't give her any kind of lead up to it.

I asked her how Lewis came to be in Sweden and why he was locked up, but she wasn't listening. 'A sort of fruit cake,' she said.

Driving back Ariadne questioned me closely about Tres. All my girls do this about my almost ex-wives; it is a measure of their interest in me and the seriousness of their intent. Diana, paralysed from the waist down, was never more than slightly ironic about them and called them both 'Auntie'. I could see that Ariadne, part of the Highgate New Wave, was going to take a firmer line. She suggested I poison them both by spreading cyanide on one side of a table knife and then cutting an apple in half. This is done in front of witnesses, the murderer eating the clean half, so that it is never discovered how the stuff is administered.

'Rachel did that,' she said, 'our domestic science teacher to this chap who was pestering her in Florence when she was on her *Ecole de Cordon Bleu* course.'

Wasn't this done in an old Matheson Lang play? I'm sure it was. About a bungalow. The Chinese Bungalow! By a coincidence I had just picked up a second-hand book in Flask Walk with the old actor's name and address (30 Avenue Road, NW3—another Hampstead worthy) written inside in his own hand and all for a shilling. Anyway I challenged her on it and she turned sulky.

'You have to be a hundred years old to remember a thing like that,' she said.

This gave me the first clue that she was lying to me. I should have got it before, I suppose, with the people thrown in the Thames with bricks tied to them, but somehow this hadn't seemed much worse than the other things that went on at the Cookham parties and which had been verified and spread in *The People*. Apparently lying amongst kids these days is the new kind of wit. You're supposed to know which is the lie otherwise you're not with it. The total effect, in a world of prep and 24 buses through Camden Town, is to make life more colourful and exciting.

'Put your foot down!' Ariadne suddenly instructed.

'Why?'

We were coming east along the Fulham Road from Putney.

'How fast will it go?' she asked.

She was sitting round, kneeling up on the passenger seat, her arms along the top of it, her chin resting on her hands, looking back through the rear window, her bottom up on her heels. Her dress was a short-short white wool crochet Dolly Rocker see-through bought at Peter Robinson, the panties M&S St Michael and the tights Kayser Bondor.

'Turn sharp left,' she said now.

I was going so fast I practically mounted the pavement outside *Le Café des Artistes* into Redcliffe Gardens.

'Now right!' she said, a moment later. And when I did she said: 'Good. I think we've lost them.'

'What?'

'We were being followed.'

'Oh yeah??' Then *clang clang clang* and I heard the police bell behind me.

'Quickly,' she said, 'shoot into this mews and stop—that's what Mummy does—'

'It's the police!' I told her.

'I know—but they're not your lot or ours. Do you usually have Jamie? We have "A" Divison.'

As I stopped the car, half out into the traffic stream of Brompton Road, three police cars chopped off my escape as neatly and swiftly as a knife-thrower's knives chunk around his wife's head.

'Crumbs!' Ariadne said, squirming with delight.

'All right—get out!' the man said.

Very stiff, very courteous, traffic stopping, everybody looking.

'Do you mind coming too, miss?'

'What about the car?'

'We'll take care of it, sir.'

Ariadne prodding me, hissing: 'Demand to see your solicitor…'

She was lapping it up. We did the fast drive with the blue lamp flashing, down to South Kensington, through to King's Road, on to Victoria and New Scotland Yard. Ariadne sat in the back with two detectives and I could hear them talking—I was in the front.

'Do you want my fingerprints?' she was saying.

'Whereabouts, miss?'

Big laugh.

Detective Chief Superintendent Jamie Kinnear was so delighted to see us it was embarrassing.

I'd never been to his office before and seeing it now I could understand why he was always glad of a chance to get up to Hampstead. These glass-fronted cabinets they're putting up everywhere and nobody protesting with Orwell dead; you grow up, you qualify, you get filed away in the fourth drawer from the top.

'You can't open the window,' Jamie told us—rather pathetically I thought—'that's the sad thing.'

They were double windows. All you could do was adjust the air conditioning and you didn't even know it was air. 'Now to get down to brass tacks, laddie,' he said, 'have you been across to see your wife in Wimbledon and in a fit of temper, shall we say, blown her boy friend's motor car to pieces with a home-made bomb?'

'No,' I said.

Ariadne gasped with sheer excitement.

'Ah now, I didna think ye had,' Jamie said. He was seething with inner ecstasies, immeasurably grateful to me for not upsetting some theory of his. 'I'm glad to have you confirm it,' he said. And getting up to dismiss us: 'Ye'll find your motor-car outside.'

'Aren't you going to tell us what's happened?' Ariadne burst out.

'Eh?' he said.

What had happened was that ten minutes after we had driven

away from Tres' house Cedric's car, parked outside on the road, had blown up.

'Fortunately, nobody was hurt this time,' he said.

This time? Then I got the picture; the reason for the delight, ecstasy, general *bonhomie*. The superintendent was looking for the man who had blown up AK-Edgar over the Adriatic. They love this repeat thing.

Possibly the work of the same killer . . . It is believed to be the same kind of weapon used . . . The body was found in similar circumstances to . . .

It all peters out in the end but never mind, they've been turning things up, having theories, earning their scratch. I mean how could Cedric in cheapjack publishing have anything to do with a plane-load of film moguls? They were two different worlds. Don't think Tres has improved herself in any way.

'One more thing, Mr Spurrajon,' Jamie said as we were finally going. 'Would you have a copy of your new book, at all?'

'Which one's that?'

He consulted a note below desk level so that I couldn't see it. 'Ah yes—*Supercon Don*—'

'That's not my character—it's one of Cedric's comic rehashes. I'm going to sue him.' In fact it was a very good big-business con story based on one of Albert's ideas when he was still a milkman. He used to be full of these fantastic ideas for making money; they were never practical but they made good plots. '*That's Unfit for Babies.*'

'That's a good title,' Ariadne said. 'What's it about—condensed milk?'

Jamie laughed: 'I see you've your mother's pawky sense of humour, lassie!'

Did you hear that? He saw a shade too late, either from my face or Ariadne's, that he had slipped up. He had a very endearing way of blushing and holding his face when he'd embarrassed you. 'Ah, don't worry, your little secret's safe with me,' he said. 'I'm not concerned with morals or juvenile delinquency.'

You feel a bit of an idiot when you've kept up a big pretence and everybody you think you've fooled has actually been helping you just to save your face.

'I'll have somebody pick up a copy of the book,' he said now. 'Perhaps you wouldn't mind signing it?'

A nice compliment, the falseness of which came across ten seconds later. I told him that I hadn't got copies yet but I had another book, equally brilliant, which I'd let him have.

'I'm afraid it has to be that one,' he said.

He wasn't being nice about my writing; he was working on the case of the sabotaged airliner. It happened to be identical with the plot of *Unfit for Babies*.

Below in the car park the coloured detective was crawling from underneath my car as we got there. He smiled pleasantly, or as pleasantly as they can, and showed me my keys; there was a new one on the ring.

'This is for the burglar alarm,' he said. 'I'll show you how it works.'

'What burglar alarm?'

'Touch the car and you'll see.'

I touched the car and it shrieked at me, the horn blaring and a bell ringing from somewhere inside the bonnet. Man Friday was grinning and talking. Ariadne was screaming and holding her ears, but all you could hear was the electric cacophony. He stopped it with the key, showing me how to do it.

'They'll never get a bomb under that,' he said. And he said, in what was meant to be a reassuring way: 'Don't forget we'll never be more than hearing distance away from now until we get him.'

You see, what Jamie had neglected to tell me, was that the bomb in Cedric's car was intended for me. The white Volvo and the white Capri are not very different—and somebody knew I was visiting Tres. Great, isn't it—I was nearly blown up. No wonder old Jamie was delighted to see me.

'Who wants to kill you?' Ariadne asked as we drove north through Regent's Park. 'Albert?'

'I don't think he would blow me up.'

'And what's in that story?' she said.

'Nothing,' I told her. 'It's just a very big con trick connected with the film business. A way of making five million pounds out of foreign investors. Company fraud.'

She said: 'But that's what this is all about. That's what Jamie is investigating. Is there an airliner crash in it?'

'No,' I said. 'I never kill innocent people in fiction.'

She put her hand on mine between the seats. 'I think you're very kind, Horace.'

It's true; I am kind.

'Look,' she said, pointing: 'there's some giraffes!'

I stopped the car, took her across to see the animals. On the side of the road there's an enclosure for giraffes, dromedaries, chimpanzees and zebras. You can see them free at the gaps in the hedge.

'Lift me up,' she said excitedly.

I lifted her up. I was excited too. If there's one thing you don't have to lift people up to see it's giraffes. A Scotland Yard 'Q' car pulled up not far away and the crew pretended an interest in the animals. I was not inhibited. They knew who I had with me. They were not worried and so why should I be worried. Jamie's attitude seemed to give me *carte blanche*. I felt more officially her custodian.

'Can I sit on your shoulders?' she said.

I bent my head low and hoisted her up and she straddled my shoulders with her long legs, her crutch in the back of my neck and wriggling gently with delight.

'I wish I had some buns,' she said.

How the young ones do like animals. The giraffes were peering around as if in search of Africa. One raised its head and gazed wistfully after a high-flying jetliner. They all seem to have their troubles the same as us. On the wooden wall of the zebra house was written in white stripy chalk:

'IGUANAS—GO HOME!'

Nine

Joanna Browne was in my bed when we got back.

'What the hell are you doing there?' Ariadne snapped. And to me: 'What's she doing here?' As though it might be a Friday arrangement.

The child was holding my arm in a possessive, wife-like way. She didn't give anybody a chance to explain anything, but rushed on to Joanna: 'This *happens* to be our bedroom!'

She then went to the head of the bed, jerked the pillow from under Joanna's head and took a tiny white cotton nightie from under it. It looked like a conjuring trick—I don't wear cotton nighties.

Joanna shot me a glance of fearful pity; like nothing could stop me going to prison now.

Joanna got off the bed, slowly and painfully it seemed. Apart from having her shoes and dress off she wasn't undressed. These she put on again, guiltily, under Ariadne's accusing stare of fury.

'I've had a bit of a VNI,' she said. 'If you'll just give me time to explain.'

'Very Nasty Incident,' I translated to Ariadne.

I noticed now that Joanna had a shadowed eye and a swelling lip and was apparently quite badly bruised. It was the result of a script conference with Mac McKilvey last night at her flat.

'Couldn't you sue the BBC?' Ariadne said, sympathising a little now. 'That's what Mummy does.'

'They're looking for you everywhere,' Joanna said, when she'd got her dress on.

This pleased and intrigued Ariadne, she sat on the bed hugging her knees and showing her arse. 'Tell me all about it.'

'Did you go home this afternoon?' Joanna asked.

'No. Did I, Horace? I've been with Horace. His wife's

boyfriend's car got blown up by a bomb in mistake for his. I was sitting in it!' And on a note of new recollection she said to me: 'I probably saved your life, Horace. They didn't know it was your car because I was sitting in it.' And to Joanna: 'What happened?'

'I went over to see if Dinah could put me up,' Joanna said. And to me: 'I've been turfed out of my flat—the bed went through the ceiling! Anyway, somebody broke in and stole your cello and three hundred pounds from Lenny Price's jock-strap while he was in the shower.'

Ariadne the child spoke with lips, mouth, everything: 'Fucking liar!' Joanna's finishing school expression came on and Ariadne qualified it: 'He was not in the shower he was trying to rape me again! Look!' She pulled down the neck of the white woollen dress and showed the rope mark.

'Is that the one you call Bruto?' I said. 'He tried to strangle her with a rope—look at that! We ought to get the police '

'A *rope* mark?' Joanna said. 'In that case I'm covered in them!' And she pulled up her dress and slip, pulled down her bra, rolled down her tights—there were ghastly red marks everywhere right up to the top of her thigh.

'You too?' I said. 'They ought to lock him up.'

She said: 'That's Mac McKilvey on two bottles of daddy's brandy. They're ordinary common or garden love bites.

All that rope business was more of her lies, then. So was Bruto. Lenny Price is one of Dinah Thing's boxers. Film stars often have boxers; well they look like boxers. They come to rehearsals, parties, hang around their flats and so on. Big, musclebound types, often quite young. They sit around, smoke and drink, chatter to each other. Sometimes, even at a select affair you'll hear a voice yell:

'Two 'arves, mate!'

That'll be somebody calling for his beer. They have names like Alf and Sid and Lenny, flash lots of banknotes, sit outside studios in big cars, stretch out on the Carlton beach at Cannes—the showbiz scene is riddled with them. I expect they are to the film business in London what gangsters are to the film business in Hollywood and New York. In a confectionery world full of money and paperweight people it is probably necessary to have heavies; not necessarily to do the dirty work but just to be on hand, like publicans keep alsatians for when they call 'time'. You never know. Norman had borrowed somebody's boxers to have me nailed to a tree. I haven't said much about this because it's too recent to be comfortable and my hands still hurt, but I will say now there was no animosity there or personal feeling.

'What 'ave you bin up to then me ol chicken,' the one said who drove in the nails. He didn't even know. It was just a job of work. One of them kept looking at his watch to see if it was opening time.

'He wanted me to play ludo with him,' Ariadne was saying. 'And when I wouldn't he started getting ideas.'

Oh yes and they play ludo in the props room. If you've been round a film or television studio you must have heard those thick voices coming from behind closed doors: 'Your move, Sidney.' 'No—after you, Fred.'

Dinah Thing had three or four of these boxers and at the time of the big scandal one of them was accused of the murder of the shopgirl they found dying in a bedroom but there wasn't enough evidence to prove anything. Everything, including her clothes and her boy friend, the prosecution said, had gone into the Thames.

'So now you know who's trying to blow Horace up,' Joanna Browne was saying.

Had I missed something?

'They think I've stolen three hundred pounds for you,' Ariadne told me.

'Not for Horace. They don't suspect Horace at his age. They're looking for one of your other dropouts—Roger, Chris, one of those,' Joanna said. 'They've gone down to Weybridge. They think you're living on a barge with a crowd of hippies. They think they sent you home to steal some cash. They think—'

'Are you writing this?' I asked her. 'Is this something you're writing? What d'you mean one of her *other* dropouts?'

Joanna looked all peculiar for a moment as if she'd just been shaken out of a good dream, 'What did I say? What was I saying?'

Ariadne said: 'I don't know anybody on a barge at Weybridge.'

Joanna Browne sat on the bed and lowered her head into her hand. 'I hit my head when I fell out of bed,' she said. Could I have a glass of water, please?'

'Did Dinah's thugs put that bomb in Cedric's car?' I asked her.

'I don't know. I don't know, Horace. I'll have to look in my little red book.' She took her book out and started flicking through the pages, read a little, then gasped: 'Oh God. I've got my mother's birthday in here!'

'Does it matter?' Ariadne asked.

I knew it mattered.

Joanna was crying, the tears streaming down, falling onto the book. 'This is fiction. This is supposed to be fiction.'

I sat down with her and put my arm around her. She was going through what is probably the most terrifying mental ordeal in a writer's life; the first time fact and fiction get mixed up. I can only convey it in terms of a pilot passing through the sound barrier for the first time.

'Take deep breaths,' I told her.

'I'll get some water,' Ariadne said.

She went out and I let Joanna's head rest on my shoulder while I stroked her tears away, kissed her better.

'Will I be all right, Horace?'

'Yes,' I said.

She shuddered, then clung to me. 'I love you,' she murmured.

She didn't really; it's all a part of it. I showed her some things on the table, remains of my breakfast.

'What's this?' I asked.

'Pepper pot,' she said.

'This?'

'Salt cellar.'

'Good.' I picked up a scrap of fried bread. 'This?'

She went to speak, got lost, was about to blurt into tears—but then got it: 'Fried bread!'

'Now press your feet hard on the floor as though you've got cramp.'

She did this with all her strength and as she did it the lines went from her face, her eyes tranquillised, her body softened against me.

'Thank God you were here,' she whispered.

I know how grateful I felt when Gordon Trotsky saw me through mine. Really she should have stripped off and laid on her stomach while I knelt across her back and worked her feet to get the *plana* circulating, though I knew this would only cause trouble with Ariadne.

Human *plana* is the invisible flux that encircles and cores through the vital organs and the spleen like magnetic lines of force through lodestone. It can become very weak with some mental instabilities and certain physical conditions (like Diana's paralysis). The *plana* can be stimulated and revived by *paramagnetic donors* like Trotsky (sort of transfusion process) or can be kept strong merely by always lying with your head toward the north pole and your body therefore subject to the longitudinal lines of the earth's magnetic field which, in Hampstead for instance, is 0.22 gauss.

'Send her home,' Joanna said, softly, giving me little cheepers all over the face and neck (small kisses).

We could hear Ariadne laughing and talking to the nurses and not bothering too much about the glass of water.

'I can't,' I said.

'She's got a hold over you, hasn't she?' I had to admit it. 'Crummy little hot arse!' she said, rather uncharacteristically, which is also a symptom of mental take-over in fiction writers.

She looked at me steadily for a moment then said:

'Have you ...?'

'What, dot dot dot?' I said. 'No. Not yet.'

'If you do you'll go to prison.'

'You don't know how old she is,' I said.

'Yes I do. She's fourteen and a half—'

I stopped her: 'Don't tell me! I don't want to know.'

'That's no defence, Horace. Spend one night with her and you'll be crucified.'

'Not again,' I said.

'Her father's a Roman Catholic priest—'

I slapped her face just as Ariadne came in with the glass of water. 'What was that for?' she asked.

'She keeps talking fiction. I'm trying to snap her out of it.'

Joanna was rubbing her cheek.

'Here,' Ariadne told her, giving the. tumbler: 'Drink this. All of it. We'll go on!'

'It's all right.' Joanna put the glass away. 'I'm all right.' And to me she said, unable to expand it: 'I wasn't talking fiction that time.'

'Mac made that up. That was Mac's idea.'

We were talking over Ariadne's head but she seemed more concerned with the glass of water she's just been getting the nurses to dope with barbiturate sleeping tablets.

'It was one of his snide jokes—I don't want any water!'

'I went to all the trouble to get it,' Ariadne said.

'He was just getting at Dinah. He knows she doesn't want anybody to know.'

'When you've finished talking about my family,' Ariadne said, 'drink this fucking water.'

Joanna looked at me as if to say: 'Roman Catholic priest!' Mind you I don't see why they should be better than any other priest.

'Are you going to drink it or aren't you? If not I'll throw it away.'

You can see the kid's point once you know what she's done. She has just told the nurses that I was trying to get her to sleep with me and could they give her something to put me to sleep. That's what all the laughter was about in the kitchen while I was bringing Joanna through her aberration. It was the beginning of a battle of wits between the two girls to shower their favours on me—which is a little ironic when you consider how little I get most of the time.

'What have you done with Lenny's three hundred pounds?'

'Drink this water and I'll tell you.'

I left them. I left them to it. I knew what was going to happen to that water; what happened to the orange squash at Joany Scattergood's party.

'Horace . . .'

Four pretty maids all in a row; Helen, Mary, Claire, Patricia in their mini-mufti with hair-dos, eye-shadow, new nails, beckoning me into the kitchen. I was halfway to the lavatory with the fourth big volume of Orwell's correspondence and writing, *In Front Of Your Nose*. As Ring Lardner, according to Scott Fitzgerald, got less percentage of himself into his work than any other writer, so I believe did Orwell get the most of himself down in his short life; and there was nothing in the universe so small that he couldn't shed a little extra light on it. Born on a desert island and brought up with nothing but Orwell's complete output you would astonish your rescuers by being better informed, adjusted, orientated and socialised than the average educated citizen and already angry about the right things. Given permission to swear and print obscenities (unfortunately he was born too early) George Orwell/Blair would have been the best writer this century; even stuck with bugger and bum he didn't do too badly.

'Come inside and shut the door,' Claire whispered.

On the lavatory wall of the thirties Orwell had the chalk but Henry Miller had the language.

'See what we've made for Wendy,' Patricia said.

'He's not listening!'

'He's not even looking!'

'His lips are moving!'

My lips have started moving when I think. Another ten seconds I could have been in the lavatory. It's the only place. It really is the only place.

'Did you get a present for her?' Claire asked.

'Who?'

It was that night's first human dignity ritual. Wendy fresh back from hospital and clear of foetus was now lying in state in a clean white nightie across the landing. The girls had made her jellies, trifles, cakes, goodies, each contributing their own personal speciality (how is it out of every ten girls seven can only make lemon-meringue pies?). There was that old-fashioned formality that even the most modern way-out girls drop into at the mention of wedding or confirmations or anything that touches their basic beliefs. They were cross with me for still being the same old Horace.

'Put your suit on (I've got a suit now) then you can come and see her,' Claire said.

'I hope you've got a present,' Patricia said.

Of course I've got a present. I've got two presents; a box of *Good News* and a bunch of violets. Who wants to fuck Ariadne anyway if she's only fourteen-and-a-half? If you're waiting for it I advise you to put the book down now and go to a Edna O'Brein book and get it out of your system before coming back. We are on one of Horace's intellectual kicks here. Lavatories always do this to me. I write speeches in my head. I had a good half-hour evacuation with George Orwell and a cup of tea which Helen provided. It's a tatty little bog and yet, like all bogs, it's home. There are great veins of red, rusty fungus erupting out of the plaster all over the walls of the lavatory and the bathroom wherever, I imagine, there are hidden pipes; it's like some monster that's trying to get out at you and at first you feel impelled to wipe your arse and get out fast, yet in the end it becomes a friend.

When I went back into my room Joanna Browne, daughter of the Earl of Whatever, was kneeling on the floor with her hair wet and water running down her face and searching minutely Ariadne's belongings while the child sat watching without anger or rancour.

'Tell me if I'm getting warm,' Joanna said.

'It's not there. I didn't touch his jock strap. If he took it off it was optimism.' To me she said: 'Would I bother to bring my piggy bank if I had three hundred pounds tucked away?'

'I'm just going to wash my hands,' I said.

I always wash my hands now, even after just spitting and pulling the chain. I saw this children's hour programme where all the germs were shown white; even if the woman had just had a quick pee the germs were massed like shaving lather all over her hands and arms and dripping onto her feet and everything she touched—like shaking hands or kissing her child—turned white and, I assume, began to petrify and rot.

They show these things on the box without any 'X' certificates or warnings to the young.

'You shouldn't watch it, dad,' Fiona used to say when she was helping to bring me round, 'if you're going to be like this every time.'

It's a kind of compulsion; to know what we're made of and what the dangers are, I mean: you have to watch.

I forget what happened next. Oh God, that's great, isn't it. You get halfway through a book and you forget what happened next. I'm trying to get to the bed scene to tell you the truth. The most appalling thing happened. I'm dying to tell you about it and yet I'm ashamed of it, too. Just the same I think anybody would like to do it if they had the courage to admit it. I doubt whether they would write about it afterwards, though.

Look, I'll tell you what I'll do; I'll skip through our formal visit to Wendy and get to bed. Nothing remarkable happened there anyway. Doctor Aubrey Parsons sat on a chair by the bed eating Wendy's grapes.

'Barry Smith is still alive,' he told me.

'That's nice,' I said.

'Let me see your scars again,' Wendy asked Ariadne. 'Aubrey says Horace just missed a vital spot. I mean I did.'

Nobody was fooled about who had cut her wrist; pretending to be was just a formality.

'I haven't got them now,' Ariadne said. 'I took them off. Look, I've got a Caesarean now.'

Ariadne's wrist scars were made of plastic, stick-on. She pulled her dress up and her panties and tights down to show us the new location of the ugly stitchy weal.

'You're not quite accurate there,' Aubrey said. 'Let me shift it a bit.'

He managed to get his hand well into her pubic hairs even with everybody watching while he removed the Caesarean scar. I thought it was disgusting, but nobody else seemed to.

'They're educational, really,' Patricia said, about plastic scars.

We ate some cakes and the lemon-meringue pie with teaspoons out of saucers and drank a glass of sherry each (medium-sweet South African). Claire gave Wendy a pink knitted bed-jacket which she put on; it seemed oddly appropriate or at least symmetrical for it had come from a young mother who had died in childbirth at the hospital but whose child had survived.

'I hope can still have children,' Wendy said.

'Oh yes, I think we'll be all right now,' the doctor said, and he was rubbing his wrist and extending his fingers as if relishing some rubber glove he had once been fond of.

Everybody seemed to know what he mean except Joanna and me. Which is funny considering that we are both writers. The whole thing seemed rather over Joanna's head and she didn't say very much until we'd left the party.

'Let me get this straight,' she said while we were in the dark hall together and Ariadne was in the lavatory. Writers have to get things straight. 'We were just celebrating that girl's abortion?'

'Yes.'

She thought about it as though she wasn't clear what to write in her little book. A good deal of tortuous thinking goes on in the matter of unwanted and terminated pregnancies.

On the one hand it is the proof that she is a woman, that all her parts work, that she could have had a baby; on the other that now surgical intervention has taken place maybe none of the parts work and she couldn't have a baby.

There is a later phase where the aborted infant would have been crippled for life and another stage where the mother might have died if she'd gone through with it.

And so to bed.

Joanna wanted me, this is what made the whole thing work. This was not only because I had seen her through her fact/fiction trauma (though this had given me a nice credit mark); her wanting me had started a split second after I had withdrawn my little finger at the party.

Questioned, she would never tell you this but it is psychologically true all the same. The knowledge of it came in separate ways, the first being when she related again her experience with Mac Gordon McKilvey last night. Because she wouldn't let him have his own single-tracked way he accused her of fancying me. He started trying to put her off in the nicest possible way as one does with one's friends' mistresses; for instance:

I don't want to be disloyal, he's a good chap, but I would say this to his face and you can ask him, I mean he knows himself what he's like—then a short list which can include impotence, homosexuality, perversion, drug-taking, masturbation, venereal disease (he may be clear now of course), bigamist or, if you're really clever, something particularly applicable to this particular girl; if she loves children, then he once kicked a child to death when he was drunk.

'I didn't believe half the things he said about you,' she told me. 'For instance—this can't be true!—did you once rape a paralysed girl while she was still unconscious?'

And sometimes (and this is cleverest of all) they pick on the one thing that is true. I explained about Diana the sculptress. We all know about Diana. It wasn't rape it was debt-collection.

'Could I be raped while I was asleep and not wake up?' guess-who said. Go to sleep, dear, I'll tell you in the morning.

'That's not a very nice thing for a child to say,' Joanna Browne said.

Ariadne said: 'You grownups are such hypocrites! You're not lying in between me and Horace to keep him away from me. You want him yourself!'

Joanna blushed. 'Take your foot off his legs and shut up!' she said.

She knew Ariadne had got her foot across between my knees; I thought she'd missed it. Another minute and Ariadne would have been tickling my genitals with her toes like the Countess used to do.

I swear I'm kinky, sometimes. How do girls know this without asking you; they just go ahead and do the very things you want them to do.

'You drink this water, then.' Ariadne had got some more doped water. It wasn't really doped. Helen had a quiet word with me while she was in the bath—we don't lock doors it's another nice family thing about shared flats.

'If she gives you a glass of water pretend to go to sleep for a little while,' Helen said. 'The tablets won't hurt you. They're for your fingernails.'

They've even got *tablets* for their fingernails!

Getting them into bed with me hadn't been easy. At least, it hadn't been easy for them; it had been easy for me, I'd just made the Ovaltine. The hundred odd arguments against all sleeping together were resolved in the typically female way that as long as Joanna was there to chaperone us it would be all right (as long as it's an orgy and not a normal couple then okay).

Mind you, I'm not one of those divorce court judges who think that going to bed together is the same as committing misconduct; ninety-percent of the country sleeps together in hate. It helps a new relationship perhaps simply because the girl has probably got her pants off for the first time. With these short-shortie nighties you can't even be sure of that and you might just as well be watching television.

'Tell Joanna about the nineteen-twenties, when you were a boy,' Ariadne said, after she'd given up trying to dope Joanna.

'I want to go to sleep,' Joanna said.

Ariadne said: 'That's what I mean.'

Very funny; so I'm a bore.

'Tell Joanna about the times your mother made you all rattle your knives and forks to kid the neighbours you had food,' Ariadne said next.

'You just told her.'

'Tell her about the General strike in nineteen-twenty-six. Horace and his brothers and sister used to dig peat out of the ground and sell it. Tell her. They used to go round after horses with a little barrow and collect it and sell it— you know, manure. Shit. Isn't that fab? I had a horse once and its penis was dragging on the ground. Do you think it's painful? I was with this chap. It really turned him on . . .'

I don't know how much of that you could stand lying flat on your back under a candlewick bedspread with two girls, one of them Ariadne. I'm sure it was all calculated. She remembered or imagined about three more incidents like this involving herself or a swimming instructor or a young teacher in Austria and then after about twenty minutes she heaved herself out of the sheets and knelt high on the pillow to reach for the lights. Joanna closed her eyes.

'I can't sleep with the light on,' Ariadne said.

We gave her ten minutes to get to sleep then went for each other so simultaneously that we bumped heads. If you really want to sex up your married life then get the au pair girl to sleep alongside you and try to make love to your wife without shaking the bed. Just after Joanna Browne's first orgasm (I mean first ever) I discovered Ariadne's urgently yearning face and peppermint breath under mine; I kissed her on the mouth and the *plana* went leaping through the three of us as if I'd just made the last connection in a high voltage circuit.

The next time I walked down Squires Mount everybody smiled straight at me as if they knew. Mrs Martin was trimming her *Cotoneaster Horizontalis* and you won't believe this but I gave her bottom a little friendly pat.

'You look lovely,' I told her.

She laughed and said 'Oh, go on!' or something. She didn't mind. She didn't mind! I could have done it months ago. I felt like—you remember Arturo Conti walking down Wardour Street? A real sod at last and everybody knowing. And respecting you for it. It was like I'd been doing all these good works under cover with nobody being quite sure then suddenly out of the blue you get the OBE.

It improved me, I could feel it, there was something honest about it. The girls felt better too.

'Oh boy!' said Ariadne at breakfast, bacon fat on her top lip, 'and I thought you were going to be all talk.'

Horace Spurgeon Fenton, writer, artist and year book.

'God is love, yes, but love,' Trotsky once told us triumumphantly, 'is *plana.*'

Ten

Sad scene everybody cry. Dawn in the Hampstead bedsit, everybody asleep, the author sitting down secretly practising typing with holes in his hands:

tHe bbiG BrOwn ʐabbit s its iN abowlof sOUp—

Ah, shit.

I wanted to get this dream down while it was hot. You can't tell a dream you have to write it and you have to do it hot. The fear and the frenzy and the heartbreak of a dream are the most difficult things to catch in literature. This big brown rabbit sitting in a bowl of soup, for instance. Just its head and shoulders were above the creamy opaque surface and it was looking round at a crowd of people, me and B— the poodle. I was being proud of the bowl with the rabbit in it as though it was something I had invented. Just to prove I could do it again I tipped it out, refilled the bowl, then tried to pick up the rabbit. That's when it went mad. Suddenly it was as big as a six foot rat and murderous. People tried to grab it, B— went for it, it swerved this way and that and then leapt at me and got me by the fingers. I held up my hand and the long heavy body of the rabbit hung down from its teeth which were embedded in my ringers. It hung there for a long time with voices shouting panicky advice and then it fell, came after me again, this time leaping at my throat, me screaming, everybody screaming, B— barking. Its teeth hit the side of my throat, it fell, came up again, hit my throat. I woke up with the hard teeth hitting my throat and discovered that it was my own fist with the fingernails pointing together like a rabbit's mouth; I jabbed my fingernails into my throat about three more times before I could stop it.

You know what it is? This is being an author. You're not supposed to go to sleep and stop work. These are secondary and advanced traumas which Joanna doesn't know anything about yet.

'Whatsa marrer?' Ariadne asked from her sleep.

'I've just been attacked by a rabbit, he said,' I said.

He said, I said... Did you get that? Sticking 'he saids' and 'she saids' in your conversation, talking in quotes. That's another thing. De Quincy called it the horrors and yet we can't even get National Sickness Benefit for it.

I gave up trying to type. You remember that western where Marlon Brando gets his gun hand smashed by Karl Malden and goes away and secretly practises it better? I wonder sometimes Karl Malden hasn't been shot dead in real life. He's done more things to more people in more movies than anybody else in Hollywood. Remember Baby Doll! That wasn't acting. That old man young girl thing really revolts me in other people. Have I said that before?

Anyway I've done the rabbit dream as well as I can and I thought I would try it on Mrs Bracknell's black museum and by a coincidence I met her later that Saturday (did you remember it's Saturday) morning in Heath Street. I didn't mention the rabbit because of what she mentioned first.

But that's getting ahead a bit. First of all we got up and we had breakfast. I mentioned breakfast, didn't I? Somewhere? I think I did. Then Ariadne, naked (not naked as though I was a man and she was a woman but naked as though I wasn't there—I mean this is morning and we're family) spotted the typewriter out and the bit of paper in it. Do you think she found this poignant?

'This is all wrong, Horace. Horace. This is not right. Are you just learning to type or something? Anyway, it should be "The lazy fox" not the rabbit...'

That and Joanna ironing everything in sight. She's had her first climax and feels like a wife—or that she ought to be one as soon as possible. Don't think I'm fooled by this first orgasm thing; if a girl can't say she's a virgin then she implies that not having had an orgasm is the same as being a virgin. It's a very bent second barrel that only hit a very slow target. But when it's genuine, when sex suddenly becomes beautiful instead of just a kick, then it must be god-sent for a purpose and not just for pleasure; it must be for making babies with. I show you what I mean:

We are walking, the three of us, up Cannon Place and round by Christ Church as a Saturday wedding drives away. The bride in the back of a ribboned limousine, her dress and veil filling the car like a big white wing-spread bird sitting on top of a little pin-striped navy-blue egg.

'I never want to get married as long as I live,' Joanna Browne says.

'Hmmmm...' says Ariadne, looking at me, warningly.

I could have done without both of them. I was in a writing mood. I didn't want to go half-arsing around the shops buying black bread and yoghourt. You spend half your time making girls and the other half trying to lose them. If I'm going to write anything half decent I have to draw all the shutters dark, play an Eddie Lang solo on the guitar of an old Fats Waller (When I say 'get it!' Ever'body mess around!) record, pace up and down for an hour, lie on the bed for an hour to slow the pulse and get into limbo —then it just might start to happen. It takes just one person saying 'How are you getting on?' the moment before I hit the first word and I have to start the whole thing again.

Have you noticed any of these requirements during the last few days as I have described them? Now it was Mrs Bracknell.

'Mr Fenton! Mr Fenton!'

She is standing amid a crowd of people on one side of the pedestrian crossing, we are standing with a crowd of people on the other side, there is a white-water rapid of murderous traffic screaming between us.

'What?'

'Your life is in danger!' she shouted.

'She's got another message for you,' Ariadne said; then to Joanna Browne and the rest of the Heath Street shop: 'She got a spirit message from Horace's dead poodle about the sabotaged airliner.'

'There's a man trying to kill you!' Mrs Bracknell was shouting now. A police motor-cycle got between us with its radio squeaking and I missed the next bit, but then got: 'He's a titled Italian!'

'Oh?' I shouted. What do you say with everybody looking at you?

Next instant some brave public-spirited soul put his foot on the crossing and stopped the traffic. Mrs Bracknell got pushed to our side of the road, we got pushed to hers, she turned to shout again but then a rather dramatic thing happened. Somebody clamped a gloved hand over her mouth and dragged her into a car which drove off up the hill and turned with squealing tyres into the road by the hospital.

'Did you see that?' Joanna Browne gasped.

'No—what?' I was glad to see her go. It had become embarrassing. A Hampstead crowd is not a normal crowd; they'll participate in anything without much encouragement.

'Come to the Quaker Church on Thursday afternoons!' a woman said to me.

I quickly pulled the girls on towards the Express Dairies.

'Aren't you going to telephone the police?' Ariadne shouted.

She must be joking. Never send for the police, it might make it worse. Especially if you feel like writing. We managed to get five small articles of pre-wrapped food for six guineas and then went and sat at the continental occasional table outside The Coffee Cup in the High Street. We were joined almost immediately by a young man who said:

'So anyway, why don't you come to a freak-out at the Roundhouse tonight, darling?'

This is what I mean by Hampstead.

He was dressed as a Dutch settler in the mid-west around 1860. I swear they're all on their way to some fancy-dress party these days. He wore a Dutch-boy cap on wavy golden hair down to his shoulders, a drooping moustache over a meerschaum pipe, a pair of merry twinkling eyes which he must have got from some catalogue.

Oddly, he wasn't talking to me but to the girls. And when he saw me watching he said:

'Perhaps your father would like to come too?'

I ignored him, drank my tea, but went on listening. It turned out that he was a top photographer for Photo-Centre in Covent Garden, Ariadne was a concert cellist and Joanna the daughter of the last man to be hanged for murder in the state of Oregon.

'He ran amok with a machine gun and killed a whole string of race horses without even hitting the jockeys ...'

'I nearly directed Casino Royale which was frightfully funny in a way because ...'

'And there I was in the middle of the concerto with my bow stuck in the "f"-hole ...'

Photography hadn't impressed anybody enough so he was now a film director. I would like to crayon the scene here for the benefit of the book jacket artist (why do they always give me abstracts I don't understand?). Joanna is sprawled back on the bench seat with her lemon-tea in the silver tumbler-holder. She is wearing 1930 wide-bottomed crepe trousers in green and a short mink fur coat. My sister Christine wore an identical outfit except the fur was rabbit when she took me to see the Western Brothers at the New Theatre in Cambridge in 1929.

> *We'll stick a flag on Snowdon*
> *And Lady Snowdon too*
> *And keep on having honeymoons*
> *Like Jim and Amy do ... (oh, let's be beastly!)*

Those cads.

Ariadne was in the new Indian maiden style with a short-short leather skirt, fringed to her crutch, an expensive scooped-necked scarlet and white striped jumper (Clobber) and a band of coloured beads around her forehead; moccasins, of course.

'We all slept together last night,' I heard Ariadne saying.

The film director looked at me with deeper interest. 'Really? You do bloody well. What are you on—Amphetamine?'

His name was Philip and he started inviting us all back to his place in Well Walk for an afternoon pot session. I felt it was time to go. I mean it interested me. I'm just afraid of upsetting my creative balance, that's all.

'... and now our landlady's been murdered,' I heard Ariadne's voice trailing behind along Flask Walk as we walked home. I just hoped she wasn't going to bring him with her.

Mrs Bracknell had not been murdered or kidnapped, except by Detective Chief Superintendent Kinnear. His man Friday, the black, was sifting through our mail just inside the front door. We have half a ton of old mail belonging to gone people. Sometimes in the winter we use it for lighting fires.

'Will you go down, sir?' he asked me. The part of the letter in his hand which I could read said, in urgent Parker 61: '—and if you're not back by prize-giving day I'm going to kill the babies and then myself. Pamela will have to go to ...' 'The Super wants to see you,' he said.

Ariadne said: 'Can I come?'

'Are you Miss Thing?' he asked her. 'There's somebody been telephoning you. She says it's urgent.'

The bell started ringing in our flat right then.

'God I hope it's not mummy. You didn't tell anybody where I was, did you? Or Lenny Price?' She was talking to Joanna as they went up to the mezzanine floor. I had an idea she did know something about that missing three hundred pounds. She had paid six guineas for the yoghourt and things—legally that could be interpreted as receiving. (*Author denies living on child's stealings.*)

I went down into the mausoleum, Mrs Bracknell's spirit world. The trick was to hold your breath taken outside then exhale it slowly; gradually the thick atmosphere, rich with paraffin, onions, vinegar and embalming fluid filled your lungs. And even amid all this smell and the debris of her husband's skeleton (everybody swore) hanging just inside the door, her cats and the parrot, broomstick, the lot, she could still entice young students down there to live at exorbitant rents.

'What are ye doing in that closet, man!' Jamie was saying as I went in.

'This is not a cupboard,' the chap said, 'this is my room!'

The superintendent took me into Mrs Bracknell's private laying-out room, or lounge-cum-bedroom, a converted rubbish-tip with no windows except a gun-slit overlooking the heath with steel bars over it.

'Tell me,' he said, 'de ye know a middle-aged Italian called Raoul Lecci who might want to kill you?'

'Is he titled?'

'Aye, he is. He's a Count.'

'My dog knows him,' I told him. 'Where's Mrs Bracknell—she'll tell you.'

'Here I am, Mr Fenton,' said Mrs Bracknell in her medium's voice; it came from a patch of darkness near the grating. I walked over to her. She was lying on top of a long padded coffin, still in her coat and hat and with her face buried in her arms. 'Bear witness!' she said.

'What's the matter with her?' I asked Jamie.

She answered herself, looking up at me with a tear-stained face:

'The police molested me in Heath Street. I'm waiting for my solicitor—no, don't touch me! You nasty little professional Scottie!'

Jamie had put a helping hand out to her. He told her: 'Madam we may have saved your life.' To me he said: 'She was shouting dangerous information in public. There's a homicidal lunatic somewhere at large.' 'Not necessarily,' I said.

You must be finding it difficult to get all this into focus. Don't be ashamed—I did. I did! Now, it seemed to me that the police had over-stepped themselves and Mrs Bracknell was being hysterical. I'm rather good at rationalising, calming people; I did it now.

'This is all really my fault,' I told Jamie. 'Mrs Bracknell has been good enough to act as spiritualist intermediary between me and my dead poodle—'

'Another time, laddie,' Jamie said. 'Tell me about the Count and Jane.'

'Who?'

'Your friend in Hollywood. That's what all this is about.'

That surprised you, didn't it? It surprised me.

There was no message from B——. It was an airmail letter from Jane:

darling darling horace. (one should guess that this girl would use no capitals—communists never do) *greetings, tried to ring you from manhattan tother night, raoul, very naughty, in london to kill you. beware the black spot!*

Jesus! And I thought it was Albert!

'Did you know her very well, Mr Spurrajon?'

'Just a minute.'

albert's fault entirely, is he really dead? if so we are partners in the richest gold mine in hollywood. if not then it's jail for life, raoul knows that your death gives him half share, also jealous about anybody who has slept with me. he must be having a busy time in london. for instance what has happened to norman freville? furnish Scotland yard with enclosed photo and following names and aliases: count raoul lecci. prince giulio camparo. john smith. horace take care! (how are your balls?) vital you meet me flight 727 Olympic london airport august all love and sex—jane. p.s. you are the only one I am warning—stay alive and gear yourself for the disposal of five million pounds not dollars.

I just folded it up. Letters like that in the film industry hardly warrant any comment. This did not satisfy the inspector, however.

'Have you anything to say?'

'What about?'

'You're a rich man, Mr Spurrajon. A multi-millionaire!'

'He doesn't pay his rent,' Mrs Bracknell said.

'This is rubbish,' I told Jamie about the wild promises. 'They always talk like that.'

Remember Arturo Conti? I've had Royal film premieres, half shares in the biggest writer/artiste agency in the world, I've even owned a documentary film company—but seldom more than five pounds in cash. For six months I had one of the best offices at MGM out at Boreham Wood; a secretary, a car to take me to and fro—never the bus fare. I remember the day I moved in with my bed (I can't write without sleeping as you know, it's all dreams with me). My youngest daughter helped me carry it in from the car —she was about fifteen and blonde, her face painted like a clown's. Half an hour later when I looked out there were faces at every window opposite—all the offices above Stage A, people at the dubbing theatre door, more out in the corridor. The gatekeepers had telephoned round—it started a legend about me which I have never deserved, as you know. I hope it will die with other MGM legends amid the rubble, for they're pulling the place down now.

'Horace!' Ariadne burst in, closely followed by Joanna who looked red as a ghost. The telephone call had been from old Daffers—remember old Daffers? Her father had a bowel stoppage and they live in The Vale of Heath?

'Her mother telephoned my mother and told her where I am—she's sending her boxers to get you!'

'Lenny Price will carve his initials on your face,' Joanna explained.

'Not a bit of it,' said Jamie confidently. 'We'll not let any harm come to Mr Spurrajon until we're ready.'

This is the kind of selfishness I bring out in people. Albert was always trying to get me shot for publicity purposes. The funny thing is they really think it's for my own good. Well frankly if Dinah's boxers were after me I don't think Scotland Yard would stand a chance to save me. My hands started hurting just thinking about it. I told Ariadne:

'You've got to go home and you've got to tell Lenny Price you haven't got his three hundred pounds and I haven't got it and you never took it—'

'Wheesht, man!' Jamie Kinnear exclaimed. 'Dinna haver! Three hundred poonds is it? Is that what it's all aboot?' He snapped his finger rudely against the letter in my hands from Jane. 'And ye're mixed up in a cool five million poonds swindle!'

'I'm not mixed up in anything. I don't know what she's talking about.'

'Do ye not?' Jamie said. 'And does the term "Alivies" mean anything to you?'

'Alivies?' I said.

Well the odd thing is it does mean something to me. In a few years time it will mean something to you, too. Or maybe you've read about it already. You've had talkies, widies, smellies. Well Alivies comes next. It was one of the big ideas Albert had in his milkman days, one of the big impracticable but plausible ones that seemed to work better in fiction than in fact. You'll find it treated more fully in *Unfit for Babies* but for now and briefly *Alivies* is this: (Albert had this printed.)

Alivies is a mixture of film and live drama. The sensational feature of them is that for première occasions in the capital cities of the world the stars of the film play their interior scenes in person on the stage of the cinema. I'll elaborate a little bit in case Edna has to grapple with it: You make the movie complete as normal. But in certain converted cinemas—New York, London, Rome, Paris on necessarily staggered occasions— the mix from exterior action (say) to interior action is really a mix to interior stage. There are certain key scenes matched on the stage in foreground while the screen takes motion picture back plates. John Wayne will hitch his horse to the rail and (mix) comes walking into the saloon actually on stage. When he's thrown everybody through the windows or shot them and finished his drink and gone, then you're back on the screen to see him ride away, his imperturbable self. It gives film stars something they want most of all, which is personal contact with the audience, it gives the audience a chance to see their favourite bedroom people hard at work, it has the sly cultural effect of bending filmgoers towards the live theatre.

'And not only that,' Albert said, sitting in his little milk float outside Tres's house on that long-ago occasion, 'it grabs publicity more than any foyer line-up could.'

He wanted to call it Realies or Alivies. This was just before his embossed wallpaper period and I thought he had forgotten it long since—especially as he was supposed to be dead.

'He is dead,' Detective Chief Superintendent Jamie Kinnear told me when I mentioned all this. 'Countess Jane is right about the swindle but she's got the wrong man. The man we're looking for is Sir Ambrose Argyle.'

Well, good old Jamie, bless his heart, let him go on thinking that. How Sir Ambrose was supposed to connect up with Alivies and the swindle he didn't go into; either because he didn't trust me or because he thought I already knew since the whole lurid scheme was laid out in my book *Unfit for Babies*. He makes a great mistake if he thinks I understand everything I write about. I don't to this day know how I promoted Albert Harris from being a milkman to being one of the foremost film producers in the western world, though I've read my account of it several times. Do you remember that agent I had in Grosvenor Gardens?

'If you were half as clever as your characters, Horace,' he told me one day when I was trying to borrow from him, 'you'd be rich, boy.'

The point is they are not my characters. I don't write novels any more. It's a long time since I had to resort to making anything up, the way things have been happening. Not everybody believes this.

'You pillory yourself unnecessarily,' my publisher told me.

He really thinks *I* do it. Shall I tell you who's doing it again now? Just listen :

'Mr Fenton,' Mrs Bracknell said before I left her room, 'do you mind if I show somebody over your room this afternoon? I think I've got a new tenant.'

She's talking about my home. I've got no other home now.

'Are you leaving?' Jamie said. 'I'd rather you didn't leave.'

I told them I wasn't going anywhere and what the hell.

'But you gave me a month's notice,' Mrs Bracknell said. It's up next Saturday—you'll have to be gone by twelve o'clock midday.'

Albert had telephoned using my voice. Amongst all his expert impersonations there were two things he was really good at: English wild birds and me.

'Well, pay up all your arrears including gas and electricity,' she said, when I explained this, 'and you can stay on.'

It was nearly time for me to drive north, which was Albert's whole idea. *Supercon Don* rides again ...

'Whom shall I say is speaking, sir?'

'Horace Spurgeon Fenton—'

'I'm sorry, sir, Lady Argyle is not at home, if you understand that. Goodbye, sir.'

I understood it. Did you understand it?

'Mention Albert!' somebody hissed.

I said: 'Just a minute. I've got news about her son Albert.'

It was all going on the Scotland Yard tape but I didn't care. Jamie was so sure I was wrong anyway. A very unpleasant thing happened then. Mrs Harris (I still call her Mrs Harris) must have come and picked up the wrong line—the one with me on it. I heard her saying:

'You keep Horace talking while I get the boys round there. I thought it was him. Pretending to be Albert. The tenth call in two days. Pretending he's stuck in Scotland with no money. I knew it was Horace. He's after what he can get.'

Stokes the butler's voice, faintly East Anglian and therefore traitorous, came distantly:

'Youm got the wrong telephone, madam.'

'Oh, have I? Well never mind, I'll talk to Horace while you ring Sidney. Tell 'em to make a right proper job of it this time, love. Don't muck about crucifying him, he's too thick—it don't sink in.'

Then, in her warmest Preston and Blackpool accents to me: 'Horace? 'ello, love. Wir exactly *are* you now?'

Do you ever get the feeling the world's against you?

A moment later, for three of them had shared the earpiece with me, Philip the settler was saying:

'What you want to do, love, is get into your car, point it up the M1 motor road, press the accelerator to the floor for three hours—'

Everybody was roaring with laughter by this time, all coming back to my room.

'Isn't he good news?' Ariadne asked me, brightly.

I was already dialling 999.

'You're too late,' Joanna Browne said.

From the hall by the telephone you could see through the double white doors out of the front hall into Squires Mount and East Heath. People were milling—*milling*—out of newly-arrived vans and cars; you couldn't see what kind of vehicles, just dozens of heads, fists, waving sticks and cudgels.

'Good God!' Philip the settler suddenly cried, turning very white. 'It's a *corp militante*!' He turned to me, angrily : 'Now look here, what exactly have you been up to, you old sod?'

'I don't know,' I said. 'What's a *corp militante*?'

'Here comes some more!' Joanna said.

A bus had just arrived. *A bus*!

'I wish we could stay!' Helen the nurse said, regretfully.

The *corp militante* is, apparently, a mobile striking force of student mercenaries; they'll fight anywhere, anytime for any cause given money or an arguable reason. The mercenary bit doesn't necessarily mean money but can mean fighting for ideals not always their own—they have vast international affiliations. In some countries, Philip told me later, the student-assisted weak unprotected minorities are actually building tanks.

'In time to come,' he said, 'they will replace war.'

In the meantime they were fighting me.

'Horace Spurgeon Fenton?' I heard a woman's voice outside. It was Mrs Benson going out with her kid; she was talking to the leader of the *corp militante* and pointing my way. 'Up the steps and through the double white doors.'

A big hulking chap in a black shirt came goose-stepping up the steps, flanked by two students carrying cudgels which appeared to be legs of tables with huge nails driven into the end. A whole mob of them were out now on the terrace of the house and yet there was hardly a sound to be heard; the discipline was frightening.

'This is what we do,' I said to Ariadne; 'you keep them talking while I get out of the bathroom window—'

Philip had already opened the door.

'Horace?' the leader said.

'Good heavens!' I said.

It was *Cedric!*

'Look here,' I said, 'I haven't done anything—this little girl came to me in all good faith—'

'Never mind all that,' Cedric said. 'Who blew my fucking car up?'

All this student power was on my side.

'The CID tell me they were really after you,' Cedric said. 'I don't want to know what you've been up to. It must be a mistake. But when they touch me they touch White Power....'

I took him inside, everybody silent, awed, listening to him.

I've never known what Cedric's politics are. In the Caxton Drake days he sometimes used to come into the Fleet Street office with bumps and bruises collected in this demonstration or that. He was in the papers once for having bashed a man over the head with his own banner. It wasn't ideological—just his short temper. He had a monthly dinner with M— 'the old man' as he called him, until his firm found out about it. Now he was a freelance God knew what he was up to. All this CRRRRK! and WHAMMMM! and POWWWWWW! was undoubtedly little more than a rather appropriate cover for it. I'm sure that somewhere in that Wimbledon timbered house were plans for world government.

Having his car blown up was something he understood and was ready for—as you can see. He was as pleased as punch that all these boxers were on their way to kill me.

'You've done very well,' he said. And to Joanna he said : 'Haven't I seen you in Trafalgar Square?'

She admitted it, but reluctantly; it was before she'd had an orgasm.

'What about you?' he asked the mice.

'We're nurses,' Claire said.

'Good,' Cedric said. 'We shall need nurses. What's the rest of the situation here?' he asked me.

Philip said: 'I've got a hundred and sixty-three tins of corned beef—Fray Bentos.'

'Good, good,' Cedric kept saying. And to me he said: 'Come outside and show yourself—don't forget your son's a hero.'

'You didn't tell me!' Ariadne cried.

I didn't know.

Outside on the packed terrace Cedric delivered one of these rabble-rousing speeches with which he had made Caxton Drake a force to be reckoned with in the world of international crime. Whether it was a strip-club murder or a wages grab Cedric would find some opportunity to advocate the partitioning of Africa or the disbanding of Parliament in favour of a junta. Now it was his blown-up car, though you'd never detect this.

'As you all know Lewis Fenton is rotting at this moment in Gothenburg jail—victim of the frightened men of Leipzig!'

'LEIPZIG!' cried the *corp militante*.

Mrs Martin and her family were looking out of their window. Children had been taken off the streets. The police had all vanished. Cedric held up my hand:

'Now they are coming for his father!'

'LEIPZIG!' came the frenzied cry again followed by wild cheering for me.

I felt idiotically proud.

Mrs Bracknell had appeared with some of her students from the basement, cars were stopping on the hill; Ariadne was looking at me with pride, holding onto one arm which Joanna held onto the other. I wished the Official Receiver was there and all the people who knew the worst about me.

'You all know what to do!' Cedric shouted, and his tooth dropped down; he pushed it back. Everybody started sitting down as if for a long wait. We went back into the kitchen and Joanna made some coffee. He wanted to know all about everything and I told him. Far from thinking that I was in desperate trouble he seemed to consider that I was sitting on a potential gold mine.

'Find out if Albert's alive and what there is in it for you,' Cedric said. I told him about the call from New York and showed him the letter from Jane. 'Horace you cunt. You may be worth millions and here you are playing with little girls.'

There was a feeling of great activity and preparedness in the flat. Members of the *corp militante* came and went with vacuum flasks, the nurses in their uniforms—Wendy had got up and dressed—were in and out preparing dressings as though for the battle of Atlanta. Ariadne and Philip the settler were out on the terrace leading the students in Bob Dylan's *Masters of War*.

Cedric no longer seemed part of all this; he manipulated the forces of ideology but only as one would use a bicycle to get from A to B. He was talking in fact now about the death of Sheila (his wife).

'She was driving me to hospital at the time—did you know that?'

'You had had your heart attack.'

'It wasn't a heart attack,' he said.

Even on the rare occasions when I think I know something it turns out that I don't. What had actually happened to him was just about the most terrifying thing that can happen to a person. When two people having sexual intercourse get stuck together.

'We were on the rug in the hall, two o'clock in the morning, Sheila and the kids all in bed and asleep—I was having one of my alcoholic black-outs. Well, I must've been, it was Sheila's sister from Sevenoaks. Her husband was there and all their kids. It was supposed to be a family reunion on their dead mother's birthday—in April.'

'The Ideal Homes exhibition had just started,' I said.

'What?' he said.

If you remember me and Tres and the kids had our last meeting at the Ideal Homes exhibition that year.

'She'd come down to get a glass of water—that's what she said. I think she'd heard me come in. She was practically naked.

Throwing it at me. Well, let's face it, that's the only way she could get anybody to take it.'

'What happened?' That wasn't me—that was Ariadne. She had just drifted in in the middle of it; by this time we had about five listeners.

Cedric said: 'I managed to bang the dinner gong with my foot.'

The picture it conjured up was hilarious, but nobody laughed, it seemed so painful. Claire gave it a name, this muscular spasm that traps a man's penis somewhere in the vaginal cavity.

'Sheila and Patrick—that was her husband—had to carry us out to the car—'

'That's dangerous!' Wendy said. 'They should've got an ambulance.'

'Yes, I know. They were afraid one of the kids might let on we weren't married. They were going to say we were married. They laid us on the back seat of Patrick's Humber.'

'Did it still feel nice?' Ariadne asked, politely.

This is when she sounded twelve years old. Like somebody who'd heard about sex. Cedric was enjoying retelling the story until now but with questions like this and with Claire saying that St George's Hospital (where they'd tried to take the stuck couple) was no good anyway, he began to cut it short. They had crashed on their way to hospital, Sheila had been killed outright and Cedric and his sister-in-law had come apart.

'Do you still see her?' Ariadne asked. These girlie inconsequentials, which I find quite natural, Cedric sees as ghoulish. He leaned closer to me:

'Is there somewhere we can talk privately?'

My room was now out of the question. Four students dressed in battle-green had a machine-gun rigged up in the window commanding a view of the heath and the hill.

'It shoots eggs,' one of them explained, 'though it can be converted.'

'You can use our small room,' Wendy said. 'We want the other one as a dressing station.'

151

Locked in the small bedroom, panties, tights and bras hanging everywhere, Cedric opened a brief case and spread printers' pulls of my *Don the Con* strip adventure all over the bed.

'I don't think you know what you've got yourself into, Horace,' he said.

He knew. Ariadne knew, I do believe; and so did Joanna Browne. I'm always the last to know.

The story, here shown in pictures but already written into *Unfit For Babies* was briefly this :

'ZONK! Don the Con with MASSIVE IDEA! ! ! !'

FOREGROUND: Don hunched over boardroom table facing Directors of Global Film Distributors.

BALLOONAGE: 'Gentlemen. You will be pleased to learn that I have obtained financial backing for ten major million-pound movies.

DIRECTORS KNOCKED SIDEWAYS BY THE NEWS: WHAM! POW! ZOOT! Explain, Don! Fantastic! What about the world economic situation?

SHOUT BALLOONAGE: 'Etcetera! Etcetera!'

SECOND FRAME: DON WITH WORLD ATLAS DON'S VOICE OVER SCENE: 'Orchard and I have penetrated and infiltrated dangerous Iron Curtain countries and Police states of the world contacting frightened millionaires unable to get their money out of the country or obtain world credit—'

MED SHOT DON'S PLATINUM SECRETARY TAKING NOTES 'We go in, use their money to make our film. Come out with the negative. Their share of the profits becomes available throughout the world!'

FRAME FOUR: CHEERING DIRECTORS

DON IS LIFTING ORCHARD'S DRESS

HIS BALLOONAGE: 'There were one or two narrow escapes from corrupted politicians !'

CLOSE SHOT ORCHARD'S BRUISED PELVIC AREA

SEE DARK BRUISES: BRACKETS: (NOTE: Bruises in reality Don's own fingermarks !)

RESUME SIXTH FRAME :

FOREGROUND DON'S BIG ANNOUNCEMENT: BALLOONAGE :
'Gentlemen ! Next year sees the birth of
GLOBAL ALIVIES!'
DIRECTORS KNOCKED SIDEWAYS: ZINGGGGGG ! ! !

'Right,' Cedric said, when he had shown me thus much of this abortive adaptation of my prose work. 'Now do you remember the trick your character Albert played to get the money?'

I couldn't quite remember. You write these stories and then forget them. I never remember anything once I've been paid.

'Tell me again in case I've forgotten,' I said.

'He went round the world taking a commission from each investor—'

'I've got it!' I said. This was Albert's con trick; I'm talking about while he was still a milkman at twelve ponds a week. 'He cleared a hundred thousand pounds in commission in return for a distribution contract. That was going to be forged on company-headed paper.'

'Well he didn't have to do that,' Cedric said.

There was a tap at the door and Philip the settler looked in; he was wearing a gas gun in a holster now.

'Leader,' he said to Cedric, 'sorry to intrude. They're here—a dozen thugs in a Dormobile.'

'They're friends of Dinah Thing, or maybe Lady Argyle's—' I started explaining.

'Just a minute, Horace, I'm trying to think,' Cedric said.

He snapped his fingers a couple of times and then told Philip : 'Okay—beat them up. Don't kill them. Set fire to their van.'

'Sar!' Philip saluted and went.

Cedric turned to me : 'Well Albert didn't have to forge anything. He's a director of Global. It's my belief he gave guarantees in the company name in return for percentage pre-production payments.'

'Good God. It is Albert, then?'

153

'It could be Albert, Sir Ambrose, Jane Chapell—what about her old man Lecci? Is he one of us or a filthy commie?'

There are no liberals in the world of KRRKKK!

When people start talking positively and forcefully and knowledgeably like this is when I realise how little I know about anything. I don't think I'm interested half the time. In a world of plenty I take just enough to make a meal.

'Listen!' Cedric said, suddenly.

A prolonged sound of breaking glass came from somewhere near. Somebody screamed—it could have been male or female. Or male turning to female. Cedric got up.

'You don't want anything to do with this,' he said, 'and nor do I.' He consulted his watch: 'I've got to get to the BBC—you pack a bag and get up to Skye. That forged postmark is your appointment day. The 13th! It's an old Cossack trick.'

He went out before I could object to this—he goes to Shepherds Bush, I go to the inner Hebrides. I followed him and found Ariadne whipping a man who was tied spreadeagled on the kitchen door frame. It was Lenny Price, her mother's boxer. Every time she brought the whip down he said something foul. Cedric watched for a moment, approvingly.

'I'm trying to make him confess!' she told us, with another hard lash across his bleeding shoulders.

'Confess what?' I asked her.

'Oh—anything!' she said, impatiently.

'You take her with you,' Cedric said. 'You may need help. Tell Albert or whoever it is there's finance waiting if the scheme is sound.'

What scheme? 'What about Jane — she's flying over—'

'I'll take care of Jane,' Cedric said.

'Where we going?' Ariadne asked. Tired of whipping Lenny Price she had now given him a glass of water.

'Just get your piggy bank and don't ask questions.'

'I'll get you, cocker,' Lenny Price said to me.

I knew I had to get away. I didn't want to get away. All I wanted to do was shut the door on everybody and get down to some writing. This is why I'm not interested in anything else. You get interested in things and before long somebody's going to get you.

Eleven

'You see that tree?'

Ariadne looked and saw it.

'That's where I was nailed.'

'Gosh,' she said.

It was in full leaf now; then it had been bare.

We walked back through the woods to the caravans. I had already seen Forsyte and got a vacant Bluebird for the night. The same old site, full of memories; the same Forsyte, full of shit. Well, not really. He was an ex-theatrical though and they're sometimes hard to take. Especially if you're feeling sentimental and they're seeing what was precious to you as part of the hilarious past. He named names and recalled incidents in a way I'd rather not repeat, then finally took two pounds for the derelict old van.

'I'm not sure everything's working,' he called from the door of his van.

Nothing was working.

Only my imagination.

Pat pat pat pat pat pat pat went the footsteps behind us across the grass as we walked through the darkness towards the dim shape of the *Bluebird Calypso* caravan and I didn't even look round. It was only later after I'd got the bed down and found the bedding and connected the calor gas cylinder for lighting and morning tea; it was only after this and after Ariadne had started undressing that I noticed that she was not wearing her pat pat pat *Doctor Scholl* sandals but a pair of knee-high boots. Does that put a shiver down your back? It did mine.

'What is it?' she asked.

She was sitting up in bed hugging her knees in the little white nightie, I was peering through the curtains out to the site. A gleam here and there indicated that others were in residence or having one night stands.

'Nothing,' I said.

'Are you sure?' There was a note of disappointment in her voice. Here was a child hungry for excitement and sex, I began to realise, was only a last resort. 'Come to bed then,' she said. 'And keep me warm.'

Keep me warm ... At twelve years old she was already a typical woman of seventeen or more. Next it would be 'Don't stand there all night and get cold'.

Are you going to cuddle me to sleep?

'Are you going to cuddle me to sleep?'

They never say what they really want.

'Kiss me goodnight' she requested.

She turned on her side facing me. I had left one calor gas mantle alight low at the kitchen end of the van—no, wait a minute, I'm thinking of the Pemberton; we were at the kitchen end in the Calypso (it's really a holiday van) so therefore the light was at the front bay window over the settee. Her back was to the light. I put my hand up under her nightie and held her breast. Her breasts would just about fill champagne glasses, which is nice. Then I snuggled down a bit and put one of my legs over hers and let my balls touch her wrist.

'Goodnight,' I lied.

'Goodnight,' she lied.

Then I kissed her. Do you know what she did? She held her breath. She held her breath while I kissed her! I don't write this kind of stuff normally; it's got nothing to do with love or the uniqueness of human relationships. You fuck and that's all there is to it. It's great, we all know it, we don't have to read about it. If you want it dressed up in cellophane and flowers (*He gave her of his love to the full dot dot dot*) then read *Woman's Own*. What's unique here is that she held her breath. I did it again and she held her breath again. Then I made it last and she came out gasping as if she'd been under water.

'Are you all right?' I asked her.

'Yes—phew!—thank—you,' she said.

Phew?

'Does my breath smell?' I asked her.

'Yours doesn't,' she said. 'Mine does. I have to have peppermints. You wouldn't stop.'

'I've stopped!'

'I mean at a shop.' She was crying. Poor little sod. 'Crickey,' she said. 'It's always -the same.'

Here was a girl who was a virgin I had no doubt simply because she hadn't got the Colgate Ring of Confidence. I'm serious. It's about the only consumer ad based on fact.

'I'm constipated,' she said, sniffing, wiping her eyes. 'That's why I have to keep going to the lavatory. It makes my breath smell.'

She coughed, then before she could turn her head away I got the faint obscenity of her bowels; it gave me instant asthma. My penis had flopped despondently, tired of waiting. Oh Christ, my kingdom for a peppermint.

'That's what those pains were,' she said.

'What does the doctor say?'

'It was chronic, in the family; doctors can't do anything. It's in our family just the same. I take big books to the loo and it works. You have to take your mind off it.'

'I think I could go now,' she said.

I slipped my hand up her nightie again but she didn't mean that; she meant go to the lavatory. I don't know whether you know what's involved in going to the lavatory or getting a glass of water on a caravan site in the middle of the night. We traipsed across the grass, me with my mac and shoes on, Ariadne wearing her school duffle and hood and Doctor Scholl's sandals. I took the grimy plastic water-can, half a candle and a bunch of torn pages from an old *Radio Times*.

'Can I leave the door open in case there's any spiders?'

For me it was an old scene. Her on the lavatory with the candle flickering, me trying to find the cold water tap outside. It reminded me of Diana; it made me feel sad. If I was going to go on doing this why not for her. She needed me—this special unique thing I have of groping around lavatories on caravan sites at night. The last year I had done nothing but bitch at her because I felt trapped. But she was trapped too. Who was looking after her now? Trotsky? No. She just used him to save my conscience. 'Don't ever worry about me,' was the last thing she ever said to me. This was the first time I had. Suddenly I wanted to rush to her.

'Are you still there?'

'Yes. Are you all right?'

It was the same dialogue, everything.

'Don't listen!' she called.

I could hear the strain in her voice. In somebody ten years younger you would be holding them over steam and saying: 'Uugh! Ugh! Ugh!' to help them strain.

'Good evening,' somebody said. You always know caravan people. I wrote this *Hiding Place* where the only clue they had was the toilet paper in the dead man's pocket. 'He lives on a caravan site,' said the detective. This man was in the usual uniform of pyjamas and raincoat and carrying a torch and toilet roll.

'You can't go in there!' I stopped him. 'My girl's in there.'

'She's in the wrong one!' he said. 'The women's is over by the lane.'

'Who's that?' Ariadne called.

'Nobody,' I said.

'I'll wait,' he said. He lit a cigarette and gave me one. 'Marvellous site, this. You're new, aren't you? You'll like this. Flush lavatories. We've had Elsans all the way down from Edinburgh...'

They talk about nothing but lavatories. It's all they ask out of life: flush toilets, a shower and the occasional friendly wave from a passing motorist.

'I did it,' Ariadne said, when she emerged.

'Good girl,' the main said.

'You haven't got any peppermints have you?' I asked him.

He hadn't but he thought he knew somebody at the top of the field in an almost new Safari seventeen-footer who had and who wouldn't mind my knocking him up. I didn't bother, though. To tell the truth I was getting impatient— we were still only thirty miles from London. It seems whenever I tackle a big issue a little issue gets in the way.

It wasn't my night and it wasn't yet over. I decided to heat some water enough for us to wash in and make some tea, but when I turned on the gas ring under the pan the light went almost out. This meant that the calor gas cylinder was almost exhausted. I went outside and traced the pipe to the cylinder again, gave it a good shake-up. It activated the gas for about ten minutes then I had to go out and do it again. It took me two-and-a-half hours to boil the water by which time Ariadne was fast asleep. The light went out while I was trying to wake her up. To hell with it. I went out again and turned off the cylinder for safety, then came back and got into bed with her.

At first the sheet had got folded in between us and she was lying on her side with her back to me, her knees up. Very gradually so's not to wake her up I pulled the folds of the sheets until she was sitting naked on my lap. I resolved to be content with this. If I could just get her a little more comfortable, perhaps. I slid my hand round to hold her breast, pulled her back a little rest my face in her long hair. The excitement, slow, warm and undramatic had brought the kind of erection that won't stay down. I had to slide my right arm, which was underneath me, up to open her knees sufficient to take what stood hard between us. Now it was better. Now it could rest. With just the tiniest movement. Now and then. Now . . . and then…

The dream came back. There was a nearness and a flesh-ness and an undressness about it that gave us at one and the same time the exquisite pleasure of love and deprivation. That perfect permanent state that we knew we had it to come … come … come…

Part Three

Twelve

'Did you sleep all right?' Ariadne asked me.

'Yes. Did you?'

'Yes,' she said. 'I don't remember a thing after I got into bed. And anyway,' she added, 'it was only on my legs and I washed it all off.' This was a form of school joke too but I saw it too late and got stupid marks.

'We'll get some peppermints.'

It was Sunday and we had already driven a hundred miles up the A1 without passing anywhere likely to sell peppermints.

Peppermints may seem trivial to you, set beside the need to stop people killing me, find Albert, discover how I come to be in partnership with the Countess Jane in Don the Con's massive Global £ million project. But they're not, really, when you come to analyse human emotions. Your next fuck is like your next book—you're bloody certain it's never going to happen. Yes, you can remember the ones before, can remember having the same desperate feeling, remember that it did, having the joy. But it doesn't help. I should not be able to apply myself, my brilliant mind, complete as a potato with all its little eyes and knobs, until Ariadne and I were lovers. Proper lovers. Last night was nice, but it was only a curtain-raiser—a nightie-raiser.

Still, it was nice. The night had done something for us and camping people will know what I'm talking about. The shared hardships and miseries of camping bring people together like war. This morning, for instance, since there was no gas, I had borrowed a methylated spirit burner and a frying pan from old Elsan the lavatory man and cooked streaky bacon and eggs and fried bread and tomatoes in the grass with the wind blowing and spots of rain sizzling in the fat.

'You see that Rover passing us?'

I saw it.

'Has it been replaced by a Ford Executive? Red?'

'What d'you mean, replaced?'

'What's *tailing* us now?' she said, exasperated.

I looked in the mirror. It was a Ford Executive—I couldn't see the colour. I can't see colours in mirrors—is that strange? All reflections to me are black and white. I looked right round—yes, it was red.

Ariadne said: 'They've been following us in relays so we don't get suspicious. There's four of them—Rover, Ford Executive, a grey Mini-Cooper with a checker-strip—'

'I've seen that,' I said.

'And a Hillman Imp—white,' she said. 'The driver of the Rover was at the next table to ours in the cafe.' We had called in a Forte.

I didn't doubt any of this. Good old Jamie was waiting for me to lead him to Sir Ambrose Argyle and the missing millions. I had a nasty thought; how long would it be before he realised which direction I was heading, the road to the isles, and remembered the postcard, got there ahead of me? I would have to shake them off.

Ariadne said, when I told her this: 'Then you'll have to change your number plate—and that's illegal.'

But I was suddenly wondering what they were doing last night when we were at the caravan. If it wasn't perhaps safer to have them prowling around while Raoul Lecci was on the loose. From Jane's letter he sounded too excitable for comfort. My brother Ronald's like that; he gets angry quickly and his right eyelid quivers. They have to be shot or hit on the head from behind.

We suddenly swished across a side-turning that tugged at my heart and left my imagination behind me at the corner. It was where, many light-years ago, I had picked up the prostitute and the tramp while taking Diana to get rock for her sculpting. They had fornicated on my back seat. That was in the old Hurricane coupe. My sadness about Diana came back; she was linked in my mind with the old car and the old roads. That was before her accident, before we got lost, trapped into the caravan site. The Hurricane had fallen to pieces practically and we had finally abandoned it on some roadside, thumbed a lift home, never gone back for it. Every old Hurricane I saw now I looked at the number plate; every invalid chair I looked for Diana.

'Bagsie that cottage,' she used to say.

'Bagsie that farm,' I used to say.

We used to Bagsie the sky, the sunsets, the spring and the autumn. It would never be the same with anybody else. I had crippled her my way, she had crippled me her way.

'I bagsie that hill with the redskins along the skyline,' she would say.

'We're still together,' I used to say.

There were three of us; Diana and me and B— the poodle in the middle. We thought the road would never end.

'What's the matter?' Ariadne asked, suddenly.

We had been driving without talking for some time, the music coming and going from the radio.

'You've gone different,' she said.

'You've been altered,' my autistic Diana said.

You don't alter, you just feel different about the way you are. Everytime you're loyal to somebody you're deserting somebody else. It has to be. By Scotch Corner I had decided to chuck it. Fuck Albert, fuck Ariadne, fuck old Jamie and the plane disaster, Cedric and Don the Con, fuck the world. I drove right round the big island and started south to find Diana and put some flowers on B—'s grave under the rhubarb.

'Where're you going?' Ariadne said.

'Back,' I said. 'And so are you.'

I had no ties this time, thank God. She wasn't pregnant and she wasn't crippled and she was still, probably, a virgin.

'Look!' she exclaimed, pointing. 'It's your number!'

It was on the AA signboard just south of Scotch Corner. Written in chalk: 'MESSAGE FOR 565 OMU'.

I stopped, reversed into the service layby.

The Ford Executive flashed past at seventy. I used my AA

key and rang the local AA and gave my number.

'There's an urgent message from B—' he said, using the dead poodle's full name.

'Was it a dog?' I said.

'It didn't sound like a dog,' he said.

It was a woman. It was Mrs Bracknell of course, passing the message on. It was vital, according to the dead poodle, that I kept my original appointment and didn't change my mind.

I always trusted B... If she barked there was somebody there. If she shit on the carpet it was because the door was shut. I drove across the centre-verge U-turning anarchistically onto the northbound carriageway back up to Scotch Corner and off northwest over the Pennine Chain on the A66, the bleakest road in England heading for Penrith, Gretna and the border with my foot flat on the floor.

'Why was that message on the southbound side?' Ariadne remembered, belatedly. 'We were heading north.'

'Dead dogs know everything.'

'Do you really believe that?' she asked me, earnestly.

When you have as little to go on as I do you're glad to believe everything.

'Anyway I think we've lost them.' She was looking back at the broad empty road behind us.

We had also lost my heart. We were going on but my heart had turned back and was travelling swiftly southwards.

Six and a half hours after leaving the caravan site in Hertfordshire we crossed the Scottish border; anyone who claims to do it quicker is flying. It was my first time in Scotland and I was expecting to see mountains, whisky, kilts, thistles, haggis; it is not like this at all. It is like a very long wide wet road at the getting-dark end of the day.

There is a road-weariness that gets into your body and mind, sweats the hair, rims the eyes, makes you careless about scratching, dribbles the mouth, gives you the appearance and character of somebody who's been sleeping rough. Ariadne looked like a car-hopping student flossie and I looked like a dirty old driver on the make. It was only fractionally inaccurate and I saw it in a hotel mirror a shade later than the receptionist who had just said they had no rooms, double or single.

'Do you mind if I use the phone?' I asked.

'The noo,' the woman said. They seem to say this for everything and this time she meant, as it turned out, I could waste a bit of time looking through the directory while she went and reported us to the manager. By a careless coincidence she had left proof of their perfidious plotting on the desk for us to read.

'Horace...' Ariadne spoke quietly, her finger on a pad by the phone. There was the printed word 'Jotter' at the top of the page and underneath:

Two dozen eggs.
4 lb best and neck of lamb.
565 OMU White Capri.
Blokie and lassie (fat, Humphrey Bogart type—girl about fourteen.)

The last items on the list were undoubtedly us and the writer had jotted the description down from the telephone —I could hear Detective Chief Superintendent Jamie Kinnear's voice in amongst the pencil scrawl.

I grabbed Ariadne's hand and practically ran out of the hotel. Were there voices calling after us? Did I hear a distant police bell? I doubt it. I drove away at high speed, left the A74 road to Glasgow and the isles, turned right, turned left, turned right, drove along some brick-surrounded road and into a coal yard.

'Now calm down,' Ariadne said, 'and let's look at the map.'

We weren't anywhere, which is exactly where I thought we were. A coal lorry gave us: SCWS. A railway wagon label said: RETURN EMPTY TO HAMILTON. It was Co-op land. The divi world of Wigan Pier. It's that bit of archaic Britain that will have to have a bomb on it before we enter Europe. Somewhere near they were shunting wagons. Gone the lovely chuff chuff chuff PSSSSSSSS! In its place jungle noises: HAOOORH!

'You want the road to Fort William,' Ariadne said, scrutinising my AA map in the handbook.

No I didn't. If they'd alerted a crummy little hotel in Larkhall, a ribbon development south of Glasgow, then they had the whole route to the Hebrides staked out. No, that couldn't be true either. If they knew where I was going they had no need to follow me.

The significance of the Flora MacDonald postcard had passed them by, they knew nothing of the false postmark, my date with Albert and a nice bit of arse on the 13th. They knew the area I was in, that's all. And how did they know that? How did they know that! Come closer and I'll tell you:

When they fixed a burglar alarm on my car at Scotland Yard they also put a radio beacon underneath—I was beeping my way north on the ten-meter hand. *Moscow* knew the area I was in.

'I'm going to throw them off,' I told the fourteen-years-old lassie. 'Instead of heading for the isles I'm going to strike for the Highlands—we'll lose 'em there.'

'You're really good news,' Ariadne said, though a little tiredly as if maybe it were a politeness now.

I drove hard up the A81, by-passing Glasgow proper and heading for Loch Lomond and the Trossachs. She didn't speak again till we were running down the back street hills into the town of Inverness. We had eaten a little stamped out meal in Kingussie, looked in at the big Odeon-type skiing hotel in the Cairngorms at Aviemore, watched by brooding police faces in both places; now I intended to end the farce, get Ariadne tanked up, have one steaming night of sex and put her on the train south before continuing on my assignment with the dead Albert.

Well, at least it was a plan. I get fed up with not having plans, sometimes. You get to fifty-one and you haven't got plans, nobody's given you a literary award or a scholarship, you've got holes in your hands and your flat is full of strangers and you're five hundred miles from home—you get fed up. I was fed up. My usual brand of animated chatter had dried up. I was leaking *Doing The Uptown Lowdown* between my teeth from an otherwise empty brain. Inverness was a nice town no doubt but it was dark. It could have been Kilburn.

'What am I drinking?' Ariadne asked me.

She was drinking rum and peppermint; I was trying to kill two birds with one stoner. We were in the saloon bar of the Dolphin Hotel (Trust Houses) at that nice time of early evening before people get there.

The glasses and bottles were shining, a log fire was glowing, the fortune-telling machine was flickering its secrets for a penny and a genteel lady sat behind the bar knitting—her name was Miss Cross and she had just shown us to a big Cromwellian type bedroom with sloping floor and ceiling and huge fuckrug of a bed with shiny brass knobs. I had dressed Ariadne in her Indian maiden outfit; the tiny fringed micro-skirt, a Paisley-type flowered jacket, sandals, headband.

'We are at the head of the Moray Firth, dyewsee?' Miss Cross said, to her knitting. She had been saying 'dyewsee' ever since we checked in. She seemed unaware, refreshingly so, of the squalidity between our ages. The police hadn't got to her yet. Nobody had by the look of her. She was nice. 'I've put two hot water bottles in your bed, dyewsee?' she said then.

Ariadne giggled and there was a slight 'hick' in it. I began to cheer up. We had started playing darts now and everytime she reached for the dart in the double-top I could see what I'd got to come. While she persevered for her double to finish the leg I issued a few swift instructions for the evening. A tray in our room instead of dinner, a bottle of Asti Spumante bubbly to liven the occasion.

'You'll find a knob on the wall for background music, dyewsee?' Miss Cross told me.

She was just being helpful. What a nice change from the usual pub vulgarity. At Loch Earn we had a barman who showed us a photograph of the hotel alsatian standing on its hind legs with a red bow of ribbon tied to its penis. Ariadne killed herself though frankly I didn't know where to put myself. Vulgarity embarrasses me as nothing else. The terrible thing is I put on a great show of enjoyment to hide my snobbishness. Beer, for instance, I know nothing whatever about. It's just acorn water.

'Will you still be wanting the Anna Neagles?'

We both watched Ariadne tottering on the halfway line, trying to aim the dart. I don't think she needed anything except carrying. An 'Anna Neagle' is a strong gin and Italian (vermouth) with a touch of Pernod and a slice of lemon. I picked up the formula in Harwich.

'Dyewthink?' Miss Cross added.

She was thinking exactly what I was thinking and yet by some alchemy of innocence it was all properly in order. The gentleman had to take the young lady when she was sufficiently smashed out of her head, dyewsee?

'Fuck!' Ariadne had missed it again.

'No,' I said. 'Send up the tray and the bottle and put it outside the door.'

'What about papers in the morning?' she said.

'Never mind the morning.' I said. 'Watch the *News of The World* next Sunday.'

We were laughing together when I heard Ariadne say behind my back:

'I don't mind but I'll have to ask my uncle.'

Two brawny Scotties had come in and gone to her instead of the bar; Hairy Arse One and Hairy Arse Two.

'How about a quick four-up instead of a two-up?' one of them said to me.

They weren't talking about darts. Two had his hand on her little leather skirt; she liked it. They weren't waiting for my decision. HA1 was already getting extra darts from Miss Cross.

'And a muckle dram for the wee lassie's Uncle Horrid!' called HA2 from the dartboard.

I laughed. I laughed at him! What's the matter with me? I swear when they crucified me I held the hammer while the boxer blew his nose.

I can't bear to offend people right up to the moment I put the knife in.

'I belong to Glasgow,' Ariadne and her new friends were singing, holding onto each other and swaying in front of the dart board, 'Dear ol' Glasgow toon!'

There were now four Hairy Arses and two frightful-looking dreg-type girls. As a country Scotland produces a drink, an accent, a wholesomeness in food and muscle that has infiltrated the world; it has also produced a scum element which no other race can touch for beastliness and violence. Glasgow's murder rate is higher per head than New York's.

'Are ye coming to the party, Horrid ol' chappie?' one of the men asked me, satirically.

I've suffered this old-school-tie type take-off thing before. I don't have a public school accent but I have always taken care to cover my East Anglian tendencies with decent modulation.

'Isn't it fab?' Ariadne asked me, blearily. 'We're going to a rave-up!'

'You've had all the drink you want,' I told her, since I was now her uncle.

'D'you think so?' HA1 said, comically waving his fingers in front of her eyes: 'I'd have said she needs another two!'

'I've ordered dinner now,' I told her.

'Food, is it? Ye'll not want for food at Charlie's!'

'I'll bring her home safely, Uncle Horrid!'

'Yes,' Ariadne said. 'You needn't come.' To her new friends she said: 'He's done a lot of driving today.'

One of the Scottie girls wearing a platinum bubble wig, a mauve jumper and tight tartan trews, gabbled something to me in pure Glaswegian; it might as well have been Norse. Ariadne of course understood every word.

'Flora wants to stay with you,' she said.

'Aye, she fancies an older man!' HA2 cried, slapping the offender's bottom.

'Quietly!' Miss Cross called. And when all looked at her, astonished, she said: 'Dyewsee?'

There was suddenly a banging on the window and a soldier appeared there, apparently sitting on another's shoulders.

'Hurry up!'

The door slammed back and more soldiers appeared:

'What y' doing then, Jock?'

'Did you get her?'

'Don't have her 'ere mate—wrap her up and bring her back to barracks, we all wanna bit!'

'Come on, lassie,' Hairy Arse Major said, dragging Ariadne by the wrist to the door.

'Okeydoke, careful!' I was glad to see in her face that element of panic which showed that she had just realised she'd gone head and shoulders too far into a situation not quite as she thought; she called to me: 'Coming, Horace?'

'Fuck Horace, we don't need Horace,' said Hairy Arse One, calling outside to his platoon: 'Get your engine started, Hamish!'

'Hamish?' cried Flora's friend, suddenly pulling back from the door. 'I'm not going to the barracks if Hamish's there—'

'What barracks?' Ariadne asked, hanging onto the door post now.

'Hamish is the one who bit my friend's nipple off,' the girl explained to Ariadne in passing.

'Don't be frightened, lassie,' said Hairy Arse Two, pulling at her and starting to kick her ankles to dislodge her from the doorway. 'The lad was only practising his atrocities for the Queen—now come on or I'll have to chop you—'

She chopped him, two swift blows each side of his ugly head. It didn't knock him out but made him release her. She flew to the bar where a soldier was gathering bottles for the party, grabbed one and knocked the bottom out of it, gave it to me with the beer swilling out; quickly she smashed three more and had one in HA2's face by the time he reached her—I was holding mine upright, the jagged glass edges towards myself for safety. What do you do in these situations? They're so undignified I always think. Authors like Hemingway and Steinbeck just swing ham fists and knock people flying; they also have hordes of burly peasants ready to fly to their succour. 'Show us your filthy enemies, Maestro. We shall tear them to little pieces and feed their revolting entrails to the dirty yellow dogs of the drains. We love you, Maestro. We are your people. The words you write come from our hearts, the ink you use from our blood—we kill your enemies, we give you our food, our shelter, our daughters, our wives—'

I don't want to overmilk it but where do they get all this from? I am fifty-one years old as you know, I have written perhaps thirty-five books (I have never killed a bull or made a tortilla it is true) and I have only ever met one person who has even heard of me. This was a dear little old lady at the *Yorkshire Post* luncheon who shattered me by saying that she had read all of my stuff—I felt really ashamed. She never offered to kill my enemies or anything.

'Kill 'em!' Ariadne was urging me now.

I've never met a twelve-years-old girl with so many alarming sides to her character. We with our backs to the bar and Miss Cross were facing, if you get the picture, a slowly advancing platoon of soldiers all intent on rape and murder. Even HA1 and 2 were soldiers. What had happened was that being Sunday and bored this press gang had been sent out to get booze and kye (cattle, that is women). Since the pubs shut in Scotland they had been around the hotels and kirks (churches) peering in windows before making their raids. They had watched Ariadne through the window before coming in to get her; the two civvy-clad scouts formed a polite spearhead but had taken a little too long. Their knives, bayonets and broken bottles were dancing in front of their braw red faces and foul mouthings about what they were going to do to Ariadne when they got her in the truck.

'I'll run ye through with me great steaming goo-gaw and two more besides then I'll fuck somebody else wi'out taking ye off,' said one young soldier who couldn't have been more than twenty. Another, with his penis already in his hand was shouting: 'I'll hae ye little leather fringe aroond me bollocks afore the night's oot!'

'Now stop it, lads,' I said. 'A joke's a joke. She's only twelve.'

'Don't talk like a cunt,' Ariadne said, without taking her eyes from the attackers. She jabbed at the nearest and he had to spring back. 'Come on, you mother-fucking sheep-stuffing Scotch elementals!' she cried.

My god I thought they were going to kill her on the spot; there's nothing infuriates a Scotsman more than being called Scotch.

Miss Cross's head came up from behind the bar: 'The bottles are not paid for, dyewsee!'

'You carry on,' I told Ariadne, 'I'll be paying for the drinks.'

Suddenly two, including HA1 rushed Ariadne at once and very expertly she jabbed two bottles into their faces; they fell back, spurting blood and clutching their eyes.

'Get two more bottles,' Ariadne said.

'That'll be another three shillings and eightpence,' Miss Cross said.

For a few surrealist moments there I was buying bottles of beer while Ariadne broke the ends off and stabbed them at the soldiers; this is what was confusing the enemy: they understood the broken-ended bottles but not the paying for them.

One of them gave up and threw away his bottle without striking a blow. 'Are ye trying to take the piss, dad?' he asked me. 'For God's sake,' he said to the others, 'we've got enough wi'out this little pissquick.'

But what broke it up finally was a couple of regulars coming into the bar, man and wife, oblivious of what was going on; they sat at the same table and had the same drink and said the same things.

''Tis a wet nightie, Miss Cross,' said the man.

'Aye,' said his wife, 'and there's more t'come I'm thinking.'

'Are y' coming or do I have to take you piece by piece!' HA2 hissed at Ariadne.

His voice brought the old gentleman round in his chair; he smiled and nodded at the soldiers: 'Have they saved the Argyll's yet?' he said.

Miss Cross was picking her way through the broken glass and puddles of beer with two glasses for the newcomers. HA1 held a bottle to Ariadne's face and whispered, conspiratorially: 'Ye've not heard the last of this!'

She put her fingers up to him. They left in untidy disorder. She put down her remaining broken bottle and smiled at me, ruefully.

'Sorry about that. They looked like good news at first.'

I asked her how she learned to fight that dangerously and she shrugged, modestly. 'At the bungalow. It went on all the time. Practically every party finished with broken bottles. I'm trying to give it up.' She laughed at me then, spontaneously: 'You were really disgusted, weren't you? We couldn't really get going with you there. Don't you ever want to kill people?'

I don't know whether you know it but it's always a mistake to plan sex. Especially for a man; perhaps only for a man. You have it in your mind that you've got to do it, there's no animal spontaneity. What you have to plan is that tonight you won't even try.

'It's late,' I said, 'you're tired, you want to have your bath, tuck into bed, get straight to sleep no mucking about.'

'What about all these sandwiches and this champagne, then?'

I'd forgotten it. It was all on the luggage rack just inside the door. Another delay was there was no private bathroom and we had to trail along corridors. It all took about an hour before we were sitting up in bed, side by side, drinking the last of the bubbly wine. We had each had a quarter hour in the lavatory; we didn't need anything now except each other.

'Are you ticklish?' she asked me.

This is one way and it's not bad. You say no you're not and they start at the feet and work up. Nothing happened for a long time, it seemed, and I felt a bit embarrassed. Then I had the idea to imagine that she was fully dressed —instantly it was all right. That's when the bedside telephone rang.

'I have a call for you from Welwyn,' said Miss Cross. 'It's a person, dyewsee?' It was Edna.

'Hello?'

'Horace? Is that you? I inarf had a job getting through. I'm in a box over the main.'

'What, at one o'clock in the morning?'

'Sue's just had a little baby girl!'

'Sue?'

'Our Sue!'

'Oh? Who's the father?'

'Cyril of course! Honest to God, what a thing to say about your own daughter!'

'Well, don't worry. They'll get married. And if they don't it doesn't matter these days.'

'They are married! They've been married two years! You daft bugger.'

'What are you ringing me for? Who is that?' I said. You get these sudden doubts about the whole thing.

'I thought you'd like to know you're a grandfather again, that's all. Christ almighty. You might ask how they are.'

'How are they?'

'You're hurting my groin,' Ariadne said.

I had to move off her; it was obviously going on.

'She had to have stitches.'

Having babies through the crutch in this day and age can't be natural.

'It weighs seven and a half pounds. They're calling it Horatia—after you. They want it to be a writer. When are you coming back? I didn't half have a job getting your number.' The pips went and she said: 'Can I transfer the charge?'

'Do you wish to pay for further time?' the operator asked; it was a man somewhere out in the night. Isn't it odd the way these disembodied voices get entangled with your life.

'Did you get that little girl home all right?' Edna asked now.

'I'm afraid I can't allow you further time,' the operator said.

I was lying now face down on top of Ariadne with one knee in her crutch to keep her interested until I could start again.

'Her father's on his way up there,' Edna said.

I quickly got the call transferred; I could see that whatever was in her muddled mind had to be gone into.

'You didn't interfere with her, did you?' she said. 'He inarf cross. He's Italian, isn't he? Very well spoken, though. He says you've got to marry her. I think he's got the wrong chap. I told him about Sue's baby . . .'

She had spoken to at least four people. At least. They had all told her different things about different things.

'Norman Freville's escaped,' she said, among her alarms and panics. And she said that her baby had turned over, her old mother had fallen down crossing the High Street and my name had been mentioned in the *Radio Times* in connection with the Unmarried Mother series. 'They've got a bloody expert now,' she said, with one of her rare shafts of wit.

'Couldn't she write?' Ariadne said.

'And Wendy asked me to ask you did she leave a cigarette lighter in your room?'

'I don't know, do I?'

'And do you know there's a man looking for you with a little occasional table? '

I'd been away from Hampstead, how long? Twenty-four, thirty-six hours maybe. No wonder I had difficulty maintaining that ivory castle state needed for writing. It was like living under an artillery barrage.

'And there's a letter from a woman in Toronto who's read one of your books. I think it was *The Virgin Prostitute*. She wants to know if you're married.'

Somebody must have been opening my mail.

'She wants to know if you've got any instructions,' Edna said then.

'Who does?'

'Your secretary—Miss Browne, is it?'

Gradually I got the picture and Ariadne went cold and fell asleep. My bowsprit became something of a double-sheep-shank, curled up and dozed around her navel.

After the battle when the students and boxers had gone and the casualties had been carried away and the nurses gone to work,

177

apparently Count Raoul Lecci had come looking for me and found Joanna Browne in residence; she had let him stay the night just, she would no doubt explain, to stop him following me and killing me. Also Mac Gordon McKilvey had turned up with Dinah Thing and a Roman Catholic priest said to be Ariadne's father on leave from the Vatican.

'Do you mean all those people know exactly where I'm staying tonight and who with?'

'Yes. They've been sitting in your room plotting your route on a map. Did you know you've got a radio bleeper fastened under your car?'

They weren't picking it up directly. Jamie was passing the information on in the hope that somebody would connect up my route or destination with AK-Edgar, the telephone calls, the black spot or the spirit of B. . . .

The call was being tapped but they disconnected Edna too late to stop her betraying them. There was a radio under my car which had to be removed and quickly; there was a murderous Italian flying north either to Glasgow or Prestwick who could be here in Inverness by breakfast time.

Also I was a grandfather again.

For the man who's still got his nose glued to toyshop windows there's no joy in seven-pound grand-daughters. You start watching your erections like a grower of prize chrysanthemums looking for the first signs of frost.

Thirteen

'They must mean Uncle Clive,' Ariadne said. 'He's not my real uncle but he's not my father, either. He's a monsignor. They're not allowed to fornicate.'

I got her up got her dressed got her out.

'I can just remember him in Durban when I was ever so tiny.

He used to take me to ballet lessons on the back of his horse.' She thought about this for a moment. 'Or it might have been a zebra.'

Miss Cross came down in her Pearl White nightgown; I paid the bill, gave her some false information about my intentions in case anyone came asking questions. Outside in the hotel park I wriggled underneath the Capri and tore off the radio beacon that had been taped onto the rear axle by Jamie's Man Friday. I wedged it under a sack of potatoes in a long-distance lorry going south while it stood in front of me at traffic signals.

'Anyway I thought that priest bit was only in Mac the Knife's script.' It began to intrigue her; she put a hankie over her hair, closed her knees, steepled her fingers to her chin and started looking holy.

In the house of my life my car is the most important room. From its window I can see any part of my life I choose. The crooked piece of Burwell High Street between Taylor's grocery shop and The Harrow, Hanover Square (my agent), the North Circular, the Icknield Way, the Channel Ferry, Paris, Heidelberg, Bognor Regis, Newmarket, Weston-Super-Mare and now Loch Ness by night south to Drumnadrochit then a swift turn west and another back north to shake pursuit; *Beauly 15* and *Muir of Ord 5*; *Steep Hill* here and *Wild Animals* there, all reduced to simple children's drawings; the *School!* warning with regional inhibitions betrayed in silhouette: a big girl may lead a little boy by the hand but a big boy may not lead a little girl.

We passed out of Invernesshire into Ross and Cromarty, went through Conon Bridge and Dingwall then ran eight miles up the shore of Cromarty Firth; the whole of it was reduced to fifteen yards of Lucas-yellow electric light on a granite surface with rain streaking down through it. It didn't matter. The swift movement across the crust of the earth when you yourself are half-a-century old, meeting the elements, conscious of the mountains, the knowledge that your six or so stars are high and clear still and not getting wet; the marriage of all this cosmic existence to the life going on at its lowest level in the utterances of BBC disc jockeys and Luxembourg commercials; the Ford 1500 GT engine singing at a steady sixty miles an hour, the Dunlop tyres.

'Are you asleep?' Ariadne asked me at one stage. I made a noise to prove that I wasn't. 'I just saw a rabbit,' she said. And then she said': 'Can we go back and help it?'

'I'll buy you a rabbit,' I told her.

This is not childlike, this could have been Diana talking. Ladies, wherever you see them and whatever the weather, rabbits are already home.

'Here is an urgent message just come in,' said the BBC man (I remembered him on one of the pirate radio ships and he had no authority for me). 'It is for motorist Mr Horace Spurgeon Fenton, believed to be driving in northern Scotland, possibly on the A9 towards John O'Groats—'

The three-way signpost at Bonar Bridge had just come up and I swerved off the A9 onto the A836 for Invershin and Cape Wrath.

'Will Mr Fenton,' the man went on as if nothing had happened, 'please stop at the first box and dial 999 for the police. This is vital if he wants to stay alive—hey there! That's drama, isn't it, folks? Mr Fenton, have you checked your king-pin assembly lately? Yuk yuk yuk!'

Yuk yuk yuk to him.

'Did you hear all that?' I asked Ariadne.

She was asleep. I was glad. How long does it take to make a name? I've written and published thirty books (including my *Caxton Drakes*) and yet they still call me a 'motorist'.

The day, when it arrived, was not much different from the night; the road got a bit longer than fifteen yards, things I thought were clouds turned into mountains, wandering sheep gave you more chance of survival and you saw that what you had been belting along at sixty miles an hour was little more than a hill-track with passing places and murderous hump-backed bridges over flooded 'burrans'.

'Where are we now?' Ariadne murmured, sleepily.

'Nowhere,' I told her, with extreme accuracy.

The rain had developed into a steady downpour, the sky and landscape had locked together and apparently the whole of the British Isles was covered in anti-cyclonic gloom. The water on the windscreen was ignoring the wipers and actually travelling *upwards*.

'I'm hungry,' Ariadne said.

The way things were it was a fairly abstract remark. What she remembered next was far more down to earth.

'Jesus!' She sat upright and plunged her hand down between her legs. 'Stop the car quick!'

You think it's at least a miscarriage when they suddenly discover what's been putting them in agony for the past hour.

'You'll have to wait for the next passing place.'

'Never mind that—I want a pissing place.'

Education counts for very little now that emancipation is complete. The next passing place came up with its little crossed post, a heap of road-flints and a litter bin. She jumped out before I'd hardly stopped, started pulling her knickers down—

'Not there!' I can't take this kind of thing. I've walked across a ploughed field just to spit. 'You're not a baby any more.'

'Look the other way then!'

'There's a car coming!'

There was a car coming, believe it or not. I had driven for hours it seemed without passing anything. Now there were headlights distantly through the gloom. This always happens.

'Come over here,' I said.

I took her ten yards along the road, jumped a sheep that was lying flat to the ground with its nose buried from the downpour in a heap of stones—my God, what a way to live.

We were interrupted by the horn blast and bell ringing of my car's burglar alarm. The police pissing about again, I thought. It wasn't. As we came up from the burn a man turned from my car, aimed a shot-gun at us and fired. In the same moment I had pulled Ariadne down the bank again. We heard the shot hitting the stonework of the bridge, rattling through the grass and

181

hummock; the sheep jumped up and ran in their peculiar jerky epileptic way as though hit.

'In the water!' I told the girl, pulling her into the fast, shallow stream. The only escape was to walk through the tunnel of the bridge under the road and follow the burn through waterside foliage beyond.

'I'm soaking !' Ariadne gasped.

'It's better than being dead !'

Above the continuing din of the car alarm a man's voice came echoing through the bridge ahead of us.

'Fenton ! I am going to kill you. You fucked my wife.'

He had cut us off. We had stopped walking. The bubbles of her urine floated past as if mocking us.

'My God !' Ariadne said, disgusted at me.

'That was ages ago,' I told her.

'Don't shoot me,' Ariadne called. 'I'm coming out !'

'Don't leave me,' I asked her.

'I have to kill you both,' Count Lecci called. 'You are a writer, Fenton. Explain to her.'

'You would be a witness against him,' I told her.

'I won't say anything!' she shouted. And then to me: 'Tell him I won't say anything.'

Oh yeah? I said: 'You stay and keep him talking till I've gone—'

Another shot this time fired through the bridge and ricocheting all around us. The only escape now was to run back through the burn the way we'd come and head for open country; the visibility in this downpour was no more than fifteen yards. Just in time I heard his footsteps running across the road above our heads. We ran in the original direction and were out between the bushes of the open moor before he discovered we'd gone. He did not follow us. It was not necessary to follow us.

To start with we couldn't run. If ever you read of someone running across the Scottish moors don't believe it. It is not like meadow grass, you couldn't draw a chalk-line on it. Imagine laying your front room carpet on a layer of blown-up pig's bladders and then trying to dance on it without breaking your ankle. What looks like a pretty mauve carpet from the comfort of your car turns out to be great coarse clumps of vegetation clinging to thick spongy peat; it is intersected by streams of water which you do not realise are there until your foot vanishes through the crack in the vegetation. The water coursing down from the mountains eats its bed from the peat, the channels get overgrown by the grass and heather and bramble so that you have to pick your way watching each foot in turn.

After five minutes of this slow progress, holding on to each other—luckily we had our coats on, not that this was going to be noticeable soon—we were still close enough to hear Raoul Lecci's feet on the flint road and the gunshots were terrifyingly close; we flung ourselves down flat but then on looking back discovered that he was blasting the tyres of my car. I counted the shots and multiplied by seven-pounds-ten-shillings—it came to thirty pounds. He then looked round for us, couldn't see us, went and got into his own car, drove it down to the next passing place, turned it round and drove back, ran onto the grass and parked, lit up a cigarette, rested the shot-gun through the car window on our side.

There was just enough increase in the downpour to enable us to run, crouching, stumbling, falling, farther away from the road. We had no choice of direction. Right angles to the road and we'd be heading for the mountains—Ben Hee, Ben Hope, Ben Loyal, Ben More Assynt, inaccessibly high places where we would die of exposure in our town clothes. To head back parallel with the road the way I had driven would get us to no habitation as I knew; there remained only the way ahead. From my memory of the AA map now in the car, there was at least, fifteen miles without a village shown. Just the same we could strike a croft or dwelling and get somebody to go for the police.

'If you hadn't thrown that beacon away they'd have been here with us now,' Ariadne said.

I didn't blame her for recriminations. She was standing knee-deep in some babbling subterranean burn, the hankie around her hair was soaked, streaks of water and hair covered her face which was red with cold.

'Upsadaisy,' I said, lifting her as best I could.

We trudged on, stumbling, weaving, soon so wet through that we no longer got any wetter. Every now and then we heard his engine go past on the road. He was judging our walking pace and driving from lay-by to lay-by to keep up, keeping his feet dry and waiting for the time when we'd be only too glad to be shot.

'There's a house!' Ariadne exclaimed. It seemed too good to be true and it wasn't true. A big square black shape coming up through the rain that we now saw was a great cubic stack of dug peat, ready for winter collection. We had passed it and were facing into the bleak infinity of water ahead when I saw an alternative.

'Stop a minute.'

I took her back to the stack of peat, made her sit down on some that had tumbled down.

'What are you doing?' she said.

I told her I was going to make her a little house.

'We can't stay here forever!'

'Just till the rain stops. There'll be other traffic along. He won't even know we're here. He'll look for us and he'll have to give up.'

I pulled the big slabs of wet peat out of the stack on what I judged to be the side away from the road. There was not a lot of time. It was one of those in-the-cloud days when visibility is doubling, multiplying, then closing up again—every ten minutes the picture changing. For one freak moment the sky opened and silver sunlight funnelled down; another time the peak of Stack Polly showed dramatically above the rain. Twice we heard his gunshots but there was no shot flying our way.

'He's shooting at sheep,' I told her. 'He thinks it's us.'

'How many bullets has he got?' she asked.

How the fucking hell should I know? 'About twelve,' I told her.

'How the fucking hell do you know?' she said.

She had just been wondering. I often mistake this for definite conversation which expects a reply. I get misunderstood a lot. She must have regretted her harshness because she said a moment later:

'Don't try to comfort me, Horace. If I'm going to die here that's it. Nobody will ever know.'

'They'll find the car,' I said.

'He'll push that into a quagmire,' she told me.

It was true; I could see him doing it, the mud oozing in under the sunshine roof, the heavy engine dragging it down, nose first. It was a lovely car. When it was first advertised in around 1962 they had nine big policemen sitting in the open boot to show how roomy it was. I wish to God they'd kept them there. And besides the sunshine roof and the GT conversion on power, I had a third windscreen-wiper operating on the rear window.

They say when you're about to die the whole of your past flashes in front of your eyes. It was dripping in front of mine. By the time I'd tunneled my way a couple of yards into the peat stack I felt really ill. It's funny, sometimes intense cold and hard work can invigorate you; you remember the snow drifts in 1926 or 7? I shifted one along Newmarket Road the size of a house—I was only nine. Other times you're caught in a shower and you think you're dying. It depends how your plana's running.

The gun went off again and three sheep came gadding past with their bald eyes staring.

'I think he's coming!' Ariadne said.

'In here, then, quickly!'

What I'd done was, it wasn't exactly a little house but a dugout with a roof on it. I put my mac on the ground, dry side up, took the girl inside then pulled the peat blocks back across the entrance, piling up a wall to cover us then drawing as much of the rough stuff as I could across the top. A tall man could have looked in at us, but I doubt whether anyone would even think of it.

'Isn't it fun?' Ariadne said now, standing on tip-toe to peer out of the top. 'If we had a gun we could win him.'

'Sit down and keep quiet. Listen for his car to start up.'

Go and sit in your broom cupboard for half an hour if you want to get some idea. It wasn't fun but it wasn't bad; very little rain came in. The wetness had made us cold but now being pressed close together and bathed in our own breath we started warming up.

'Fenton!' The voice was too close for comfort. The foreign tone was not so much Italian as American. But it was no doubt Jane's husband. From the moment she had said (we are sitting in the bath, remember, in Shepherd's Market) 'I am thinking of adopting you' she had brought me nothing but trouble. 'I know you are there!'

'Oh crumbs!' Ariadne whispered.

'Stand up or I fire!'

I started standing up but Ariadne was clutching my neck.

'One . . . two... three—'

We buried our faces in each other's bodies as the gun went off.

'Baaaaaaaaaaaa . . . !' said the recipient of the shot.

He was killing sheep right left and centre.

'All right, Fenton!' He was off again. 'I know you are inside that sod!'

'Does he mean me?' Ariadne whispered.

He shot the gun into the stack of peat. None of it penetrated.

'I shall set fire to it and shoot you as you come out!'

'He's joking,' Ariadne said. 'You can't set fire to rain.'

'I go to get the petrol. . .'

He was so close we could hear his footsteps swishing away across the moorland, the sound of his buttons against the gun butt.

'Come on!' Ariadne hissed.

'No ... He was bluffing.'

In the darkness of the hidey-hole she was looking at me with terrible uncertainty. I was uncertain too. Have you seen peat burning? It burns with such intensity it burns green and blue.

'Horace,' she said, 'will you take my confession?'

'I'm not a Catholic'

'You're another human soul. If we die together in fire you will be cleansed. God will believe you then.'

The rubbish they pile into them at these expensive schools. I told her to go ahead but talk quietly.

'I killed my baby,' she said.

'No, come on, stop mucking about. If we are going to get killed, which we're not, you don't want to confess a load of bloody lies.'

She wasn't lying. She crossed her heart and hoped to die. This was the real truth about Ariadne Thing. When she came to it I remembered the headlines. Funny you don't connect headlines with people. My bankruptcy brought me more glaring publicity than all my literary output together, yet the neighbours and tradespeople didn't connect me with that Horace Spurgeon Fenton.

*Mr Fenton at work in the Hertfordshire wood*s ran one caption to an idyllic photograph in the *Daily Mirror* of me typing away in the wilds. This was organised by them on the back lot of MGM studios to back up a load of crap I'd fed the judge about having to keep my car for work purposes—you probably remember it now I've mentioned it. In the same way I remembered Ariadne's headlines:

BABY'S BODY IN LAUNDRY CHUTE
FILM STAR'S EVIDENCE

She still had cuttings mixed up with toffee papers and bits of fluff in her school coat pockets. I managed to read the one above by the light of my cigarette lighter. I never mention smoking, do I? I smoke all the time, or I seem to; not long panatellas or things my publisher wants from me though. *Peter Stuyvesant* mostly; they're so weak you can't taste them at all but the brand and the package is vaguely American which is why I use them (in America I'm told nobody's ever heard of them). My lighters are all Ronsons that Edna and Tres and the kids buy me and I keep losing.

Mr David Alexander (that was Dennis's real name) in reply to counsel's questions said that Miss Tweak (that was Ariadne's real name, Millicent Tweak) arrived in the middle of the night at his apartment in Miss Dix's (that was Dinah Thing's real name) house at Shepperton while Miss Dix was on tour in South Africa. He said that he put her up in the guest bedroom.

Mr Samuel Quorn: Did you not perceive (see) that Miss Tweak was about to give birth to a child?

Alexander: No, sir, I did not. She was wearing a duffle coat. They are pregnant anyway.

(laughter)

The brackets are mine.

Don't be dismayed if you are confused, gentle reader. You are supposed to be confused. It's the way they're running the century. Nobody is who you think they are, nothing what you think it is.

'Dinah flew back from Africa and came to visit me in Holloway Prison,' Ariadne said. 'That's when I met Mummy for the first time. She asked me to incriminate Denis in the prison visiting room. He was innocent really though the police were glad to get him for lots of other things. They hanged him with his own braces because they couldn't make anything stick. Nobody would talk or they'd get a brick tied on them at one of the parties. That's the whole truth and nothing but the truth so help me God.'

'You don't say that to a priest you say that in court.'

'What do you say to a priest then?'

'What about the baby?' I asked her.

'It was it or me,' she said. 'I was all by myself in Dennis's guest room. I broke the cord with my fingers though I think it was already dead.'

'Who was the father?'

'One of the village boys—that why I ran away to London.'

'And Dinah Thing was looking for an illegitimate daughter for publicity purposes?'

'Yes. She was fed up with Dennis.'

I don't know whether you can get any of this; I can't make it a lot plainer, anyway. Ariadne (Millie Tweak) came from the village of Steeple Mudsen in Hertfordshire, just off the Icknield Way. I should have known she was an A505 girl; I felt that I already knew her. Once driving the long straight Roman fen road between Over and Dry Drayton I passed a beautiful slim long-legged long-haired girl dressed in a scarlet coat and carrying a brown paper carrier-bag with the words BROADRIB — PORK BUTCHER on it. I saw her for a mile before I passed her and I saw her in my three mirrors for another mile afterwards. I have seen her ever since and I shall always see her. She was an Icknield Way girl.

'What are you doing?' Ariadne asked. I was stroking her hair. 'You don't half have moods,' she said. Then she succumbed a little, weary with talking and ready for death. 'I'm glad I got that lot off me chest.' Her dialogue was getting nearer the Icknield Way now, further from Television Centre. 'One other thing,' she said. I had undone her bra and got her tights down to her knees now, stroking everywhere. 'God knows I've never broken my word all this time. Mummy's forty-one. Dinah Thing I mean.'

'Forty-one?'

'If we come out of this alive, Horace,' she said, 'promise you'll never tell anyone.'

The whole thing was a confession and I've always treated it as such. Even now I may wipe if off the tape before starting on the draft manuscript.

In the confined space and with Ariadne on her back cocooned in school duffie, scarf, jumper and skirt it was like looking for a pearl inside a sack in the dark.

'Promise,' she said.

'Wait a minute,' I said.

We did it several times afterwards but never as perfectly as in the rabbit hole of dirty wet peat and with her muddy boots round the back of my neck. It amazes me sometimes —not everytime I admit—but sometimes when the plana's running high how you can take away the undercarriage, so to speak, by shifting your hands to the pelvic position so that the dynamic centre of gravity is sharply centred at womb level, both bodies leave the ground, the legs perfectly balancing the upper parts and the whole rocking on a fulcrum which, at certain stages, is no more than the two wrist bones. Once having levitated into this magnificent optimum floating position the control is perfect; the angle of penetration continuously variable by both parties, the length of stroke adjustable to such exquisitely fine limits that the male orgasm is kept just one ten-thousandth part of a degree under while the female climaxes one, two, three sometimes—not everytime I admit—four times; and each time her climax comes at that precisely engineered second when the stroke has gradually reduced in inverse proportion to her need so that suddenly and for that one second of ejaculation the penis at maximum strength and hardness jams into the womb.

The mutual balance at that moment is akin to the man on the tightrope over Niagara Falls who has just dropped his balancing stick.

Ariadne screamed: 'I did it! I did it!'

'Good girl,' I said, just as old Elsan had congratulated her on another achievement.

Then before it's lost, and like starting a Yo-Yo from the bottom of the string, we got it rocking again. She had five orgasms and on her fifth I had mine.

This, gentle reader, is what is meant by marriage. If you haven't got this then wait for the kids to go to sleep and creep out of the house in different directions. Don't stop walking for about a year then see where you are and who's around.

'Somebody's licking my foot,' Ariadne said, presently.

After such a session involving every Alpha particle and taking almost an hour, you will swear that you haven't been to sleep but somehow your watch will have jumped the odd day. It was now much lighter and less rain was getting in. Ariadne's foot had somehow gone outside. Now we could both hear clearly the pleased whiny breathy sound of a dog saying 'pen and ink, pen and ink, pen and ink'. It seemed safe to assume—may I have that again? That is a cliché. Isn't it odd how they hit you when you never use them. Every cliché of word, thought or action that you use is a bit of your life thrown to Old Sloughfoot. Safe to assume, reasonable to suppose—these are words that fraternise together like hollow little clerks on the 9.15. What I'm trying to say is that the shooting had stopped sometime during our fucking.

When we looked out of our peat hide there was a lovely old sheepdog and a lovely old Scottie shepherd looking back at us. There was the feeling of swift recent movement and it was anybody's bet who'd just been lying flat licking Ariadne's foot. Friends of mine who remember either George Haufmann at the electronic factory or Colin Braine the photographer's agents at Artists Parker will know the kind of man this was. If you met him in the street you'd think he'd dressed up as Father Christmas for a laugh. Later you realised that he was perpetrating the most elaborate fraud upon himself as a form of public flagellation on our behalf. Theirs is the kind of beard that makes everything grown since 1960 merely cosmetic. Given a crop it would make God's eyes water at any harvest thanksgiving. The eyes, bright, penetrating, wicked, saintly, were the eyes of a prophet; one, however, who has through no fault of his own arrived a little after the event and too late to do more than help.

'Och!' he said.

We both said 'Och' and started climbing out of our burrow. The rain had cleared and the sun was trying to break through a complicated composite of mountain cloud. I was alarmed to see that Count Raoul Lecci's motor car, the new Fiat launched in this country almost solely on its copulating passenger seat, was still parked in the nearest passing-place. My Capri on its flat, blown-to-ribbon tyres was parked on the next one. We had not got very far and neither, as we saw a moment later, had the count.

'Horace!' Ariadne cried, pointing. 'Look at those poor sheep!'

'Aye,' said the shepherd.

There were five dead sheep and one poor wounded brute in

an area of moorland between the peat stack and what appeared to be a burnt-out crofter's hut (we should waste time digging shelters?) We wandered from corpse to corpse and the eyes of the wounded sheep followed us, though it didn't appear to be able to turn its head.

'I'm sorry about all this,' I told the shepherd (I wish I could be more effective in moments of high drama). 'I know who did it—he thought they were us.'

'And I thought he was a leaping red deer,' said the shepherd.

Count Raoul Lecci lay dead in the wet grass.

There was a can of petrol standing by the door of the little stone building and a handful of thatch from the roof lay nearby. Not difficult to imagine the scene which had taken place here in the pouring rain while we had been galloping obliviously on the heights nearby. The old shepherd, dead-tired, rescuing lambs on the mountain, the shots outside undoing all his work, the mad voice crying: *I shall set fire to it and shoot you as you come out!*

'There is no need for your guidselves to get involved at all,' the shepherd told us over a cup of strong hot tea laced with whisky. 'Martin—that's the sergeant over by Lairg— warned us of his coming.'

I reminded him about my stuck car but he already had that worked out and heaven knew what else. By a stroke of good luck the tyres were interchangeable with the Fiat's and although it was a long job he did most of the work and by the time it was done the sun was out on the heights of Stack Polly and we were feeling good. I don't think it was out, actually, but it seemed to be out.

'Ye'll find the best hunter's hotel in Scotland ten miles down the valley—the Altnacealgach. Tell them auld Tammie sent ye.'

On a generous afterthought he insisted on putting one of the dead sheep into the boot of my car and his last act of all was to thrust an unlabelled bottle of whisky into my hands with a friendly glance at Ariadne's legs and the remark both cryptic and prophetic that we'd no doot be needing the wee drap of nourishment. He didn't wait for me to start the car but turned abruptly and went about what seemed to be the beginning of a busy morning.

'I feel I should have given him something,' I told Ariadne. I'm always feeling this about people. I used to give my hairdresser on Rosslyn Hill a shilling tip until one day I saw him driving a Bentley through Squires Mount.

'Don't be daft,' Ariadne said. 'He's got a fortune there. Look at this but don't make a fuss until we've gone.'

She was holding, below the level of the car door window, a bundle of hundred-dollar American notes. She had found them in the cubby-hole of the Fiat while auld Tammie and I had been busy changing tyres.

'There was five thousand dollars. I took half. It's only fair. We brought him here—he shot him.'

I couldn't, of course, let her keep it. She couldn't understand me. She pointed out that the shepherd had got the car full of expensive luggage and clothing, three very valuable cameras and a box-full of home-made bombs.

'It'll all come out at the inquest !' I told her.

'What inquest?' she said.

Auld Tammie, holding Count Raoul Lecci's ankles, was dragging the body behind him like a wheelbarrow and heading for Stack Polly and the quagmires in between.

Fourteen

I'm cutting out dirty great chunks now.

Well I must have talked about five hundred pages onto that tape recorder because of the holes in my hands.

'Are you hungry or have you eaten?' the lady at the hotel asked us. I told her we were starving. 'Good,' she said. 'We cater for starving people.'

You might think I've made this up. All I can say is, go to Altnacealgach by Lairg and find out. It's the only hotel in the.

United Kingdom I should think that wants to get you food when you're hungry instead of between this and that time. Bathwater? Anytime. Drinks? Go into the bar and help yourselves. Just sign the book. It's a hunting, fishing, pony-trekking, boating paradise amid the highland glens. And they not only do packed lunches and flasks of soup for their customers they have a special line in doggie wraps.

'One dog, a greyhound, that was with an English family who stayed here last year,' the girl Helen in charge of our welfare told us, 'trotted back two weeks later by himself— all the way from Middlesex.'

And that is what I call a real testimonial.

'We're on the run from the police,' Ariadne told her. Everybody stopped eating and looked round at us. I grinned at them. Ariadne was too busy with the roast pork to notice. 'At least, Horace is. Mummy's after me.'

'They'll not find you here,' Helen said, comfortably.

There was a kind of chorus of 'hear hears' and the laughter of agreement from the diners. I got the feeling they were all Jacobites.

We sat at a family-sized oval table with eight other people, the men all tweedy refugees from town jobs; there was that anti-establishment set upon them you get with the middle-aged and elderly when the commuting's over and the grave is in sight and suddenly they see the trees. There were two or three touring caravans parked outside,. cars trailing boats and dinghies, all the things they'd meant to do now assembled for the last fling.

'She wants to take me on another world tour but Horace thinks I'm too young,' Ariadne was telling them as their interest increased. 'I'm a concert cellist, you see. I studied under Rostropovich in Moscow, Tortelier in Paris and Leonard Rose in New York. Horace is my manager, though in fact we were secretly married in Las Vegas on my fifteenth birthday— that was two months ago.'

'Can you play the *Flight Of The Bumble Bee*?' some body asked; it was the only question from all that mass of lurid information and it just about summed up the dangers. They were non-existent.

'My cello cost a thousand dollars from Nathaniel Cross in Philadelphia,' Ariadne was saying.

I believed her. She was so convincing you couldn't doubt any of it.

'You must be very proud of her,' a woman said.

I was; I really was. Every life story she told was better than the last.

'When I've unpacked I'll show you my cuttings,' she was promising a red-faced old chap at her other side. This was going to be interesting; the only cutting she had to my knowledge was her murder trial and she only showed that when she was about to be killed. Somebody suggested she gave us a concert in the lounge after dinner that night but she told them the police had her cello at the moment (It was under my bed). 'They say they're looking for drugs but they're having a marvellous time. They beat up the boys and strip all the girls. All the drop-outs in London are rushing to join the police force.'

'I've heard about that,' Helen the waitress said.

The conversation shifted to police atrocities the way it does between law-abiding people in a bureaucratic society where nothing is up to them. Apparently the landlord of the red-faced man's local pub was a retired policeman who entertained the saloon bar with stories of police brutality.

He told us about a bunch of blacks the police had picked up for some suspected offence or other which they were denying. 'The sergeant told them they were all going to be shot,' he said. 'They blindfolded them, stood them in a row in the police station yard and on the word "Fire!" clapped two dustbin lids together. They nearly all passed out with shock.'

'They're not like policemen any more,' a woman said. 'It terrifies me if I see a police car. I make Charlie stop until they've gone.'

'They could get you for that,' the red-faced man said. A car went past outside and everybody stopped talking and eating until the noise had dwindled.

'When you're in the mountains it's different,' a woman said.

It really was a safe feeling and I recommend the Highlands for everybody who's getting twitchy about the welfare state. I had stopped worrying about Scotland Yard, the airliner sabotage, Freville and Lecci were dead, Ariadne was no longer under age and I was looking forward to seeing Albert alive and well on Skye. On top of this I was a grandfather again, Edna's baby had turned over and Tres was making fruit cakes. And on top of this according to the Countess Jane Chapell I was a millionaire. I looked at my watch; Cedric should be meeting her about now at Heathrow Airport.

Against all this wellbeing was one niggling worry that had come out of Edna's long-winded telephone call to the Inverness hotel. Who was looking for me at East Heath Road? And why was he carrying an occasional table … ? Funny, isn't it, it's the main essentials of my life that seem to worry other people—it's the tiny incidentals that worry me.

'Aren't you coming into my bed?' Ariadne asked.

They had given us a large twin-bedded double room at the back of the hotel. The front looked out onto the loch, the road, the moored rowing boats and the hills to the south; from our window we were looking straight up the side of a mountain, the top of which, severed by a white scarf of cloud, resembled a half-submerged hippopotamus. I pulled the curtains together, shutting out the view and darkening the room, for it was now three o'clock in the afternoon. Then I got into my own bed and turned my back on her. 'Horace?' she said, soon.

'Aren't you tired?' I asked her.

We had been so starving that we'd gone straight into the dining-room, following the delicious smells, without bothering to take our cases to the room, wash or change our wet clothes; apparently this is what they expected of their fishing hunting clients. The people who had been eating and talking with us were now floating around out on the loch, burping peacefully, knitting, watching their lines for trout and salmon. Occasionally you could hear a distant 'baaaaaaaaa'; this was the red-faced man calling to the sheep. His wife had kept trying to stop him doing it at lunch.,

'Don't you love me now?' she said next.

She was trying to romanticise it now. What about Millicent Tweak biting through the umbilical cord in some squalid showbiz bedroom; was that love? I didn't have to say this, she was already tuned in.

'That was all a lot of lies,' she said: 'Don't make me suffer for it. That's what happened to Jody Paynton. She kept telling everybody her father had gone bankrupt—you remember Paynton's Parquet Flooring? One night she went home from school and her father had shot himself. The bankruptcy rumour had got back and crippled his business.'

'And yet you all go on lying?'

'You have to. If you tell the truth they think you're a freak or something.'

'You told me the truth,' I told her.

'I didn't. I made it up.'

'You showed me the press cutting.'

'Of course I did. That's part of it. One girl had herself tattooed.'

This was too much. I tucked down and got comfortable. To go to sleep what I have to do is lie on my left side until my heart jumps, then turn on my right side, put my face up on my crooked elbow, spread my feet to distribute the weight evenly (thirteen stone) and fling my left arm right round behind me to keep my lungs open; then it usually takes about two hours. Not this afternoon, however; when she spoke again I nearly went through the ceiling.

'Come and cuddle me,' she said.

'Oh my God,' I said. 'Don't do that!'

Then she said: 'I'm only about twelve.'

My penis twitched.

I'm such a dope; my body believed her against all the evidence. To hell with her, I went to sleep.

What woke me up was the sound of my own car door slamming. With all the millions of cars on the road today it's surprising that a driver knows the sound of his own door, isn't it? It's to do with the characteristic acoustics of the car. For instance when one of the Capri doors slam the sunshine roof lifts up and snaps down again; and also now of course the horn goes off and an alarm bell rings. Also, I have to admit, mine was the only car parked round the back of the hotel practically under my window. When I knelt on the bed and pulled back the curtains to peer down I saw two men searching the boot while a woman's legs stuck out from the passenger door as she rummaged in the cubby holes.

'Where did you put that money?' I asked Ariadne.

She didn't answer. She wasn't there. I looked at my watch (Ingersoll, seventeen jewel lever, Swiss made— Welwyn Stores). The time, believe it or not, was eight-thirty in the evening.

One of the men withdrew his hands from the boot and I could see that they were covered in blood—the dead sheep. I had decided not to give it to the landlady or mention Auld Tammie; anything that led back to the corpse of Raoul Lecci was bad, I felt.

As he wiped his hands of blood on a tuft of grass he happened to glance up and see me. I quickly drew the curtain together again and sat back with my naked heels against my naked bum. I knew instinctively that they were police; with a woman policeman because a girl child was involved. Luckily when I know things instinctively I'm always wrong. While I was undressing for my bath before going to bed I had seen blood on my shirt and knew instinctively that I had been shot by Count Lecci without knowing it at the time; then I couldn't find the bullet hole and decided that Ariadne had been shot. But she hadn't either. It's a great relief sometimes to have a capacity for error.

There was a tap at the door which opened and Helen the waitress looked in, covered her eyes. 'Sorry sir,' she said. Then she grinned at me and said: 'Your wife's downstairs.'

'Oh Christ!' I said. I was thinking of the fat legs protruding from my car. Was it Tres or Edna? 'I mean that one,' she said, pointing to the indentation in Ariadne's pillow. 'Carlotta.'

'Oh, Carlotta.'

'She's having her dinner. She wants to know will you be long?'

Dinner? Lunch was still giving me a stomach like a bolster. I told her I'd skip dinner and join her in the lounge for coffee afterwards.

'Shame on you,' she said. 'You'll have to eat while you're here. The air's as strong as wine.' I told her I didn't get enough exercise and she said: 'Would you like a room with a double bed for tomorrow?'

I couldn't believe she was being suggestive and she wasn't; didn't see the connection, added: 'Can you hear that din? Somebody's knocked against your car and started the alarm. Have you got the key to stop it? I'll do it meself.'

To get the key I had to get off the bed naked and reach for my trousers; she looked out of the window meantime, then took the keys from me without looking.

'Thank you, sir.'

She went out, closed the door. This impersonal thing is a great art. The way they come into your room in the mornings and seem to walk backwards and sideways putting down trays, pulling curtains, keeping up a cheerful chatter and never letting their eyes go on the bed, never letting their minds go off the weather.

When I went into the lounge bar an hour later I didn't know what to expect, but then luckily I never do. I had heard Ariadne's gay chatter as I came down the stairs and there she was entertaining a dozen replete fishermen and women and kids and dogs. She was dressed in her best short-short pinafore dress and looked about twelve again.

'So the Judge said: "Do you mean you live together as man and wife?" Horace said: "Good heavens no—we're perfectly happy!"' And as everybody laughed round at me, she said to me:

'I'm telling them about the time you were charged with procuring.'

'Oh yes?' I said, and tried to laugh it off but then I saw that she had the press-cuttings; or rather, they had; bits of newspaper were passing round the room from group to group and I managed to get hold of one.

'That's my concert in Detroit,' Ariadne said. 'You remember.'

'Carlotta Gomez takes City by storm,' said one headline. 'Schoolgirl Cellist Sensation,' said another. I said: 'Haven't you got those with pictures of you on the platform?'

Red-face's wife thrust some into my hand: 'There you are. And what a happy moment!'

The happiest thing about that moment was that a child was passing a bouquet up to Carlotta Gomez as the photo was taken covering the face—Ariadne had chosen it for the purpose, of course. I found out as time went on that they came in sets, these con-tricks. I mean it wasn't just a question of deciding who you were going to be and collecting the material, there were lots of sets of material already circulating that had been used several times by other lying girls in other schools and towns. They were called Purports (purporting to be this or that— get it?). I've seen them advertised since in *Morning Advertiser* and the Sunday personals—you've probably seen them in your daughter's school magazine

Strip Club Girl Purports for sale or will exchange for
genuine prison record...

That probably rings a bell. It never caught on with boys, Ariadne told me. Men are too conceited to want to be anybody else. But there's something else about this scene in the lounge which you've probably got to without my having to mention it *Millicent Tweak was a purport.* No wonder all the names were different. Never mind that, the excitement was back, Ariadne was about twelve again and I was a monster. The blood I had found was explained; neither of us had been shot. Her wild scream of triumphant 'I did it! I did it!' had nothing to do with orgasms except as a side-issue; she meant that she had lost her virginity at last. What's more the first doctor Dinah Thing got to examine her would say so.

'Ariadne, I've got to talk to you,' I told her, *sotte voce*.

She looked at me with her calm schoolgirl eyes for a moment and then that dust of a smile bent her lips a little. The panic in my voice had communicated. 'You've just got there, haven't you,' she said; but not as a question. 'Now fix me a large Old Grandad whisky on the rocks and one for yourself. That's what I used to drink at Framis's in Manhattan,' she added to her nearest neighbour as I went behind the bar and started groping. And when I'd got them she touched glasses with me and said, with a certain ominous relish: 'Now we'll drink to it!'

'I expect you spoil her, Mr Cavendish,' a motherly soul told me, indulgently (Cavendish was Carlotta Gomez's husband and manager. Blurb writers please note it is not my real name).

'And you're going to spoil me a lot more,' Ariadne promised. She wriggled round on the settee and pulled her knees up then whispered: 'See if you can see up my dress. Mr Rawlinson keeps looking. I couldn't get my knickers dry.'

Novelist and Scriptwriter Purport available, I thought. *Would exchange for ticket to New York* . . . Thank God nobody in the Highlands knew us.

'Horace!'

A woman had spoken my name and it wasn't Ariadne because I was watching her lips for her next threat. The woman standing over us now had a very familiar look about her, like somebody you buy your cigarettes from every day but don't recognise on the bus. She was short and fat with brightly made-up face and vividly-dyed blonde hair. Her legs, I was now certain, were the ones that had been sticking out of my car.

'You got here then?' she said now. And squeezing herself down by Ariadne she said: 'Is this your little girl?' Then to me: 'Wherever have you been, Horace? We tried your agent, your publishers, all the television companies— didn't Count Lecci find you? He had some money for you and a little piece of paper for you to sign. You see we're trying to clear up poor Sir Ambrose's affairs—you got accidentally written into one of his foreign contracts.'

Red-face's wife said to Ariadne: 'You see—you'll have to to go now. You can't break a contract. Besides, think of all that money!'

'What?' my visitor said; she looked round at all the nodding knowing faces and seemed alarmed. Then to me she said: 'How many people know about it?'

'Somefink wrong, Popsie?' a man said. It was one of the men who had been searching my car. And it was Popsie. I had worked in Wardour Street with Popsie for several years when she was Arturo Conti's secretary and the chief cog in his wheeler-dealer movie machine.

I don't know why I hadn't recognised her for she hadn't changed; she was evidently still manipulating the finance, pulling the strings, removing the evidence. She said to me: 'Has Jane Chapell been in touch with you?'

'No,' I told her, promptly.

'Yes she has, Horace,' Ariadne said. 'That's who you've got this five million pound partnership deal with in Global Alivies.'

People who had been quietly watching television at the far end of the room now turned towards us with their backs to the set. Ariadne added, for their benefit, swiftly going from one purport to another: 'We're going to build a concert complex in the Bahamas as part of the Human Rights campaign.'

'I thought you meant recently,' I told Popsie. The boxer said: 'You want we should take a little ride somewhere quiet?' He was talking to Popsie but looking at Ariadne and me.

'I'd rather you saw my agent,' I said. 'You're very wise, Mr Cavendish,' one of the guests said; this was a youngish man whom Ariadne had called Mr Rawlinson. He had stopped looking up her legs and now took out some business cards. 'I don't know whether you would like some financial advice—tax, foreign investments and so on.' His wife stopped him. 'George! You shouldn't do that. We're on holiday.' She apologised to us all: 'He never stops working.'

Popsie said: 'We can't talk here, Horace.' And to the thug she said: 'Tell Lenny to get the car round.' 'He's still eating.'

'I'll get him,' Popsie said. She went through to the dining-room and the boxer followed her. I didn't have much time. I turned to the other guests:

'They're going to murder us and drop our bodies in the loch—somebody get the police.'

A big shout of laughter went up from everybody except Ariadne who had suddenly seen the whole thing. 'Oh crikey!' she said.

We were halfway to the door now, everybody smiling at us and waiting for more humour. 'You get my car keys from Helen,' I told Ariadne. 'I'll be out at the car.'

Popsie came back, her face sharp with inquiry: 'What's that?'

'We're going up to get our coats,' I told her. She said: 'You won't need coats.'

Behind her, still picking his teeth, stood Lenny Price the boxer.

'Hello, Lenny!' cried Ariadne, anxiously, just as though she hadn't flayed him with the whip while he was tied across our kitchen doorway. He just spit and a toothful of meat stuck on the middle of her forehead.

At that moment it was more frightening than a bullet hole yet nobody but us seemed aware of it. Ariadne turned to the guests, desperately:

'Somebody get the police! They're, going to kidnap me and hold me to ransom!'

It got another laugh and Popsie took hold of her arm: 'Come along, dear—no time for joking.'

Helen suddenly appeared behind them, looking at me: 'You're wanted on the phone, Mr Cavendish. It's the police at Lairg.'

I went through pulling Ariadne with me and nobody stopped us though Popsie, Lenny and the other man crowded behind us.

'In the office,' Helen said. She took us in and shut the door to keep the others out. The phone was not off the hook and she told us why: 'Your keys are in your car, sir. There's a ladder against your bedroom window. I'll keep them talking while you get away. Don't take any luggage—we'll look after it.'

As I say, I doubt whether there's a hotel in the world that could offer this kind of service and understanding. Then explaining it all with no more drama than if she was booking hairdressing appointments, she said:

'I had a message from faither.' She opened a pigeon-hole in the desk and a pigeon flew out; then she showed me the scrap of paper it had carried from Auld Tammie. He was her father, apparently (faither). 'This gang came looking for the Other One after you left. They suspected nothing. He had tidied up.' All this was contained in three strange Celtic symbols of squares and interlocking oblongs.

'That reminds me,' I said falsely; 'I've got a dead sheep in the boot of my car.'

'Keep it sir,' she said. 'You may have the need of it yet.'

I asked her about roads and ferries to Skye and she told us that we had to make the distance of thirty miles by eleven o'clock to catch the last ferry from the Kyle of Lochalsh to Kyleakin.

'It's nae much of a road. Ye'll need to keep your wits about you.' She went to the door and listened, then quietly unlocked it and looked out. It was all clear. 'They'll be waiting at the entrance. Up you go and good luck!'

Ariadne spoke for the first time since we'd come in. I think she was suffering from shock, poor kid. She said to Helen: 'Aren't you going to phone the police?'

Helen looked at me. She understood only too well.

'We'll manage without if we can,' I said.

She shook hands with us, politely: 'Good luck, Mr Fenton. Good luck, Miss Thing.'

She had reverted now to the names I had signed in the register. In the end you see, gentle reader, you can't improve on what you put in the register.

We crept up the stairs, went into our bedroom and locked the door. Popsie, Lenny and his pal were already there; they made us lock the door.

'Where's my money?' Lenny asked Ariadne.

'Not now, Lenny,' Popsie said. 'Time for private business later.' They had already searched the room, tipped out our cases, been through my pockets. To me, Popsie said: 'What's your connection with the *Corp Militante*?'

I said, grasping at straws: 'You touch us and you'll see.'

Then she said: 'Where's Albert Harris?'

'He's dead,' I said.

'Don't be tiresome, Horace,' Popsie said. 'Where are you heading for?'

'Where's my fucking three hundred quid!' Lenny said again; this time he was squeezing Ariadne's throat.

'I'll give it to you,' I said. 'Only it'll have to be in dollars.'

There was a short silence as though I had said something significant and then Popsie said: 'Where's Count Raoul Lecci?'

I told you, Popsie,' Lenny said. 'That old shepherd had something to do with it and that dead sheep.'

The other man who had kept the respectful silence of a paid underling, now brought my dirty shirt into view. 'There's blood on this.'

Ariadne looked at me and I looked at her and Popsie looked at both of us: 'Perhaps we should save that to show your mother?'

Ariadne said: 'You're not working for my mother, are you?' Then to Lenny: 'What are you doing with this lot?'

Popsie suddenly had an idea: 'Get them undressed.'

'What, both of them?' Lenny said. Then he said to his chum: 'You undress Mr Fenton and I'll undress Ariadne.'

I said: 'I'm not going to undress.'

Popsie said to Lenny: 'Break her arm—'

As he started to do this to Ariadne I capitulated: took off my tie.

'What's the idea of this?' I asked Popsie.

Ariadne said: 'That's as much as I'm going to take off while they're looking!'

Popsie motioned the boxers to look the other way.

Ariadne and I became naked.

'Now get into that bed together,' Popsie said.

Ariadne said: 'I won't do anything, you dirty old cow!'

Two naked people in a single bed don't have to do anything; I had to hold on to her to stop falling off the bed.

'Now just stay there,' Popsie said, 'while I fetch the camera.'

Lenny said. 'Wait till your mum sees this.' And the other man said to me: 'Five years you'll get for this, old 'un.' Oddly enough as Popsie walked around us with a small camera taking flash pictures we both started to show our best sides; I mean there might have been a book jacket picture amongst them.

'Right,' Popsie said, when she'd finished her reel, 'now you'll tell us what we want to know.'

'Nobody's going to believe pictures like that,' I told her. 'They're obviously taken under duress. Who'd be mad enough to get himself photographed nude with a twelve-years-old girl?' Then, conscious of where my hands were, I said: 'Anyway, she's not twelve— she's nearer twenty. Tell them about your child,' I told Ariadne. Popsie cut across all this with her question:

'Where's Albert?'

'Waiting for us on Skye,' I told her.

'Good,' she said, 'then that's where we're going. Get dressed. Come on, boys, we'll wait outside.'

As they went out I heard one man say to the other: 'Did you see that fucking great bump on his chest? My dead brother had one of those. . . .'

'Don't stop to dress,' I told Ariadne when the door had closed. 'Bring your clothes with you and don't forget the money.'

'You are dopey,' she said. 'The money's in the car.'

I don't know whether you've climbed out onto a ladder from a hotel bedroom window with a naked girl, yourself naked too? Most people have, I expect. I've never been able to surprise anybody yet. You always get this 'That reminds me when I was in Durban' thing. Before you know it your own anecdote's drowned out. That's why I write. Nobody can stop you. They can put you down but they can't stop you.

'Good luck, Mr Fenton!' somebody shouted as we got to the car. The kitchen staff were crowded smiling around the big window of the kitchen; the landlady and Helen were waving behind somewhat proprietorially.

'They're really good news, aren't they?' Ariadne got into the car, throwing her stuff on the back seat. Then she said as her bottom touched the cold damp leather: 'Oh! My bum!'

Even the car seemed to be with us, starting at the first press of the button. As I drove out from the side of the hotel onto the road I saw Mr Rawlinson on his knees letting down the tyres of the gang's Humber. He waved and smiled as we drove off and I gave him a peep on the horn. People can be really nice and often they're not as dumb as you think they are.

'Be getting dressed,' I told Ariadne.

I came out fast at the T-junction and squealed left on the road to Ullapool, quickly getting up to seventy—which for me is mild hysteria.

'Oh boy,' Ariadne kept muttering as she tried to get herself dressed but kept rolling this way and that at every bend. 'This is really super!'

We now had less than an hour to make the last ferry to Skye and it was beginning to rain again.

I was machine-gunning one of the lumbering old Gotha bombers on the fast dive into Ullapool when Ariadne noticed the fighter on our tail.

'Do you think it's them?' she said.

I looked in the mirror and saw four bobbing lights, two on top of the other two. You always get this and I think it's a trick of vibration on the mirror. It couldn't be the gang if they'd stopped to change their wheels or blow up tyres. I told her it might be the police; if Rawlinson was alert enough to do their tyres he could have phoned the law. I didn't want the police particularly either.

It wasn't just that we had a dead sheep with dangerous associations in the boot and two and a half thousand dollars in unexplained currency; it was the fact that the police were the police and the dinner talk had frightened me.

I went down to hit the seafront (Loch Broom) and turn sharp left away from the town and striking steeply up the twisted road and over the new bridge to the high edge of the cliffs overlooking the harbour. By the time we got to the top the following car was crossing the bridge below us. I didn't want to crash being chased by nobody and was looking for a layby of some kind; I saw three tracks into the woods on the left but passed them before I was aware. I slowed down and caught a flash of the following lights in my mirror. For a moment I doused my lights altogether.

'Horace!' Ariadne shouted.

It frightened me, too; I couldn't see a thing. I put my lights on again just in time to take a sharp bend left away from the cliff and in the same moment saw at the end of a short straight a track dropping down off the road. I risked what lay out of sight and shot down the track, doused my lights and braked. The following headlights came over the top of us, missing us, as the car came along the short straight. We were not hidden by anything except our steep angle down from the road. The lights veered round following the road and a moment later, rather astonishingly, the car went past our side-window. Had it been daylight we should have known that we had dropped down into one of those corner-cutting layby's used for storing road mending materials. I only had to release the brake to coast back onto the narrow road.

'It wasn't them,' Ariadne said. 'It was Mr Rawlinson.'

'Did he see us?'

'I don't know—I didn't see him.'

This is the kind of conversation that makes nonsense of a book, yet if you try to sort it out it's dull, isn't it?

'Catch him up,' Ariadne said. 'Perhaps he wants to tell us something.'

I wasn't interested in anything he could tell me. I just wanted to get across to Skye tonight and meet Albert tomorrow. What I wanted and what I felt sure he could do was take the whole situation off my shoulders so that I could go home and write. I had become increasingly certain with the appearance of Popsie and the Wardour Street boxers encouraging this belief, that I had got caught up in one of Albert's vast obscure enterprises and that was all. Murder only seemed like murder and death like death; you paid some money, as Scott Fitzgerald said about 1920 New York snow, and it turned into something else.

Two things happened before we got to the ferry; first we almost ran into some beautiful deer but I managed to stop in time. A splendid pair of adults and three young animals strolling slowly across the road. Ariadne now wanted to capture one of the young deer instead of catching up with Rawlinson or getting the ferry. She was out of the car chasing them into the fir trees before I could stop her. It took very little to ignite her headlong desires and she went from matricide to music, author's mistress to nature girl at the flash of a pair of antlers. After a few minutes she came back, rubbing her scratches and holding a torn pinafore together.

'Why don't we track them?' she said.

The second thing that happened was we ran out of petrol. I didn't tell her immediately but let the car coast on down the side of the hill; when we came to the bottom and tried to climb was when she would find out. There was Popsie and her boxers somewhere behind us and an impassable loch somewhere in front and the last ferry due to leave in eleven-and-a-half minutes by my watch.

'Hasn't it gone quiet?' Ariadne said.

'We've got no engine,' I told her.

It's a strange and rather pleasant feeling to coast a long way down hill in a car. Glider pilots must experience the same sensation after power flights. The rush of wind, the speed of the world going past, the exhilaration of having gravity working for you like an everlasting force of nature. Instead of lessening, the steepness of the hill increased and I was forced to brake now and then to maintain control.

'What's that down there?' Ariadne suddenly asked.

It was the ferry. In a little puddle of light far below us, it seemed, a car was moving slowly towards a ramp, men were walking about; then it was lost by the next rise of trees. We both realised that there were no more hills to climb; that we were winding down the side of a mountain on a series of long 'S'-bends and that we could reach the ferry without an engine.

'That's a bit of luck!' Ariadne called out; she had her window down now and was holding her hands out to catch at the leaves overhanging the road.

The next time we sailed over the ferry the last car was going aboard. I could see now that the deck of the small boat had been swung round at right-angles to the hull so that one end formed the ramp touching down on the shore. The car was the Galaxie and it was the only one there. It was unlikely that Rawlinson was looking for us; he would hardly cross to Skye and be unable to get back to his wife and family until the next day. His family must be with him and they happened to be on our route.

'Blow the horn,' Ariadne said. 'Let them know we're coming.'

We rounded the last bend and hit a level stretch of road alongside the water and the car slowed down. We were doing about thirty-five, I suppose, and had ample momentum to travel the last few hundred yards. The ferry dock now was hidden by foliage though you could see a halation of light above it. I pipped my horn just to please the girl; I hate using my horn and never do it. The times I've crawled through Flask Walk behind deaf old ladies rather than make them jump. Then all at once a frightening thing happened; Ariadne got a trailer of vine caught around her hand and couldn't let go. For a few seconds I didn't know what was happening, she was beating at a lot of foliage as if it were alive or alight. I snatched at it with one hand and got it caught first on the gear lever and then round her neck. Suddenly we ran out of creeper and the whole garland pulled the dead engine into gear with a horrible grind and strangled her.

I got my foot hard down on the brake and shot forward nearly breaking my neck against the windscreen. Instantly with both hands I pulled at the creeper, dragging just sufficient through the window to release Ariadne's neck and stop her eyes from popping and her tongue from lolling out.

I knew instinctively that she was dead (which means she wasn't) and that when Popsie's photographs were produced in court it would be impossible to deny that I had murdered her to stop her talking. My only chance, it seemed to me in that first moment, was to keep the car where it was with the creeper joining us to the roadside bushes, run to the ferry and get a witness. I mean, who was going to believe what happened? How many people over the age of five grab at the bushes as they're being driven through a country road?

My horn started tooting when I was running along the road towards the ferry. I looked back and my headlights flicked off and on. I ran back and Ariadne was getting out of the car rubbing her throat.

'Where're you going?'

'See if I can find a doctor,' I lied.

'Cripes!' she said. 'My fucking throat!'

I knew she was going to be all right. The ferry chose that timely moment to poop its pooper. I told her to sit back in the car while I tried to stop it leaving. In fact she followed me for I could hear her flip-flop sandals behind me like an echo as I ran. It was a pleasant sound and my tears of relief only now came with the delayed shock; when I saw the ferry already ten yards from the bank and moving quickly away the disappointment was diffused by the relief of her being alive. I gave it a shout more as a formality.

'I say!' I called. 'I say!'

'Jesus!' Ariadne panted, coming up right to the water's edge. 'What's the good of saying "I say!" ' Then she cupped her mouth and considering what her throat had just been subjected to gave a god-almighty hog call: 'Come back! You lousy bastards!'

The boat gave another outraged Scottish toot and went on its way. Then, amazingly, Popsie's voice came across the water:

'Horace! Horace! Is that you?'

I clapped my hand over Ariadne's mouth to stop her

211

answering. I don't have to explain what had happened. Rawlinson had let down their tyres and they had taken his car. We had been chasing our pursuers for the past twenty miles and but for Ariadne's accident would have caught them. We could hear their voices arguing as they tried to turn the ferry back but they were dealing with union men and had met their match. The last ferry was the last ferry.

'Listen.' Ariadne was listening.

There was a girl singing somewhere near at hand in a high, sweet and unforced voice and she was singing—if you can believe that much schmoltz with the ferry lights blinking away across the black water—*The Skye Boat Song.*

'Speed bonny boat like a bird on the wing
Onward, the sailors cry.
Carry the lad that's born to be king
Over the sea to Skye . . .' she sang.

She didn't get quite as far as that in fact but as I had to look it up it was worth the whole verse. Flora MacDonald as I first saw her was tall and quite beautiful and draped in a fishwife's shawl. She stood leaning over the front garden gate of one of a row of cottages by the quayside. The front door of the cottage behind her was open, illuminating both the woman and a large BED AND BREAKFAST sign.

I said good evening to her and Ariadne asked her if she could use her loo.

'It's welcome y' are, dearie,' said the girl (I nearly put 'quoth' because she did quoth it). And as Ariadne popped through the gate and into the cottage she said to me: ' 'Tis a long drive back ye'll be having. Would ye no rather bide the neet?'

'Bide the neet?'

'It means stay the night,' she said, in a quite different and rather debbie accent; it turned out to be Purley. She was a young teacher at Bennington who had taken the cottage for the summer and was finding the rent a bit too much. She had adopted the folksie act and the singing to attract people who had just missed the ferry. From what I learned later she was beginning to enjoy it more than teaching.

Before deciding I asked her what time the first boat came back from Skye in the morning.

'Skye?' she said. 'That's not Skye. Skye ferry at Kyle is another seven or eight miles on. This is Strome ferry. It's just an inlet'

Nobody had mentioned there was a ferry before we got to the ferry. When we went inside she showed me a map on the wall. Popsie and her heavies had just crossed the neck of an inlet to Loch Curran and there was no way back by road other than a hundred mile detour almost back to Inverness. I had little doubt they would press on to Skye and wait at Kyleakin for us to cross over tomorrow.

Flora MacDonald, naturally enough, was fascinated by the Legend and History of Bonnie Prince Charlie's Flora MacDonald and was intrigued that I had a rendezvous at the monument of her namesake on Skye. I was in the middle of explaining this when she realised that Ariadne was still in the lavatory. I mentioned her constipation and bad breath as you do when you hope people can suggest something; at Bennington they must have a thousand Ariadnes. She said: 'I'll mix her some senna tea.'

'Horace! Horace!' Ariadne was calling out from the bog; it had been built as a conversion from the kitchen.

'Shall I go?' Florence said. 'Perhaps we should sit her over some steam.' She had got the idea that Ariadne was my little daughter and I couldn't bring myself to put her right; I mean, she knew these girls and the kind of men who hang around the netball field.

'I'll just see,' I said. 'She's a bit shy.'

'And I'll be making the cocoa,' said Flora.

What it was was dramatic. On the lavatory wall amongst the squiggles made by doodling sitters was one that had caught Ariadne's attention; it was the drawing of an aeroplane crashing into a squiggly line no doubt meant to represent the ocean (although the squiggly line was a part of some ancient doodle of somebody else's, if you understand me; one doodle often inspires another). Then with elaborate illumination of the double-block shadowed capital letter variety was written: AK-EDGAR. . . .

If you can beat that.

Ariadne, still pulling up her outer knickers over her tights said: 'Albert's been here!'

And he had.

Fifteen

'He called me Gringo,' Flora told us. 'I think he was partly Mexican and terribly funny. And rather naughty!'

'That's Albert,' Ariadne said, who had never met him; adding to me: 'Isn't it?'

It was.

'Hey, Gringo,' Albert used to say when he came in with the milk delivery and found me moping over my typewriter. 'You got some marny? I ain't got some marny too. Oho, Gringo,' he used to sigh. And I used to sigh: 'Oho, Pancho.' And I used to tell him though he didn't believe me, if ever he got rich he would find it dull. 'These are our happiest years,' I used to say. I really meant that: In the depths of poverty with Tres suicidal or fighting off the gasmen depending on her mood and Edna making tea for the bailiff I would console myself that Paul Getty wasn't happy either.

'Did he seem worried at all?' I was cross-examining Flora over the cocoa.

'Oh no! He kept making me laugh. Are you sure it's the same man? Big, gingery, bright blue eyes, terrifically virile. He got his finger stuck in one of my cups—I had to break it to get it off. I mean the cup.'

That was Albert. If you remember everything of Albert's was over-size.

'When was this?' Ariadne said.

'I beg your pardon?' Flora said, blankly.

Isn't it strange or haven't you noticed that if you say something quite predictably ordinary in a new and fresh tone of voice people don't know what you're talking about. If you're constipated you find that after successful evacuation your brain lights up. Ariadne was now completely on the ball and that's why she had noticed Albert's doodle. She sat there on the tatty rag-piece rug holding her mug of cocoa and being as efficient as she had been about that transatlantic call from Jane.

'What was the date?' she asked. 'When was Albert here?'

'He said his name was Pancho Gonzales,' Flora said. She laughed: 'Though I'm sure it wasn't. I think I can get the date out of my receipt book.' And when we both stared at her, she said: 'He bought a knick-knack.'

Flora didn't have anything as organised as a guest-house register but she did keep careful note of everything she sold in the way of china flim-flam, good-luck tokens and Scottie folk-crap. She had bits of Robbie Burns written on yellow-varnished wood with a hot poker (one would assume) and wee Grannie Mutchie's with pokie bonnets and Highland lads in kilts all in shiny china, tartan mugs and knotty crummocks (walking sticks) and all the rest of the rubbish that tourists soak up instead of the sunshine. There were jars of ointment made from seaweed and perfume from the heather, local tweed and Highland craft knitted ties and scarves, portraits of Bonnie Prince Charlie and photographs of the Hebrides and the western coast.

'He bought two postcards,' Flora said. 'Fivepence each.'

Ariadne got up from the floor and ran her hand inside my jacket (brown corduroy, nine guineas, Hampstead Man's Shop) and took out the postcard from Albert.

'This one?' she asked Flora.

'Why, yes!' Flora looked at the card and then at me. 'Then you must be his famous author friend? I posted them for him.' And she said to Ariadne: 'The other one was to his girl friend in Acapulco. She's a countess—at least, that's what he said. He's a bit of a spoofer, isn't he?'

I found a number of answers in the dregs of my cocoa. Why Albert, who had no interest in history before (circa) the beginning of the financial year, should have picked Flora MacDonald's monument for a rendezvous—he hadn't; our hostess had picked it for him. In fact he had got the idea sitting in this room. Why Jane was flying (had flown) to England: to attend our board meeting tomorrow on Skye. The footnote on this came from Ariadne who had also got there, probably two steps ahead.

'They're here to wipe you out, Horace,' she said.

'Who? Albert and Jane?'

'No, Popsie and the boys. It's what Dennis used to do with the opposition. Lenny Price is an expert. They blew up AK-Edgar, now they're after the survivors. That's you and Jane and Albert. And that five million pounds. I bet they're glad we knocked off Raoul. There won't be so many to go shares. You know what I mean?'

It was another Purport, she had the American accent to go with it, yet it was so convincing it gave me the shivers.

'Don't stop,' Flora MacDonald said. 'It's exciting. Is this one of your stories, Mr Fenton?'

Flora had warmed towards me and I towards her; I had already divined with a familiar leap of pulse that Flora was a fruit of my favourite scrumping grounds, another rebel princess from the weald of culture. She knew about literature and quoted Macaulay on Addison to illustrate where my books stood in relation to society.

'Do you mind if I go to bed?' Ariadne said after twenty minutes of this.

'Albert told me what you were trying to do,' Flora told me, after the girl had been put in a back bedroom.

It was typical of Albert that he would use the bits of me he most disdained—the serious writing bits—to impress somebody like Flora. 'I think you should go after the Hawthornden,' she said. (My regular readers will have to be told that this is a literary prize.)

What I particularly liked about her was that her dress was a decent, dignified, feminine length and her singing voice, slightly corny but willing, reminded me of my mother. I asked her if she knew my mother's favourite, *Come Feather Your Nest*, and she sang it for me:

In a home for two, love,
Come feather your nest,
Where only true love,
Can weather the test.
No time for waiting,
No use hesitating,
The whole world is waiting,
Come feather your nest—

She stopped her trilling soprano at a sudden fierce thumping on the ceiling; it was Ariadne. Very embarrassing, we were guests after all.

'That's all right,' she said. And she said: 'She's really an actress, isn't she?'

It would have been silly to deny it; this girl knew girls. I asked her to guess Ariadne's age and she gave me the most heartening estimate I'd had so far.

'Eighteen,' she said, decisively.

Being a school teacher she had noticed nicotine in the palms of Ariadne's hands, from holding cigarettes to hide them; she had seen cracked fingernails which apparently only happens after years of poisoning with various acetates. 'And her ears have been pierced,' Flora said. 'All the fourth formers did that three years ago—that makes her eighteen. Has she any tattoos?'

'Yes,' I said. Then I said: 'I don't know.' But it was too late. I wasn't going to mention this but Ariadne has what look like a pair of cherries on one buttock.

Flora laughed. She said: 'It's all right, Horace. You are a writer.' She knew of course by this time that I was not Ariadne's father. 'Tattooed girls are between eighteen and twenty-one—I just missed it.'

Girls are slaves of fashion which sometimes scar them for life. We talked for two hours, I got another cup of cocoa and before going to bed I invited her to my publication party (which I just invented) in Hampstead for my forthcoming *Unfit For Babies*.

'I'd love to come. It's just right.' she said. 'I shall be on my way south.'

As it turned out, Hampstead was as far south as she got.

Urgent message from Clive (I've got this new underground type publisher called Clive—at fifty-two I start going underground): can he have the ms from the printer. What I'll have to do is condense the next twenty pages into a couple of paragraphs— after all what you want to know is what happens at the end. I can't bear dragging readers through long books. At the same time I don't want to lose any good sentences—they watch you like a hawk.

'You chuck your best stuff in the waste-paper basket,' the editor of *John Bull* told me once.

When I'm rich and famous and dead they'll publish my waste-paper basket.

Anyway, there's a lot of stuff about Flora getting us away in the morning—getting us some petrol, checking the gang had gone on to Skye, giving me a *Joan The Wad* as a farewell token.

'You fancy her, don't you?' Ariadne accused me while we were on the ferry. I couldn't deny it; but I did deny it. Now what I haven't said about this trip is that we took some marvellous pictures and of course I wrote pages of beautiful travelogue crap to prove I wasn't making anything up; that I'm cutting out: the pictures you can see if you send a stamped addressed envelope.

The sky was doing pretty things over the far Cullins— that can all come out. Oh yes, here we are: this crazy Scotty wedding we got dragged into—that's on the plot line and getting us closer to Albert (isn't it marvellous he's still around?).

No, just a minute—here's a bit I want to keep; you're bound to want to know if I had sexual intercourse with Ariadne in Flora's cottage now that she was eighteen. This is a good bit; it makes me laugh now but it didn't at the time.

'See how many times you can go in and out before you have to stop,' Ariadne said after I'd crept into her bed and possessed her. 'I say thirty-three. That's my locker-number in gym. What do you say?'

She's no sooner discovered sex than she has to start finding ways of making it interesting.

The wedding I'll leave in full:

We were driving the narrow roads of Trotternish—that is the top, high-flung right arm of Skye looking at the map—and searching for the Flora MacDonald monument when we encountered the wedding party. A group of people, men, women, children, Sunday-best dressed and with buttonholes, trailing across from a tiny stone kirk (church) to a big farm barn. The two buildings were the nucleus of what laughingly passes for a village in the highlands; a scattering of dwellings, roofless butt'n bens, tiny store with POST OFFICE written over it.

I had stopped to ask the way of an elderly bent man wearing a kilt.

'Are you strangers to the isle, then?' he said. And when I told him we were he called after the crowd now entering the barn : 'Margaret ! Margaret ! We have the strangers for ye!'

And to us he explained: 'Ye'll come in and take a drink with the happy twa. Tis a local tradition, you understand. A blessing from across the water. Without it no journey will be safe for them.'

'That's awful,' Ariadne said. 'What a good job we came along.'

It was a funny sort of wedding. To begin with there were no cars there, just a horse and cart with white ribbons on it and two old bicycles garlanded with *Philadelphus Virginal* (double white mock-orange or *Syringa*). Inside the barn, which was bigger and cosier than it looked from the outside, was such a spread of food and drinks as I've never seen—this is where I think Ariadne's appendicitis started for she gorged herself on such things as game pates, salmon, trout, over-hung venison, black-bun, potted-head (ugh!) and thing that had been found crawling in Staffin Bay—all washed down with a locally brewed whisky-punch which would have found a better use in flame-throwers.

'Today in many a clachan in the Isle of mists and rain' a man was reciting as he stood in front of the wedding-cake, a kilted hairy leg up on a chair and his hand on some girl's arse: *'They tell at winter ceilidh this story o'er again; And many a timid cailleach, when the evening shadows jail, Avoids the place that bears the name "Destruction of the Wall".'*

Nobody seemed very interested in the wedding or the bridal pair; everybody too busy singing and reciting and projecting themselves with song and verse about what a great place Skye is and how many people have been butchered there.

The kilted kiddies were now going with:

'Pity me, without hands three, Two for the pipes and a sword free.' And a tiny lassie piped up: *'Horror covers all the heath Clouds of carnage block the sun; Sisters weave the web of death, Sisters, cease, the work is done.'*

'Are you coming?' I asked Ariadne.

She was dancing with a brawny young Highlander who was listening enraptured to one of her purports. Then she said: 'Oh, Horace! Have you tried the prawns pickled in wine?' She was drunk and swaying.

'I better take ye oot, lassie,' I heard her partner say. I watched him lead her out of the barn with great misgivings; I wondered if he knew the risks he was running. Nearby a parent of one of the bridal pair was trying hard to start a blood bath with his speech of blessing:

'Here's to the twae o' ye—long may y'r lum reek!' he was saying, wildly, hurling his drink everywhere; it was a little nut-brown character who had brought us in. 'I hae the assurance of those various obscure relatives who managed to get here today that the wine is not poisoned nor the food contaminated—'

A bottle whizzed past his head and he merely ducked.

'And neither, during the fiery plunderings of the nuptial bed, will our hosts rise us—as did the bloody Campbells against their guests the brave McDonalds—to repeat the massacre of Glencoe!'

A knife stuck quivering beside his head into a beam of the barn wall. He snatched it out and prepared to return it only to find it had been thrown by the little girl who had just recited the *Valkyries*. In that moment when it was uncertain whether or not he would kill her, I heard the high shrill sound of Ariadne's voice screaming somewhere outside in the bracken:

'Horace! Horace! Help!'

'Have no fear!' the little man turned and said to me, comfortingly. 'It's young Muradoch. He'll impregnate her with the guid blood—none of this extraneous fucking plasma!' he said, turning the insult to the crowd waiting to drink the couple's health. Oddly, they all drank to that and hurled their glasses at each other with great gusto and joy. I hurried out.

As I came out of the barn Murdoch came running from the bushes without his kilt, his big red hands clasping his balls to cover them, his face flushed with shame. 'They took my kiltie!' he was crying.

I saw then Popsie's Galaxie steaming off over the hill; never mind his kiltie, they'd taken Ariadne. 'Get the rest of the men and follow me,' I told him.

I got into my car and drove after the gang. What a foolish, brave thing to do. Nobody followed, needless to say for abduction, sack and sacrifice are the colours of the land.

Bloodthirsty Dee each year needs three;
But bonny Don she needs but one.

Now that I was looking for Ariadne I found Flora MacDonald's monument.

At first I thought it was a cairn of rocks marking a height on the inland side of the road with a lane leading away towards it. By this time—I had followed the other car for about a mile—I began to realise that they wanted me to follow them and that I was alone and unarmed; they didn't want Ariadne, they wanted me. They were after my five million. If they didn't get me the Fraud Squad would. What was the answer? Albert, I thought; and I turned up the lane.

The lane forked and where it forked, in the apex, stood a long, low stone croft with a signboard in the garden: THE FLORA MACDONALD MUSEUM. She must be the most famous mistress of all time. You too could have a Flora MacDonald, I thought.

The right-hand fork was signposted to the Flora MacDonald Monument. It turned out to be a cemetery containing many graves and headstones and monuments. The Scots seem to honour the dead more than the living.

Albert wasn't there.

Well, what did you expect? Why would Albert be hanging around a place like Skye for the past fortnight? The phoney post mark on the hand-delivered postcard gave the thirteenth as its only clue—hand-delivered? By whom? Well of course Albert was in London like everybody else. He had just come up for this date for reasons of his own. So where was he?

It was a vast landscape from this hilltop dead-centre. Mountains and loch to the south, glimpses of the ocean and the island of Raasay to the east, and Atlantic to the west and the tip of the Waternish Peninsular enclosing Snizort Bay, Albert behind Flora's monument. Suddenly two long arms came up either side of the stone column like a ballet dancer behind a ballet dancer and each hand had two get-stuffed fingers sticking up.

'Hey, Gringo!' he said.

'Hey, Pancho!' I said.

Albert stepped out and grinned at me.

Sixteen

'Where's your nympho?' Albert asked me.

Reunited, here we are sitting on gravestones in the mist in some primitive high place in the Hebrides; we could very well both be dead, now I come to see it properly.

'Popsie and the boys have got her,' I told him.

'Good,' he said. 'We can talk.'

You can tell the only way he had changed was in appearance. He sat there like the old man of the sea; big ginger beard, his hair curling on his shoulders, dressed in dirty-white Arun sweater and with green denims tucked into sea boots (he'd come by boat). He was now smoking a pipe but he kept spitting and hating it, banging it on things. There was an overall feeling that I shouldn't be surprised to find him alive, which I couldn't quite wear. It was as if I'd kept a firm appointment.

'You're supposed to be dead,' I told him. 'Your mother's putting flowers on your memorial stone.'

'Yes, I know. I'm a bit disappointed there.' I detected that he knew all about his mother. Then he said: 'I notice you're not keeping it watered. Mary put some flowers on last week. Remember Mary at the White Hart?'

I said: 'Have you been to Golders Green cemetery?' It's a bit unfair if the dead walk around criticising their graves. The last word in narcissism.

Albert was commuting to London regularly; by boat to Benbecular, flight to Glasgow and then to Heathrow.

'I want you to go the same route,' he said then; 'you can do it in three hours from here.'

I told him I'd got a car.

'You can fly back and pick it up later. I want you to collect some stuff from Mum.'

I told him about Ariadne—he stopped me as if it was very tired news.

'Oh, Horace,' he said. 'Dinah's doing her nut and so is the BBC. Did you know the series has been called off?'

He was talking as though he'd just got in from the world and *I* was the hermit.

'The press got hold of it—well you can guess how big it is to them. Either you're screwing a schoolchild or Dinah Thing, the country's National Health Service Unmarried Mother is an old theatrical bag of forty-four.'

'The papers know about me and Ariadne?'

'Mac the Knife sold it to them—you know Mac Gordon McKilvey? He was script editor on the series—'

'I know that, I'm working on it myself.'

'Play it right and you can take it over,' Albert said. He shifted to a better gravestone and stabbed his pipe at me in the old familiar gesture, giving me instructions. 'After all, you've got the kid. Stick Dinah for a thousand at least. At *least*. She's got the kid's father on her neck now— this Roman Catholic priest (Father Thing) just flew in from the Vatican and she's having to make excuses. Arry's in the country, she's having an operation, she's on a Continental holiday with her school—make it two thousand. Make her old man pay another thousand or you'll tell the Pope.'

I began to feel better already. From being in the shit I was beginning to feel in a position of power.

'The newspapers you can take for two thousand pounds each. Defamation of character. Did you see the Sundays? They're trying to connect you with the AK-Edgar sabotage and God knows what else. I've got Leonard working on it now for you.'

'Leonard Wray? He doesn't know you're alive, does he?'

'Of course he does. He's been up here on a fishing holiday. We've formed a new holding company for Global Alivies and you've got no connection with it. Therefore you've got no connection with the air disaster.'

'And no connection with the five million pounds?'

Albert laughed. 'You can come in if you like but it would mean attending a board meeting once a month— ten o'clock in the morning.'

'Forget it,' I said.

'I have.' He got up from the gravestone and gave me an affectionate punch on the shoulder. 'How are you?'

'I feel better already,' I told him.

'Come and have a drink and I'll put you in the picture.'

'What about Ariadne?'

He said: 'She won't come to any harm. They're not after her or you. They're after me. It's the Consortium.'

'No it's not,' I told him. 'It's Popsie and a couple of thugs.'

Albert laughed and took hold of my arm. 'You don't change, Horace. Come on.'

When we got to my car he held his nose and pulled a face. I told him about the dead sheep and he backed away.

'Oh my gawd,' he said. 'Let's go back in the boat.'

He had this lovely light-blue and white motor launch moored down by a rough footpath below the cemetery. On the way to it and after we had cast off and all the way out of the bay and round the point he was asking after my familiars who had once been his familiars too. I told him about Edna's baby turning over, the new grandchild, Tres making a fruit cake.

'That's nice,' he said.

It seemed a relief for him to talk to somebody like me sometimes. He admitted as much while he was tying up at the hotel landing stage; admitted that extreme wealth brought extreme complications, that the dream was better for the soul than the reality, that he missed his milkman's round and he missed me. He paid me a back-handed but rather nice compliment as we walked up across the lawn from the boathouse.

'The thing is,' he said, 'nothing you say is worth thinking about. I find that relaxing.'

It just hurt me a little that he hadn't inquired about the holes in my hands.

'Mr Fenton!' a woman called from inside the hotel as we crossed the terrace.

Albert put his hand over my mouth and whispered: 'Not you. I meant to tell you. I'm booked in here as Horace Fenton the writer. Don't panic. You be my brother Spurgeon—okay?'

I followed him into the hotel, still trying to adjust. He was talking to an elderly, grey-haired lady standing by the tallest, loveliest Tiger Lily I've ever seen potted.

She was saying: 'I think it was the police. They wanted to know was there a Mr Fenton staying here. I told them of course there was not. And anyway you were much too busy writing to be disturbed. She smiled round at me: 'This must be your father.' And to me she said: 'I expect you're very proud of him.' And to Albert she said: 'Will it be bannocks and tea on the terrace, Mr Fenton?'

The hotel stood just above sea-level on the lowest shelf of the steep shore which, at that point, had been terraced into gardens from the coast road down to Flodigarry Bay. The building itself was part mansion restored from some old stronghold of the MacDonalds of Sleat and part Victorian additions. It had been made attractive with plenty of french windows and white casements with brightly-painted shutters ready to keep out the elements. The beautiful Tiger Lilies were part of a family of tubbed and potted shrubbery and flowers which contributed to à charge of three-guineas-a-head for bed and breakfast. For full board, Albert told me over the tea and bannocks (cakes) it came to about sixty pounds a week. With the boat and the airline commuting he was running at about a hundred and fifty pounds a week.

'It'll all go down to location research,' he said. 'What do you think of this place as an atomic submarine base for world domination?'

'You can't afford that, can you?' I knew he was talking about a projected movie and he knew that I knew. 'How are you going to make another movie when everybody thinks you're dead?'

He said: 'I've got a big press release coming up. I shall fly the press here from all over the world as soon as I've got out of schtück.'

This was the first time he had mentioned the fact that he was in schtück. The way he was living you would never suppose he was in schtück.

'How bad is it?' I asked him.

He thought about it for a moment, then said: 'Have another bannock.' It had to be pretty bad for him not to be able to talk about it. He liked talking about things he had done.

'Can I ask you a personal question?' This was one of our clichés. He looked at me and I said: 'Tell me truthfully—did you sabotage AK-Edgar?'

He shook his ginger locks and said, grimly: 'No. But I sabotaged everybody in it.'

Vote of thanks to Horace who now proposes to replace ten pages of laborious exposition with a crisp paragraph.

What Albert had done was divert some five million pounds of Global money to an unspecified business. To do this he had forged a distribution contract in the names of the other directors, now conveniently dead. Now assuming that the fraud had been discovered by old Jamie, whoever was found alive in that list of crash victims was going to be the guilty party. God, I must have been waffling to take ten pages over that.

'But Jamie thinks it's Sir Ambrose,' I told Albert; and I gave him all the trimmings. His face brightened in fascinating little clicks as I spoke—corners of his mouth clicked up, eyes crinkled and blinked like a bride. Then what he did was, he kissed me.

'I knew I did the right thing when I threw you in,' he said.

He made me feel like a bit of isinglass in cloudy wine. All those corny clues that sent the dogs bloodhounding across Hampstead Heath had been Albert-instigated and deliberate.

'What's that ship out there?' he now asked; having disposed of AK-Edgar he was now free to get on with the job in hand. He was looking out to sea with a pair of binoculars.

I told him it was the *Arosa* and he hung the glasses back on his chair. They had been there before we sat down. How long had Albert been sitting on this chair, eating bannocks and waiting for a ship? This Treasure Island element deepened when Miss Crombie came hurrying out with a piece of paper.

'The tide levels have just come in, Captain,' she said.

Albert thanked her and scanned the paper. Miss Crombie then said:

'If you could move some of your equipment, your father could have the annexe.'

'Och aye, och aye,' said Albert, waving her away.

It was nice. Whatever criminal thing Captain Fenton was up

to, it was nautical and nice. Seabirds wheeled and screeched and the sun came out and the clouds piled themselves up on someone else's distant horizon.

'Will ye hold it a wee minute, Mr Spurrajon?'

All the cavalcade of police cars that had been following our bleeper, the red Ford Executive, the Rover, the mini-Cooper with a checker stripe, the white Hillman Imp, were now parked at rakish angles around my Capri outside the MacDonald burial ground. It looked like the last frozen moment of a Hollywood car chase—except that until old Jamie spoke there were no people; now he and his band of criminologists came ghost-like from behind the gravestones; Man Friday, the black sergeant, had been doing a brass rubbing on Flora's monument.

'I see you sneaked away from Hampstead without anybody noticing,' Albert said, with comic bitterness. And: ' 'ow d'you do,' to old Jamie.

'I was at your funeral,' the superintendent said; as one might say 'I was at your party'. He was anxious to project a pawky humour in the presence of a professional.

'Oh yes—how did it go?' Albert asked him.

'It was verra enjoyable,' said Jamie.

There seemed no amazement at finding Albert Harris the well-known dead film producer now alive and cracking jokes. Nothing could have depressed or amazed Jamie and his murder squad at that moment for they had just discovered the decaying body of Sir Ambrose Argyle in the boot of my car and this had confirmed all their theories; the well-turned purport, the substantiated lie was all that justice required.

'I thought it was just a dead sheep,' I told Jamie.

'It was, laddie, it was,' he said. 'Some practical joker rrrrang the changes on you.'

'Same chap who let our tyres down,' said Lenny. Yes, *Lenny*.

'The same feller who let down the tyres on our motor vehicle,' said his boxer colleague, using the kind of words he thought the police would understand. It was the first and last time I heard him speak.

'In very bad taste,' said Popsie. Yes, *Popsie*.

'Champagne anybody?' Albert called.

We all had more champagne.

Dinner in the Flodigarry Bay Hotel that same night; all of us jolly at a long table in the long window overlooking the bay, an American moon fighting the dregs of sunset for splendour. Nothing, as you may well gather, was as it seemed.

You may notice that Ariadne, poor child, is not present. Ariadne is in Portree hospital having an emergency appendectomy, thanks to the prompt action of Popsie and her friends who, finding her in a state of collapse outside the barn, whisked her away in the nick of time; they traced me back to this hotel to inform me, arriving just as we turned up with the police and the dead body of Sir Ambrose Argyle.

'That's ours,' Popsie said. She was talking about the corpse. It had been flown from Rome to the American air-strip at Dunreay atomic power station—by special arrangement with an Icelandic airline, the only one who would touch dead bodies and lead-lined caskets. Popsie and the boys were driving it south for private burial at the widow's (Albert's mother) instructions.

At Altnacealgach they had found a dead sheep in their boot, had connected me with the body's disappearance and had chased me to Skye.

Now hands up anybody who disbelieves all this rubbish? Okay, I'm with you. Never mind, it sounded good and it fitted. If things fit it's all right. It fitted old Jamie's theory— I mean he knew Sir Ambrose was alive but he didn't know that he had got off the ill-fated airliner in Rome and had been lying low all this time; finally as low as you can get with a heart attack in the middle of the Villa Borghese gardens.

'This is going to upset Mother,' Albert said.

It meant another long trek up Finchley Road to Golders Green crematorium. Another bit of polished marble.

Nothing about the late departed Count Raoul Lecci—he

wouldn't fit. Nothing about forcing me to sign over my rights in Alivies; that certainly wouldn't fit. That was Albert's little power game and had nothing whatever to do with the superintendent's fraud investigation. The closest Jamie came to it was when he congratulated Albert on missing the flight, though how it happened was not his department.

'I'm surprised they didn't call you for the inquest?' Jamie said at one point.

Albert poured him another glass of champagne.

'There she is. Isn't she beautiful?'

Captain Fenton, all bannocks and binoculars, watching her grace *M.V. Countess*, gleaming white paint and redwood coming into the bay; her wake on the sunlit water trailed a wide arc around the headland. Seems odd to have yachts and sunlit water in my books—a touch of the Daphne du Mauriers; I like to keep things skin to skin. The most beautiful thing about this yacht was she was full of millionaires—just like AK-Edgar. Another beautiful thing was that she belonged to Albert—just like AK-Edgar. It came out the way the truth often does eventually; by necessity. I was helping him to shift his equipment out of the annexe. It was gambling equipment: roulette, baccarat, chemin de fer. This was where he had diverted the five million. Albert had gambling franchises on Skye, Acapulco, Malta, Nassau, Dubrovnik—

'It was near Dubrovnik they found the wreckage of AK-Edgar,' I told him.

'Is that right?' Albert said.

I just looked at him until he told me more. The Mafia resenting competition, Sir Ambrose getting the message while the plane was refuelling in Rome.

'He could have warned the others, that's what makes me mad,' Albert said. 'Shirley Chan* took him off sick. The bomb went aboard with fresh ice.'

*Shirley Chan is an air hostess who is doing something in Hong Kong for Albert right now.

His compassion for the Global directors lasted as long as it takes to screw a leg on a green-baize table. Now there was just Albert—and the Countess.

'Horace Spurgeon Fenton—my favourite author!'

And Jane's well-known kiss was on the back of my neck.

'You were going to meet me!' she said.

Albert told her about our new identities and brought her up to date on what had been happening in about five minutes; I learned more in that five minutes than in the entire time since I'd found the black spot on my typewriter.

'Popsie and Mum have been trying to muscle in on us,' he told her.

'Fuck them,' said the Countess.

'And your old man had a go at Horace,' Albert said.

She said to me: 'I tried to warn you. He found one of your letters.'

'Anyway he's dead now,' Albert said.

Jane covered her mouth, but only momentarily. 'Poor Raoul.' Then, half-admiringly, she said to me: 'It wasn't a duel?'

'No, nothing like that,' Albert said. 'He fell in a swamp. You'll never prove you're a widow.'

'Luckily it doesn't matter,' Jane said. 'My divorce came through just before I left.'

'Any trouble?' Albert asked her.

'Not really. I was followed from London to Belfast by a big man with a moustache—he looked like a policeman.'

'That was Cedric,' I told her. 'He's after a cut.'

Jane laughed. 'He got several cuts. I let him follow me to the docks then I put the crew onto them'.

The next time I took my laundry to Tres, she told me that Cedric was in a Belfast jail; though Lewis was now home and playing with a group while Fiona had gone into a Salvation Army hostel.

Raggle taggle of endings here if you can stand it. The best of what was on the tape; though quite a lot towards the end is missing and there's a mingling of strange voices and a pop song which I certainly never recorded with a noise that sounds like a dog barking in an empty room— some weird kind of breakthrough.

Memory will serve as well, however. A very fraught morning arriving at Portree hospital to be told that I should have to wait for Ariadne's visitors to come out before I could see her.

'Her parents are with her,' the sister said. They had to contact her parents before the operation to safeguard themselves. I got out fast. Months later a childlike letter came to me from America.

Dear Mr Fenton,

I just thought I would write you a short note. You remember me and giving me a lift to Scotland that time. We are living in Burbank now. Mummy's got a part in a western series. It is called Hooves Across Montana. If you see it look out for me in a stage coach that gets tipped over a gulch. I would like one of your books to show my friend. If you send one will you send it to her address and mark it personal not to be opened. Don't write anything in it. I'll say I got it from the library. Hoping you are keeping well, Yours faithfully,

Ariadne Thing.

P.S. My breath is better now my appendix is out ! ! !

It's a bit sad, isn't it? Not simply the relic reality that makes nonsense of your hot memories, though that's sad enough; but sadder still how unintelligent your friends and loved ones turn out to be when they try to write a letter. Even Albert, fluent, articulate, witty, wise-cracking Albert writes a self-conscious stilted formal letter, unsure of punctuation and with exclamation marks instead of jokes.

The day I left Flodigarry Albert gave me twenty-thousand pounds in five-pound notes and got me to sign some documents; this was Arturo Conti over again—the sort of thing that only happens in the film business.

'Don't spend it all at once,' he said, 'in case I want to borrow some of it back. Though it is yours. I don't expect I shall need any. We're making a bid for Paradise Island* now—it belongs to Frank Sinatra.'

The money was packed into a cardboard Hush-Puppy shoe box; I had watched Jane count it in. I think it was Jane who had insisted on my getting a cut. She always thought I could write a modern classic if I had the freedom of mind.

'Can I buy a country cottage?' I asked him.

Jane said: 'Don't ask him what you should do with it. Just spend it.'

'Sure,' Albert said. 'It's yours. Just don't go mad. You never know when the bottom's going to drop out of everything. Though I don't expect I shall come to you for anything.'

'But you might,' I said.

'Yes,' he said.

'So it's really still yours,' I said.

'Well, yes,' he said.

We all laughed.

Driving down from Scotland I kept thinking of my independence and the novels I would write.

I planned to write *Hitler Needs You* at last, about me and my friends and my family and the radio factory in the thirties, all happily pursuing our lives and oblivious of what was happening in Germany—the people Hitler needed most.

And I planned *The Wind In The Snottygobble Tree* which was a fantasy about an underground state, a sinister story of a plot to kidnap the Pope and replace him with a stooge. I thought of the great twist of the Pope turning out to be Lucky Luciano—that the Mafia had got in first. You can only indulge the luxury of writing these things on spec if you've got money and don't have to waste your precious time on things like the UM series.

*Bahamas

'Did you enjoy the holiday?'

Claire the nurse in the kitchen in her nightie and hair rollers, three in the morning.

'Yes, thank you,' I said politely, the way we do no matter the baby's died paddling and you were involved in a six-car pile-up on the way home. 'Very much.'

'Wendy's gone off without leaving her rent,' Claire now told me. The worry was keeping her awake; she had to find an extra three pounds the next day for Mrs Bracknell.

I gave it to her.

Claire I had always fancied more than the others; because she was the prettiest and because she was least interested in me.

'Are you absolutely sure?' she said. And she said: 'I'll make you some coffee.'

I got her to make me some tea and bring it to my room.

Joanna and Mac McKilvey had been sleeping in my bed; there was nothing you could put your finger on but the thought was a little revolting.

'I'll change the sheets for you,' Claire said.

While she remade my bed I found a half-full bottle of whisky in my cupboard with an economy label stuck on the side. 'Thanks, pal,' it said. I sloshed it into a couple of tumblers.

'I shouldn't be here!' Claire said.

We were sitting on the bed drinking whisky. She said:

'Do you mind if I start taking my rollers out?'

I said: 'Do you mind if I get undressed?'

As she took out her hair rollers and I got into pyjamas and we both snatched at occasional snorts of drink and dragged cigarettes and built up that most marvellous conjecture, was it going to happen or not, she put in a few discreet questions about Wendy. She had an idea I might have slept with her. I put in a few discreet answers. The idea is to reassure each other that you don't talk about whatever it is you're likely to do next.

'It's not really dry even now.' She was shaking out her hair.

'Let me feel.'

I was having a feel when Lewis came in with a girlfriend; bang crash slam and there they were, a four-o'clock-in-the-morning couple, half-boozed and riding on the tail end of some big trivial party joke.

'I didn't know you were back, dad!'

'Hello,' the girls said to each other.

Joanna and Mac the Knife were not the only ones who had been using Horace Spurgeon Fenton's Hampstead pad as a shagging ground. I'm too easy going, that's my trouble. Flora MacDonald was going to change all that.

'I'd better be going,' Claire said.

She was already going.

It was another of those vicarious nights.

Whatever had been going on had not improved my standing with the neighbours in Squire's Mount. Sunday morning coming back from the village with the Sunday supps I got a bucket of cold water in my face. Mr Martin cleaning his car in the street. It came at me out of the sun in one solid-silver pail-shaped lump. No apologies, no explanations; just this grim, silent, disapproving grown-up stranger going back indoors to get some more.

'You've had some callers,' Lewis told me.

His new girl friend was cooking the breakfast. I had slept on the floor again, suffering, pretending sleep, nearly getting there but not quite.

He told me about the chap with the occasional table.

'He just carries it round with him,' Lewis said. 'He's a psychiatrist. Doctor Thatterday. He was looking for a chap called Freville—didn't you use to know him?'

I didn't remember.

Other people had called. There was a card, a telephone number, some half-forgotten messages. Lewis was going on about would I like to join a jazz-band he was getting up with his clarinet friend Ted and some others. It was a nice idea and worth practising my guitar chords for; except for being a writer I'd rather be a jazzman than anything else. Good jazz of the Mezz Mezzrow, Bix Beiderbecke, Eddie Lang kind sends my *plana* leaping as nothing else can. It has the plaintive, lifting sadness and the urgency of not dying.

The card was an anniversary card, a little pink floral wreath, unsigned. It had a Cornwall postmark and the date was just three years after Trotsky took Diana and B— away.

Itty shitty bit right at the end.

Sitting in the bog reading the toilet roll. Marvellous to be back home with the rusty monsters hanging over me again and yet with twenty-thousand pounds in a shoe box. It's the right way to enjoy hideous discomfort.

Three weeks casual labour London Zoo, Regent's Park.

It was Freville's mad, cramped writing. The nurses must have run short of paper and used one of his escape and stay free plans. It was a bit I hadn't read before, in towards the middle of the roll.

Clean out cages, sweep paths, carry animal fodder, run errands for keepers and staff. No cards needed. No identification or records, queue up for pay each night.

That was clever. That would have fitted into the movie very well. There are not many ways you can earn a living without getting caught by the bureaucrats.

I unrolled some more bumpf.

Will have to leave soon. Getting too fond of Toby. Better not to form associations of any kind. Can't resist the way he clings to his food bucket and won't let go. Bites if you persist. Reminds me of Doctor Thatterday and his Regency table.

Toby is a bear. Thatterday is the psychiatrist—it all fits, doesn't it? Now listen to this:

New job. Two weeks casual work, London Airport Cargo sheds . . .

And that fits too. Norman Freville was working at the airport when AK-Edgar took off, filled with men who had stolen his business. That fits better than Albert's Mafia in Rome fits.

It gave me a funny feeling. To go with this funny feeling, from my room and from some East Side New York studio in February 1931, the month before I left school. I could now hear the New Orleans Ramblers with Jack Teagarden singing *I'm One of God's Children* (who hasn't got wings). It had the heartbreaking sadness of dogs trying to talk.

Signs and portents, creakings, murmurings of fate, the rattle of the dustcart, the slurping of old Sloughfoot, the wind in the snottygobble tree, call it what you will.

Then I wiped my arse on it.

What's one purport more or less? If it's all in the mind it's the truth. If it's all in the register it's the truth. The dragon of the mind has only one head and the lighting is never of the best in the house of horrors.

This day's madness came and went. Claire ran her Sunday night bath and I made Sunday night cocoa for two. The possibility was too near to be exciting. My romantic imaginings were already involving the unattained. Helen the waitress drifted through them and once or twice Flora MacDonald gave in to me after a short song.

reinkarnation

bringing great books back to life
www.reinkarnationbooks.com